AN AVALON MYSTERY

THE BRIDE WORE BLOOD
Vicky Hunnings

When death investigator Detective Shark Morgan is summoned to investigate the tuxedoed body sprawled across the steps of the antebellum church just off Hilton Head Island, he is unsure if he is dealing with a tragic accident or murder. Either way, millionaire real estate developer Marcus DeSilva is very dead.

As Morgan and his partner, Dell Hassler, begin to peel away the layers of deceit and deception surrounding DeSilva's life, one name keeps cropping up at every turn: Marissa, the widowed bride, a woman with a shadowy past, whose face has haunted Shark since he first saw it filling his television screen on the local evening news. Is she simply another unfortunate victim, or is the violence that seems to be following in her wake more than just coincidence?

THE BRIDE WORE BLOOD

•

Vicky Hunnings

AVALON BOOKS
NEW YORK

PRINTED IN THE UNITED STATES OF AMERICA
ON ACID-FREE PAPER
BY HADDON CRAFTSMEN, BLOOMSBURG, PENNSYLVANIA

In loving memory of my mother, Gladys Rouse,
who taught me that when one door closes, another opens;
and that you have not failed until you stop trying.

Acknowledgments

This book could not have been written without the encouragement and support of my parents, Robert and Gladys Rouse; my sister, Debra Rouse; and my son, Brad Hunnings.

Immense thanks to my writers' critique group: Kathy Wall, Peg Cronin, and Linda McCabe. They not only taught me the art of writing, but also convinced me I really could begin a new career. Without their mentoring, this book would not be a reality. I am especially grateful to Kathy, who spent hours helping me edit when she could have been working on her own novels. Such friendships are priceless.

Pat and Harry Skevington have encouraged me from the first draft of my first short story, and along with Helen Evans, have offered their unique perspectives in helping to proof and polish my manuscript. For these special friends, thanks seems such an inadequate word.

And finally, to Erin Cartwright of Avalon Books, thank you for taking a chance on a novice.

Chapter One

Sunlight streamed through the stained-glass windows in the overflowing Pinckney Colony Methodist Church as the minister proclaimed, "I now pronounce you man and wife."

The groom lifted the delicate veil with both hands, smoothed it back from the radiant face of his bride, and then slowly lowered his mouth to hers. Lost in the feel of velvety lips, he held the kiss longer than was strictly appropriate and broke it off only when the crowd began to chuckle. Marcus stared into Marissa's twinkling green eyes and whispered, "I love you."

Reverend Alan Hart smiled at the groom, whom he had known for a long time, as the couple turned and faced the congregation. "Family and friends, it is my distinct pleasure to present to you Mr. and Mrs. Marcus DeSilva." The organ thundered into the recessional as Marcus searched across the upturned faces for one in particular. Disappointed at not finding his son, he gently pulled Marissa's hand into the crook of his arm and led her down the aisle to the doorway of the tiny church.

After the last guests had kissed Marissa's cheek and shaken Marcus's hand, the couple snaked their way through the crowd on the steps and joined the throng that lined the walkway to the waiting white limousine. Marissa turned and threw her bouquet of perfect yellow roses over her right shoulder. The flower girl caught it, squealed with glee, and ran to display her treasure to her mother.

Marcus then raised his eyebrows, and with a devilish look on his face, knelt and moved his hand up under the slim skirt of Marissa's satin wedding dress. Slowly his fingers searched for the garter resting high above her left knee. His eyes never leaving hers, he slid it seductively down her leg and over her shoe, then placed it in his mouth. Turning to the crowd, he began to growl. Several people chuckled and snapped his picture. He rose, turned his back, and heaved the garter toward several teenage boys, who scrambled to retrieve it as the crowd laughed.

While the guests emptied their little bags of birdseed into their hands, Marcus glanced over his shoulder at Reverend Hart, then leaned over and whispered softly to Marissa, "Ready to make a mad dash for the limousine? I'm anxious to get this reception over with and get on our way to the airport. We don't want to miss our flight to Rome. How long do you think we have to stay at the reception?"

"Just give me a second to catch my breath," Marissa said, gazing fondly into Marcus's eyes. "I promise we'll make it to the airport in time for our flight."

"It can't be soon enough," he said, squeezing her arm.

A sharp crack penetrated the muted conversation and laughter of the guests. Several of the men instinctively turned in the direction of the dense woods across the road, although no one seemed particularly alarmed.

"Hunters," someone muttered, and others shook their heads. "Too damn close."

The echo of the shot had barely died away when screams froze everyone in mid-sentence. Marissa knelt over Marcus, who lay sprawled in the doorway, bright red blood staining the front of his white tuxedo shirt.

"Oh, God, someone help him!" she cried to the stunned crowd as she tried to staunch the spreading blood with her hands and the pristine skirt of her wedding dress. "Marcus, Marcus," she screamed as if her repetition of his name could somehow bring him back.

Reverend Hart, hands folded in front of him, whispered the Lord's Prayer. A few of the male guests, who had realized immediately what was happening, flung their arms protectively around their wives to shield them, not only from further danger, but from the grisly sight of Marcus, his life's blood pumping away on the steps of the church. Anxiously they scanned the woods across the road. Had it been a random shot, or would there be more gunfire?

Women began to cry hysterically, and their frightened children took up the wail. Several men, overcoming their stunned inertia, rushed forward. Dr. Charles Vincent, a well-known cardiologist, was in the lead with Marcus's sister, Rachel Wells, close behind.

Dr. Vincent knelt and gently placed his hand on Marcus's carotid artery, checking for a pulse. He found none. He leaned his head down to see if DeSilva was breathing. Vincent adjusted Marcus's head and checked again for respirations. Then he started CPR. Placing his hands in the proper position, the doctor began to compress the victim's sternum.

"Does anyone here know CPR?" he shouted to the crowd of onlookers.

"I do, I'm a fireman," a young man said, quickly pushing his way through the milling crowd.

"One, two, three, four." Dr. Vincent counted as the fireman positioned himself at Marcus's head. The fireman hyperextended the neck, and when Dr. Vincent reached ten in his count, pinched Marcus's nose and blew into his mouth.

They repeated this procedure for several cycles of the count. Dr. Vincent noticed that each time he compressed the chest, more blood pooled on the concrete step. Finally he motioned for the fireman to stop and raised Marcus's left eyelid to check the pupil, which was already fixed and dilated.

Marcus DeSilva, millionaire real estate developer on Hilton Head Island, was dead.

"Please, don't stop," Marissa begged, tears streaming down her face. Beside her, Rachel sobbed loudly.

"I'm sorry, Mrs. DeSilva, but he's gone," Dr. Vincent said, resting his hand on her shoulder in a gesture of comfort.

"Nooooooo," Marissa wailed as she leaned down and put her cheek next to her husband's.

"Marcus, Marcus, please don't die," she implored.

Dr. Vincent turned to Reverend Hart. "Can you take Mrs. DeSilva and Marcus's sister into the church while I call the police?" The minister reached down and pulled Marissa gently to her feet.

The doctor removed his jacket and placed it gently over DeSilva's face. He turned to see a few people already getting in their cars. "Can I have your attention please?" he called. "I'm going to contact the Sheriff's office. Please remain here until they come. They'll probably want to interview everyone." He whipped the small cell phone from his pocket and dialed 911.

The crowd was in a state of shock as they waited for the authorities to arrive. Despite the doctor's request, a few more slipped quietly away. It seemed like an eternity, but in fact it was only a few minutes, before those that remained heard sirens in the distance.

A deputy sheriff, tires spewing gravel, wheeled into the parking lot, followed closely by an ambulance. Two paramedics flung open the doors, almost before the unit had come to a complete stop. Clutching large orange bags loaded with their equipment, they raced toward the inert figure on the step.

"No need to hurry," Dr. Charles Vincent said, shock apparent on his face. "He's dead. Shot in the heart. Probably died instantly."

The paramedics removed the jacket from the body and, despite the doctor's assurances, checked for a carotid pulse.

Beside them Deputy Tom Sayles gasped in surprise. "Christ Almighty, Doc, is that who I think it is? And what do you mean shot?"

"We heard a gunshot in the woods, figured it was just some deer hunters. But then we heard his wife screaming hysterically and turned to find Marcus slumped on the step."

"His wife? I didn't know Mr. DeSilva was married."

"He wasn't until a few minutes ago."

It suddenly dawned on Deputy Sayles exactly what the doctor was saying. "You mean this is *his* wedding? Damn," the deputy said under his breath as he turned and surveyed the crowd.

Nervous at being the first officer on the scene, and a rookie besides, he squared his shoulders and took a deep breath. "Okay, listen up! Nobody is allowed to leave until they've given a statement," he announced. "I'll get several more officers here, and hopefully we won't have to detain you for too long." Turning back to Dr. Vincent he asked, "Are you familiar with the church? Is there someplace with an outside entrance where everyone can wait?"

"The only place large enough are the Sunday school rooms in the back. Do you want me to take everyone there?"

"Yes, please. And stay with them until my backup gets here."

"Sure, but you should know that a few people left before you got here."

"Great," Deputy Sayles muttered under his breath and then announced, "Okay. Everyone follow Dr. Vincent and wait where he tells you."

As the guests moved hesitantly forward, he pulled out his hand-held radio, and requested the dispatcher to send him some help, along with the coroner, and the death investigator.

The older of the paramedics dropped his cigarette butt on the church step and called across to Sayles, "Hey, Deputy, you want us to cover this guy up?"

Sayles turned just in time to see the medic, leg raised, ready to crush out his cigarette. "Stop! What the hell do you think you're doing?" he yelled. "What if this is a homicide? You could be screwing up a crime scene. Pick that butt up now!"

"Jesus, don't get excited! I thought it was an accident."

"Well, until we know that for sure, let's just keep the area clear."

Sayles looked up with relief as the first of his backup units arrived. Within minutes they had taped off the crime scene and begun interviewing the guests. Sayles also sent two officers across the street to check out the woods. He was just congratulating himself on getting the situation under control when a red 1965 Mustang convertible roared to a stop beside the church.

The tall man who unwound himself from the bucket seat had light brown hair with just a hint of gray. Running down the left side of his cheek, a white scar stood out sharply on his suntanned face. In blue jeans and a red T-shirt, Detective William Morgan, Beaufort County's death investigator, looked as if he had just come from the beach. Approaching one of the deputies, he asked for the Primary on the scene. The lanky officer pointed to Sayles.

"What have you got?" he asked Sayles, deciding the unfamiliar deputy must be one of the new guys. Morgan reached for his cigarettes, forgetting for a moment he had quit—nine days and eight hours ago.

"Boy, am I glad to see you, sir. Marcus DeSilva just got himself shot—and at his own wedding."

"Jesus, you're kidding!"

"No, sir."

"Well, what happened?"

"According to the witnesses, a shot rang out from the woods over there and the next thing anyone knew DeSilva was down with a bullet in his heart."

"Accident?" Morgan asked, hoping to be able to return quickly to his boat.

"I don't know, sir. I figure that's for you to sort out."

"You sure know how to ruin an afternoon of good fishing. So tell me where we stand."

"I've got three deputies interviewing guests in the Sunday school rooms in the back, and two checking out the woods."

"Good work. How about the coroner?"

"That should be her car pulling in now."

Morgan turned to see blond Anna Connors, the only female coroner in the state of South Carolina, striding rapidly toward them. He and Connors had been dating pretty steadily for the past couple of months. Anna smiled and nodded her head. "Sayles, Shark."

Detective Morgan smiled at the confused look on Sayles face. "Everyone calls me Shark. It's a long story."

"Oh, okay sir. Should I call you Shark too?"

"Absolutely, if you want me to answer you. Go see how those guys are doing in the woods."

Sayles nodded and strode off.

"So, the stiff is Marcus DeSilva? An old girlfriend by any chance?"

"Don't know, Anna. May have been an accident. Possibly some hunters over in the woods," Shark replied.

"You wish," she said, stooping to examine the body. It took only a few minutes before she stood and announced, "Single gunshot wound to the heart from a large caliber bullet. Died instantly, I imagine. I'll know more after they do the autopsy."

"Since that has to be done in Charleston we probably won't get a report for a couple of days. Care to speculate now, accident or homicide?" Shark asked.

"That's a tough one. Could go either way. With Marcus's history, who knows? Anyway, I'm done here so just tell the paramedics when you're finished shooting all your pictures. They can load him up and transport him to Charleston. I'll call and tell them he's coming."

Anna paused and looked around to see if any of the other officers were within earshot. Then she smacked Shark playfully on the arm and said, "You didn't call me this weekend. I was hoping we could go see the new play at the Arts Center."

"Sorry. I was busy. Excuse me, I need to get back to work." Shark edged away from her and motioned to Sayles. "Where's the widow?"

"In the church with the minister, I guess."

Detective Morgan made his way inside. Sunlight still lit the interior in the soft blues and yellows of the stained-glass windows. Candles overflowed the altar, and yellow ribbons drooped on the ends of the front three pews.

Shark hadn't been in a church since his father died. He didn't like churches much, knowing it was a holdover from his youth when he'd been forced to go every Sunday. Shark didn't know if he believed in God anymore either. Not since Laura died. And it was hard to imagine a God who would let human beings inflict the atrocities on one another that he saw every day.

He walked slowly to the front of the church where the minister stood talking quietly with two women. One was obviously the bride, and he wondered if the other was a close friend or relative. No one looked up as he approached, so he cleared his throat to let them know he was there. All three turned their heads in unison.

"I'm Detective William Morgan," he said quietly. He glanced at the bride and stopped short. It was none other than the woman who had been invading his dreams for weeks—the beautiful new television anchorwoman on the local six o'clock news.

The minister stepped forward, intruding on his thoughts. "I'm Reverend Alan Hart. This is Marissa DeSilva and Mr. DeSilva's sister, Rachel Wells."

Taking a deep breath, Shark forced his eyes away from the newly widowed Mrs. DeSilva and directed his words to the sister. "I'm sorry to impose at a difficult time like this ma'am, but I need to ask all of you a few questions."

Reverend Hart spoke up quickly. "Officer, I don't think we can help you. We didn't see anything, just heard a shot in the woods, and then Marcus slumped over. It *must* have been a stray bullet. It's posted 'No Hunting,' but I hear shots over there several times a day during deer season."

"You may be right, Reverend. But until we do a complete investigation, we won't know for sure. We always have to start with the assumption it was a crime."

Shark steeled himself to look over at Marissa DeSilva. She had removed her veil and tossed it carelessly onto the pew beside her. Her nearly black hair lay in soft curls down her back, contrasting sharply with porcelain skin that looked even paler than on TV. Her makeup was streaked, and her green, bottomless eyes were red-rimmed from crying. He tried not to stare at the tiny mark just above her left upper lip, but he had fantasized so often about kissing that small imperfection on her otherwise flawless face. Reluctantly he shifted his gaze to Marcus's sister.

The family resemblance was uncanny. Her tall, willowy figure provided the perfect frame on which to hang a rust colored silk suit that accentuated her dark hair and eyes. He could tell she'd been crying, but a steely control held her shoulders still and her head erect.

"Mrs. . . . Wells, is it? What did you see when the shot was fired?"

"Detective," Reverend Hart interrupted, "I'm telling you, we didn't see anything. I didn't even know something was wrong until we heard Marissa scream."

"I just can't believe any of this," Rachel Wells said, dabbing at her eyes with a white silk handkerchief. "Please,

I'd like to go back to my hotel. I have people to notify. I need to find B.J. Oh, God, how am I going to tell him about his father?"

"You mean his son isn't here?" Shark's head snapped up at the first interesting piece of information he'd heard.

"No, he didn't show up. He and his father haven't gotten along very well since the divorce. But Marcus was hoping B.J. would come today."

"He promised." Marissa spoke around a throat full of tears. "Marcus wanted . . . Rachel, we have to find him! We can't let him hear about this on the news!"

"*I'll* take care of finding B.J., and I'm *sure* you won't mind if I make all the arrangements for my brother."

No love lost there, Shark thought as he observed the interplay between the two women. It wasn't so much what was said, as what wasn't.

Into the strained silence, Marissa whispered, "Of course not."

"Fine. Detective, I'll be glad to answer any questions you may have later. But I really need to get back to the hotel. You can reach me at the Westin," Rachel said, rising from the pew.

"Well, if you insist. I'll call you in the morning and set up a time to come by." Shark pulled a small notebook from his pants pocket. "Do you need someone to drive you back?"

"Thank you, but I'll have the limousine take me," she said, moving down the aisle.

Shark was surprised at how suddenly in control Rachel seemed as his eyes followed her to the front door. He turned back to find Marissa staring off into space, her face frozen in a blank mask. "Mrs. DeSilva, shall we talk here or would you be more comfortable at home?"

Marissa drew a long shuddering breath. "I don't know how I can help you. I didn't see anything. But, if you'll take me home and let me get out of this dress, I'll answer any questions you may have," she said, studying him for the first time. She wondered what instrument or creature had cut that scar on his face. She glanced up into piercing brown eyes and felt he could read her innermost thoughts. Quickly, she broke eye contact. She hoped she would never have to be subjected to them on the other side of an interrogation table.

"Of course," Shark said, as he reached out to help her up. She picked up her veil and took his hand. As soon as her skin touched his, Shark felt a warmth spread through his body. He turned brusquely to Reverend Hart. "I'll need to talk to you later. I'll be in touch."

The minister enveloped Marissa's free hand in both of his. "I'm so very sorry, my dear. Call me if you need anything. Come, I'll let you out through my office." Reverend Hart led them through a doorway to the side of the choir loft. Shark was grateful that Mrs. DeSilva would not have to pass the body still sprawled on the front steps of the church.

Once outside the church Shark asked, "Would you like to have a lawyer present while we talk?"

Surprised, Marissa glanced at Shark, then lowered her eyes. "A lawyer? No, I have nothing to hide."

There was no further conversation as they made their way to his car. "Would you like me to put the top up?" he asked as they approached the convertible.

"No. This is fine. The wind will feel good," she answered without looking at him.

The silence continued as Shark drove down the country road and turned left on Highway 278. As they neared the bridge to Hilton Head Island, the wide salt marsh, barely visible at high tide, captured his attention. He marveled, as always, at the beauty of the barrier island with its miles of pristine beaches and dozens of world-class golf courses. It was no wonder it attracted over two million tourists each summer.

Out of the corner of his eye, Shark watched Marissa. The lace at the wrists of her cream-colored gown extended in a

V onto the backs of her slender hands that wiped unconsciously at the crusty bloodstains on her slim skirt. The
huge emeralds at her throat, perhaps a wedding gift from
Marcus, looked like green ice against her pale skin.

As they crossed the bridge onto the island Shark asked,
"So, where do you live, Mrs. DeSilva?"

"*Please*, call me Marissa. Mrs. DeSilva sounds . . .
wrong somehow."

"So where are we going?"

"Oh, I'm sorry, Brigantine Street in Palmetto Dunes. I
moved all my things to Marcus's house when I sold my
place a month ago." Her voice cracked, and she turned to
stare off into space again.

Ten minutes later Shark flashed his badge at the guard
gate at Palmetto Dunes Plantation and sped through.
Marissa pointed out the turns, finally instructing him to pull
into a circular driveway in front of a large, three-story
stucco house. Two sets of wrought-iron gates, one leading
to a garage area, and the other to what he assumed was the
front door, barred the entrances. A small semi-circle of
manicured grass surrounded by pots of red and yellow bou-
gainvillea and numerous sago palms bordered the driveway.
He figured the gardener probably made more money than
he did.

Marissa unlatched the gate and led the detective up six
wide marble steps. On the landing she paused, as if afraid
to go in. Off to the left, in a covered courtyard, a large
fountain, shaped like a dolphin, spurted water. Ivy grew up
the walls, and multiple planters overflowed with hibiscus,
lantana, and verbena in riotous color. A marble bench sat
invitingly in front of the fountain. Shark decided it looked
like something you would see in one of those magazines
of beautiful homes that he never believed anyone actually
lived in.

They climbed a dozen more marble stairs. Marissa
tugged on the door, but it refused to budge. "Oh no, I completely forgot! Marcus gave Mrs. Gonzales two months off,

and she left for Uruguay this morning. We can't get in. Marcus and I had planned to go straight from the reception to the airport." Her voice trembled on the verge of tears again. "Are you good at picking locks?"

"Not really. It only looks easy in the movies. Don't you have a key hidden in a flower pot outside like most people?"

"Not that I know of. Wait, I do remember the house-keeper telling Marcus once that she had to use the key from the poolhouse when she locked herself out. But I have no idea where it is."

"Well, searching is one thing I *am* good at."

They made their way around the side of the house on a marble walkway where Shark noted more flower beds and a huge patio and pool. Across a short expanse of marsh grass he watched a pelican dive into the rolling surf for his dinner. Most of the back yard was taken up by the pool-house, an oversized gazebo practically as large as his entire place in Beaufort.

The door was locked, but with a little work and his Visa Gold card, Shark finally managed to gain entry. He opened the door with a flourish and motioned for Marissa to enter first. Ahead of them a full-sized kitchen and a living room with fireplace, stretched across the back wall. To the right a regulation-size billiard table sat next to a small bar. He guessed the two closed doors on the left led to bedrooms. In the background he could hear the muted sounds of the pool filter.

"This may not be as easy as I thought. Lots of good hiding places here." Shark began methodically opening drawers and cabinets in the kitchen.

"Do you want me to help?" Marissa asked, her face blank as she stood surveying the room.

"No, why don't you just sit down."

Marissa perched on the edge of the couch, her eyes fixed on the flat expanse of the ocean outside the window. Again her fingers picked unconsciously at the dried blood on her skirt.

Twenty minutes later Shark returned looking triumphant. "Well, I found a key, so let's go see if it works."

Marissa glanced up, surprised to realize she wasn't alone. "Oh. Sure."

At the front door Shark asked if there was a security system. "Yes. The pad is on the left just inside the door. The code is seven-four-nine-one."

Shark turned the key, quickly stepped inside and punched the proper buttons, a little surprised that in the midst of all the day's chaos, Marissa DeSilva had remembered the code so quickly.

Marissa paused in the doorway. She looked confused, as if entering the house for the first time. Shark watched her slowly ascend the stairway just to the right of the entrance, the train of her gown dragging behind her. He waited until she had disappeared around the curve of the wrought-iron railing, then began his search.

The living room was huge, with two overstuffed couches back to back in the center of the room. One faced a large wooden armoire that housed the entertainment center. The other sofa, turned to a wall of windows, looked out on the pool and ocean beyond. A large marble fireplace took up most of the right wall. Over the mantle hung a gold-framed picture, a sailboat fighting an angry ocean.

With a glance at the staircase, Shark made his way to an antique wooden desk and systematically rifled the drawers. He had no warrant and no real cause, except for his innate curiosity and the opportunity. Finding nothing of interest, except for several pictures of Marissa in a very tiny bikini, he moved on.

Shark entered the kitchen. *So this is how the rich and famous live*, he thought, running his hands along rows of cream-colored cabinets with open plate racks. Two ovens, and the largest refrigerator he had ever seen, took up one entire wall.

The eating area right off the kitchen surprised him. Instead of a formal dining room, eight casual chairs surrounded an oval wooden table. In the center a large silver and glass globe held a white candle nestled in sand and seashells.

Over a matching hutch hung an oil painting that immediately caught his attention. Shark wasn't big on art, but the vivid colors drew him in. It was an outdoor scene of an old woman with a red kerchief on her head, bent over, tending to her flowers. The realism of the sky, trees, and flowers was mesmerizing. It was almost as if he could reach out and pick the purple irises.

Marissa found him there, a very modern man lost in a palette of colors that had ceased to exist.

Chapter Two

Shark turned at her approach. Obviously fresh from a shower, her face scrubbed free of makeup, Marissa was dressed in a pair of white jeans and a V-neck navy pullover, minus what Shark couldn't help thinking of as the crown jewels. Now she wore only gold hoops in her ears and her wedding rings. He thought she looked more beautiful than she had in her elegant dress, and she seemed a little more composed than she had earlier.

"I'm sorry I took so long. I had to call the country club where the reception was going to be held, and the travel agency so they could cancel our honeymoon reservations. I still can't believe any of this." Marissa dropped onto the couch, a short distance from Shark, and stared at the floor. "How can this be both the happiest and the worst day of my life?"

Shark turned slightly to face her. "I can't imagine the emotions you must be experiencing. I can only tell you that I lost someone very close to me, and I wasn't sure I would survive it. But you do. You're never the same, but you get

16

through it, even though it doesn't seem like it now." Shark looked away, swallowing his grief, as he had for all the years since Laura's death.

Marissa's lips trembled on the verge of tears. Shark was afraid that if he didn't keep her moving she wouldn't be able to control her emotions and he wouldn't get the information he needed. "Why don't we walk on the beach while we talk? Maybe the sound of the waves will be comforting," he suggested. Marissa didn't reply, just rose like a robot, and led him out the patio door to the boardwalk, turning left when they reached the beach.

They ambled slowly, Marissa skirting the edge of the water, which was receding. October was always a beautiful month on Hilton Head, breezy and pleasant, with most of the wicked humidity gone, along with the tourists.

The silence lengthened as Shark searched for a gentle way to begin what could only be regarded as an interrogation.

"Detective Morgan, what will happen to the hunter who shot Marcus?" Marissa asked softly, giving him the opening he needed.

Shark paused for a moment, stalling to gather his thoughts before answering Marissa's question. "Look, if I'm going to call you Marissa, why don't you call me Shark."

"Shark?"

"Yeah. That's what everyone calls me."

"Why?"

"Because I spend most of my free time shark fishing. That's why I'm dressed like this today," he said, looking down at his well-worn jeans and scuffed shoes. "And to answer your question, I just don't know. It was remarkably bad luck if it was a stray bullet. Do you know anyone who would want to kill Marcus?"

Marissa gasped, turning to Shark, with what looked to be genuine horror in her wide eyes. "Oh my God! You think someone did this on purpose?"

"We really don't know. That's why we have to conduct a full investigation."

Marissa dropped to her knees as if her legs would no longer support her. Shark was sure she hadn't considered this to be anything but a terrible accident. Until now. He eased himself down on the sand beside her. "Look, I'm not saying it was definitely intentional. At this point I just don't know."

"But who would do such a thing? And on our wedding day. It's too cruel," she said, her voice catching on a knot of unshed tears in her throat.

Shark looked away, uncomfortable with her pain, then turned back and without thinking, gently raised her chin. He felt somehow as if he knew her, even though she only appeared in his living room two nights a week. He forced her to look up at him. "I don't know who could be so cruel, but I intend to find out. If it was a tragic accident, that's one thing. But if it wasn't, then it's my job to find out who did it. And I will."

"So that's why you're here. You're a homicide detective?" She recoiled from his touch as if she had been burned.

"I'm a death investigator. We don't have a homicide department, per se, since there are so few homicides in our jurisdiction. It's my job to investigate all suspicious deaths in the county," he answered matter-of-factly, stung by her rebuff. "So I need to get some background on Marcus, interview lots of people, and see who might have had a motive to kill him. I knew Marcus myself, casually. You can't live in Beaufort County and not have run across Marcus DeSilva. Tell me, how did you two meet?"

Marissa wiped her eyes with the back of her hand, apparently fighting to get her emotions under control. She rose abruptly. "Let's walk," she said, striding out across the beach.

Shark got to his feet, brushed the sand off his pants, and trotted after her.

"I met Marcus at an AIDS benefit at the Hyatt about three months ago. I was covering it for the TV station where I work. I interviewed Marcus on camera. At the end of the evening, he asked if I would join him for a cappuccino. I'd noticed he had a pretty blond on his arm all night, so I declined. He asked me why, and I told him I didn't think his date would approve. When he wanted to know if that was the only reason, I said I thought that was a pretty good one. Then he grinned at me and said he had already sent her home in a cab, so I didn't have any excuse."

"So did you go?"

"Yes. He took me to his house, fixed me a cappuccino, and we talked until sunrise. The next day he sent me three dozen yellow roses. The card was addressed 'To my future wife' and said, 'I fell in love with you at sunrise this morning. Will you marry me? If not, how about dinner at eight?' Then he set about wooing me. Flowers every few days, dinners, dancing, jewelry, sailing on his yacht. Those things were nice, but what really made me fall in love with him was the fact that he made me laugh, every day. Six weeks later I agreed to marry him."

"Sounds like Marcus. He had the reputation that once he set his sights on something, he didn't let anything or anyone stand in his way. Do you know who the blond is he was with that first night?"

"Paige Bishop, the interior decorator. Apparently they had been dating for a few months and I'm afraid she thought *she* was going to be the next Mrs. DeSilva. Do you think she had anything to do with this?"

"I don't know. I'm just trying to figure out who might have wanted him dead. I know Marcus had dated lots of women since his divorce several years ago."

A flock of seagulls, pecking at the remains of a horseshoe crab, forced Shark and Marissa to detour around them.

"Rachel Wells said Marcus's son wasn't at the wedding. Do you know why?" Shark asked, changing direction.

"B.J. and Marcus didn't get along well after the divorce. B.J. was only thirteen and blamed Marcus for the breakup. Apparently he walked in on his dad and his secretary one day, and told his mother. They haven't been close since. But Marcus thought they were beginning to overcome some of the hard feelings, since B.J. went off to college last year. He was really hoping he'd be there today."

"So how do you and B.J. get along?"

"I've only seen him twice. He's up at Clemson. You know, I'm a lot younger than Marcus. In fact, I'm only nine years older than his son. B.J. wasn't very kind to me both times I met him, which infuriated his father. So I guess I'm not really surprised he didn't show up today."

"What about Marcus's business partner, Gene Branigan? How did they get along?"

"Gene is no longer his partner. They had an argument about something right before Marcus and I started dating. Marcus bought him out."

"Do you know what the disagreement was about?"

"No. Marcus never said, and I never asked. I do know Gene called several times recently, but Marcus refused to talk to him. I thought it was kind of odd. I gathered they used to be best friends."

"Tell me about Marcus's sister," Shark said, as he stepped around an oozing jellyfish that had washed ashore.

"I don't know that much about Rachel. She lives in Atlanta, and her husband died a few years ago in some kind of accident. Marcus was her only sibling. Their parents died several years ago. They talked frequently on the phone, but I only met her once before today. Marcus and I were going to a Braves game, and she met us for dinner beforehand."

"Does she work?"

"Her husband owned a large travel agency. I think she has someone who manages it for her, because all she talked about that night at dinner were the charities she's involved with."

Shark stopped and picked up a starfish that had been stranded by the outgoing tide and tossed it back into the water. "Tell me about yourself."

"Not much to tell, really. I grew up in a little town called Hazard, Kentucky. My parents died when I was a senior in high school. I attended the University of Kentucky and got my degree in communications. I made the mistake of marrying a jerk in my junior year of college, and we divorced right after graduation. I was offered a job at a TV station in Lexington covering town meetings and boring stuff like that. But it was at one of those meetings that I met a wonderful man who owned a small horse farm. The attraction was mutual and a few months later we got married. But then he died."

Shark almost stumbled in the sand. He tried to keep all expression off his face as he asked, "What happened?"

"He fell off his horse. I didn't know enough about horses to keep the place going, so I sold everything except our house here in Sea Pines. I'd always loved the island when we visited. A few months after I moved here, I got bored, so I took a job as fill-in news anchor a couple of days a week on the local station. Sometimes when they're shorthanded I cover local events."

"Did you ever meet Marcus when you and your previous husband visited the island?"

"Not that I recall. We usually just stayed close to the beach and ate most of our meals at the restaurants in Sea Pines."

Shark glanced up at the shoreline and realized they had walked quite a distance. "Do you know anything about Marcus's will?" he asked casually.

Marissa looked over at him, her eyes wide with surprise. "No, actually I don't even know if he has one."

"Do you know who his lawyer is?"

"I think Baker and Silverstein handled his business affairs. I don't know if they handled his personal matters as well. Do you think we can turn around and head back? I'm getting really tired."

"Of course."

As they turned, Marissa crossed in front of Shark, so once more she was nearer the ocean.

"So how long did you and Marcus plan to be gone on your honeymoon?"

"Two months. I resigned from the station because Marcus wanted me to be able to pick up and go with him on a moment's notice, whether to the house in Vail, or sailing the Caribbean on his yacht. I've never traveled much, and Marcus wanted to take me to all his favorite places. He particularly liked Greece and Monaco."

"Were you sorry to give up your career?"

"I had mixed feelings. I enjoyed the work, but I was excited about starting my new life with Marcus. I still can't believe he's dead."

Again Shark heard the unshed tears in her voice. "Will you go back to the station?"

"I have no idea. I can't think about that now."

They lapsed into silence as they made their way back up the beach to the house. Shark had run out of questions, although he wasn't sure how much useful information he had gotten.

When they walked into the house, Marissa went straight to the picture on the desk of her and Marcus, studied it a moment, and collapsed onto the couch, tears starting to slide silently down her cheeks.

"Can I get you something to drink?" Shark asked, uncomfortable in his role, but feeling the need to help somehow.

Marissa accepted his clean, but rumpled handkerchief and blew her nose loudly. "Maybe a little iced tea. There's a pitcher in the fridge. And please get something for yourself, a Coke or whatever you want."

When Shark returned carrying the two glasses, he found Marissa staring off into space. He had to call her name twice before she looked up and took the glass from him. He watched her, absently twisting a lock of hair around her fingers as she sipped her tea. He had great difficulty keeping his eyes off that damn mark next to her full mouth. He liked her. She had seemed honest in her answers, and he wondered if they might have become friends under different circumstances.

"Do you have anyone who can stay with you tonight? Maybe Rachel?"

"I don't think so. As you could probably tell, she and I aren't close, and I haven't made a lot of friends here. I have a couple of acquaintances from work, but I think I prefer to be alone. I have several calls to make, and I need to talk to Rachel about the arrangements. I hope she got in touch with B.J. I'm so glad she's taking care of everything. I don't think I could make any decisions right now. Going through it with my last husband was difficult enough. I think I must be a jinx or something. I'm not even thirty yet, and now I've become a widow for the second time."

Shark didn't respond, just let her talk. There was little enough he could say in the face of all her pain.

"I just want to go to sleep so I don't have to think about this anymore. I don't think I can bear it. What am I going to do?"

Shark had no answer for that either. "Are you sure you won't let me call someone to be with you?"

"No, I'll just take a Valium and try to sleep."

"I'll need to talk to you again, but I promise not to call too early in the morning. Thank you for being so cooperative."

Marissa walked with Shark to the front door. He pulled out one of his business cards, turned it over, and wrote his home phone number on the back. "Call me if you think of anything that might shed some light on this. Or if you just need someone to talk to."

"Thank you. Detective Morgan, please find who did this to Marcus."

48751

"I'll do my best." He turned, reluctant to pull his eyes from her sad face, then stepped over the threshold and walked slowly down the stairs.

As soon as he got in the car Shark reached in his T-shirt pocket for a cigarette, and cursed when he remembered he didn't have any. He started the car, then picked up his hand-held tape recorder and began dictating.

At the office he looked up Diane DeSilva's number. Marcus's ex-wife. He spoke with her briefly, and was surprised that she had been unable to locate B.J., despite checking with his roommate and friends.

Where the hell is the kid? Shark wondered, settling in to transcribe his notes into the computer.

Marissa sat listening to the telephone ring unanswered in Rachel's hotel room, when her doorbell rang. She opened the door to find Jason McCalvey, the general manager from WWOJ, standing on the step. She wondered how he had gotten past the guard gate and into the plantation.

"Marissa," he said, stepping inside and pulling her awkwardly into his arms. "I'm so sorry. I came as soon as I heard. You know I'd planned to attend the wedding, but I had a last-minute emergency at the station and I was late getting away. When I got to the church there were police cars everywhere. I couldn't imagine what was going on. When I found out about Marcus, I couldn't believe it. What can I do to help you?"

Extricating herself from his embrace, she walked into the living room and perched stiffly on the couch facing the ocean. Jason followed, sitting close and reaching for her hand.

"I'm not sure there's anything anyone can do right now." Marissa dabbed at her eyes with the tissue clutched in her free hand.

Jason, tall with the slim build of a distance runner, was dressed in an expensive gray suit and white silk shirt. With his salt and pepper hair, he always looked distinguished.

Marissa had never seen him when he didn't look as if he had just stepped off the cover of GQ. Jason had asked her out several times before she'd started seeing Marcus, but she had always refused. She wasn't keen to get involved with someone she worked with, someone who also had a nine-year-old son.

"Marissa, what a tragic accident! I still can't believe it."

"It may not have been an accident. The police just left. They think someone may have murdered Marcus."

"Murdered him? But who would want to kill Marcus? He's one of the most respected businessmen on the island."

"I don't know. I guess that's what the police will try and determine," Marissa said, withdrawing her hand.

"I know you haven't had an opportunity to make a lot of close friends since you moved here, but you can't go through this alone. You need someone to lean on. Let me be that someone. You shouldn't be by yourself right now. I could stay." Though it wasn't a question, Jason waited expectantly.

"Thank you, but I really prefer to be alone right now. Besides, you need to be home with your son. I'll be all right."

"I can get someone to stay with Derek. You know I'd do anything for you."

Marissa couldn't deal with the need in his eyes. "I know, and I appreciate that. But really, I have some calls to make and things to take care of." She stood and moved to the door. Reluctantly, Jason followed.

At the front door, he hesitated. "I know this probably isn't the right time to bring this up, but your job is still there, if you'd like to come back when this is all over. You know how disappointed I was when you decided to quit. Promise me you'll think about it."

"I can't think about anything right now except getting through the next few days, but I appreciate your offer."

"Please let me know as soon as you've completed the funeral arrangements. I want to be there for you," he said, as he leaned over and kissed her on the cheek. "Call me if you need anything, anything at all."

The ringing phone gave Marissa a welcome excuse to hurry Jason out the door. She spoke to Reverend Hart for a few minutes, assuring him she was holding up. After she hung up, she unplugged the phone. She didn't feel like talking to anyone else right now. She went into the kitchen and opened a bottle of wine, a 1991 Merlot, one of Marcus's favorites.

One thing you could say about Marcus, he knew how to pick a good wine.

Chapter Three

Sunday morning Shark called the Westin, set up an appointment to meet with Rachel Wells, and found her at a table out by the pool at 11:00 A.M. Rachel was reading the *Island Packet*, the local newspaper, and Shark noticed the headline announced DeSilva's death.

"Good morning," he said, as he pulled out a chair and joined her. He removed his sunglasses and put them in his coat pocket.

"Detective. I'm having a Mimosa. Would you like one?" she asked curtly. Rachel was pleased to see he was dressed more appropriately today, in beige chinos with a pink Oxford shirt, open at the collar, and a blue blazer.

"No thanks." After an awkward silence, the detective finally said, "In case I didn't say so yesterday, I'm sorry for your loss. How are the arrangements coming?"

"Marcus wanted to be cremated, which we'll do after the body is released to us. We're planning a memorial service, and then the family will scatter his ashes at sea, as he requested."

"Did his son turn up yet? I'd like to talk to him when we're finished here."

The waiter came, and Shark ordered coffee.

"I spoke with Diane several times last night," Rachel replied. "We haven't been able to get in touch with B.J. yet. I called and left messages at his dorm, but he hasn't contacted me. I expect to hear from him soon. Diane and I still don't know how we're going to tell him about his father."

"Where do you think he might be? Do you want me to have the police up there try to find him?"

"Absolutely not. You know how college boys are. He's probably shacked up with some girl for the weekend, or off on some jaunt with his buddies."

"What kind of a car does B.J. drive?"

"He has a black Jeep Cherokee. But please, don't send the police to tell him. Let me or Diane do it."

"I'll give you the rest of the day. If you haven't heard from him by five, I'm putting an all points bulletin out for him."

"That's fair enough. Are you so hot to talk to him because you think maybe Marcus's death wasn't an accident or something?" Rachel asked, her eyes fixed on his.

"As I explained to Mrs. DeSilva, we'll have to look into all possibilities before we can rule out homicide. Why, do you know anyone who would want to kill your brother?"

Rachel paused. "I can't think of anyone, except maybe his previous business partner, Gene Branigan. Gene called me a few weeks ago. He was very upset and said Marcus wouldn't take his calls. He wanted me to intercede on his behalf."

"Did you?"

"Hell no! He made his bed. I figured if Marcus didn't want to talk to him, he must have had a good reason."

Shark acknowledged delivery of his coffee and took a cautious sip. "Do you know what the falling out was about?"

"Not really. I do know Marcus thought Gene might be skimming from the business. Whether he had proof or not, I'm not sure."

"I understand they used to be best friends."

"Yes, since the second grade. They were inseparable as teenagers. They both played basketball and football, even went to the same college as roommates. I was beginning to wonder if they were gay, or something, as much time as they spent together. But then Gene got married about a year before Marcus, and that seemed to separate them a little. After Marcus married Diane they became a foursome. A few years later, Marcus started the development business and hired Gene to be his general manager. At some point he let Gene buy into the business. But after he thought Gene was skimming, he bought out his share and didn't talk about him anymore. I assumed that was the end of their friendship. I know Marcus was really hurt over the whole thing. He never expected that Gene, of all people, would take advantage of him."

"Interesting. Now tell me about Paige Bishop," Shark said, as he drained his coffee cup and looked around for the waiter to signal for a refill.

"I've known Paige for several years. As you probably know, she's the most successful interior decorator on the island. She travels all over the world buying antiques and pieces of art for her clients. She recently redecorated the Hilton in New York, and they want her to update many of their older hotels."

"I'll keep that in mind if I ever want to redo my bungalow, but what I'm really interested in is her relationship with Marcus."

"They started dating several months ago, and seemed to be an item, until Marcus met Marissa. I think Paige thought they would get married. I know she was terribly upset after Marcus stopped calling her. She and I have lunch whenever she's in Atlanta on business. I thought she'd make a perfect wife for Marcus. Attractive, well educated. Then he met

Marissa, and Paige was history." Rachel drained her Mimosa and motioned for the waiter to bring her another.

"So what can you tell me about Mrs. DeSilva?"

"I only met her once before the wedding yesterday, but trust me, once was enough. One morning Marcus called and told me he'd fallen in love with a woman he'd met the night before and that he was going to marry her. I thought he was drunk. He described her as the soul mate he'd been looking for all his life. A few days later, when we talked, he said that he was completely smitten with her and that he still planned to marry her."

"How did you feel about that?"

"I thought he must be going through that male thing men seem to get around fifty. Anyway, a few weeks later they came to Atlanta, and I joined them for dinner. Marissa is attractive enough, but I wasn't really impressed with her. Did you know she grew up in a little town in Kentucky, of all places? A few weeks later, he told me they'd set a date. I told Marcus he should slow down. Live with her if he wanted, but take his time. He said he knew the first night that he wanted to spend the rest of his life with her. I advised him to at least get a pre-nup, but he became furious, told me to mind my own goddamn business. I reminded him how much his divorce from Diane had cost him, but he said Marissa didn't need his money, that she had plenty of her own. Said her last husband had left her well off. After that we didn't talk much about her anymore."

"Were you and Marcus close?"

"Yes, we were. We didn't see each other too often, but we talked on the phone at least once a week and e-mailed back and forth every few days. Marcus was very supportive after my husband died. I don't think I could have gotten through that without him. After the death of our parents there were just the two of us, and we're only four years apart in age. Now there's just me," she said, her voice cracking.

"How did your husband die?"

"In a skiing accident in Austria four years ago."

"Mrs. DeSilva said he owned a travel agency in Atlanta."

"Yes, the main office is in Atlanta but we have six other satellite offices in the surrounding suburbs."

"Did you take over the business after your husband died?"

"I tried, but I found it terribly boring. So I hired someone to run it, and I spend most of my time involved with charity work."

"What was the relationship between Marcus and B.J.?" Shark asked.

"B.J. never forgave Marcus for the divorce. He found out that his father was seeing other women while he was still married to Diane. It caused a lot of problems in their relationship. Marcus kept trying to break down the barriers that B.J. put up, and felt he was making some progress, once B.J. got away from his mother's influence."

Shark asked the waiter to bring him a glass of iced tea. He'd had enough coffee to last the rest of the day. "What can you tell me about Diane, Marcus's ex-wife?"

"They were married for fourteen years. Diane and I always got along well. I was sorry when they divorced. She came out all right financially, got to keep the house in Sea Pines, and Marcus gave her a lump sum payment of two million dollars. She took the money and opened an exclusive dress shop in Shelter Cove. She does well as far as I know. I haven't seen her in about a year."

"Do you know anyone else who might have wanted your brother dead?"

Rachel paused. "It's inconceivable to me that *anyone* would have wanted Marcus dead. Now, if you'll excuse me, I'd like to try and call B.J. again."

"I think that's all for now," Shark said as he stood. "I assume you'll be staying on the island until after the memorial service?"

"Yes, of course." Rachel, too, rose. "Do you have any idea when they'll release Marcus's body?"

"As soon as the autopsy is completed. I'll try and find out for you."

"Thank you. I'd appreciate that," she said, turning abruptly and striding away.

Shark sat back down, wondering if Marcus had been as tough a cookie as his sister. He took out his tape recorder and dictated the highlights of what he had just learned from Rachel Wells. He found it strange that nobody had been able to locate B.J. DeSilva. He clicked off the recorder, took out his cell phone and dialed Marissa's number. Strange, but he already had it memorized.

"Hello," she answered in a quavering voice.

"Hi. It's me, Shark. How're you doing?"

"Not so good. I couldn't sleep and now I have a terrible headache."

"Have you eaten anything today?"

"No. I don't have any appetite. Where are you?"

"I just finished talking with Rachel here at the Westin."

"Has she reached B.J.? I haven't heard anything from her."

"Listen, why don't I pick up a couple of sandwiches and come over and fill you in?"

"You can come over, but you don't have to bring food. I don't think I could eat anything."

"I'll be there in just a few minutes."

Shark stopped at the pizza place in Shelter Cove and picked up a couple of sandwiches and salads. *Maybe she'll at least eat a salad*, he thought. He refused to question his motives. About ten minutes later he arrived on her doorstep and rang the bell.

Marissa answered in a pair of pink sweats. Even with no makeup on and her hair tousled, she took his breath away. "I brought food." He held the bags up for her inspection.

"No, really, I can't . . ."

"When did you last eat?"

She paused for a moment, "Breakfast yesterday, I think."

"Well, that's probably why you have a headache," he said, edging past her and depositing the food on the table right off the kitchen. Marissa slumped into a nearby chair, her head gripped in both hands.

"If I could just get rid of this headache. I've had it all night."

Shark unwrapped the food and placed it in front of her, then sat down and attacked his sandwich. After a couple of minutes she began to nibble a little. As he ate Shark filled her in on some of the things Rachel had said, deliberately leaving out her obvious hostility toward Marissa. By the time he was done she had finished about three-fourths of her sandwich and half the salad. He was pleased to see that color had begun to seep back into her cheeks.

"I wish they could find B.J. I'd hate for him to hear about this on the radio or read about it in the newspaper. That would be a terrible shock."

"I know. When I get back to the office, I'll see if I can get a plate number on his car and put out an alert."

"I can't believe Marcus is going to be cremated. The thought of that gives me chills," she said, a shudder rippling through her body.

"Rachel said that was what he wanted, and then to have his ashes sprinkled at sea."

"I don't know. That's not something we ever talked about."

"I'm not surprised. That's not what you normally discuss when you're planning a wedding."

"Did the deputies find anything in the woods when they searched?" she asked quietly.

"No, nothing. They said there was some trampled grass but nothing that looked recent. And they didn't find any shell casings."

"So what's next?"

"Interview people and find out who has an alibi and who doesn't. Look into the backgrounds of those closest to Marcus to see who might benefit from his death. Talk to his lawyer and see if there's a will. That's all we can do since no one saw anything, and there wasn't any physical evidence at the scene."

With no more legitimate reason to stay, Shark reluctantly headed for the office.

As soon as his car was out of sight, Marissa pulled on tennis shoes, picked up her sunglasses, and let herself out the back door. She decided after she was done walking the beach she would make herself presentable and confront Rachel about the arrangements.

She strolled along beneath a bright blue sky scattered with puffy clouds that looked like marshmallows. The temperature hovered around 75 degrees. Fall was beautiful here, but she did miss the changing of the leaves. The overpowering summer humidity was gone, thank God. She relished the feel of the cool ocean breeze. The beach was almost deserted, and she felt so alone. Marcus had been her only real friend on the island.

A huge brown lab came racing toward her, carrying a wet stick. He dropped it at her feet, then looked up at her expectantly. She picked up the piece of driftwood and heaved it into the water. The dog bounded after it and ran back to his owner.

After Eric, her second husband, died she had been anxious to sell everything and escape to the house in Sea Pines. But she had found making friends on Hilton Head wasn't any easier than any of the other places she'd been.

Marissa gazed out at a shrimp boat hauling in its laden nets. A flock of sea gulls followed the boat in hopes of an easy meal.

Marissa had found there was almost a class system on the island. There were a small number of blacks whose ancestors had lived on the island for years, and a new influx of Hispanics who seemed to work mostly in landscaping and construction. Then there were the food and beverage workers and middle class, many who couldn't afford to live on the island, but commuted here. And there was definitely an "upper crust," which was the crowd Marcus ran with. All they seemed to care about was who had the biggest home and yacht, or who drove the most expensive car. She had been treated like an outsider, until she hooked up with Marcus.

Marissa wondered what she should do now. Should she stay here and wait it out, or go someplace else until things were resolved? Would the police even let her leave with a possible murder investigation underway? She would just have to wait and see how things played out.

After a shower, Marissa dressed in a black pantsuit, picked up the keys to her white Miata, and made her way to the garage. She glanced over at Marcus's gleaming black Porsche. *Maybe I'll start driving that*, she thought as she backed down the drive. *It's really more my style*.

A little after two o'clock, Marissa knocked tentatively on the door to Rachel's hotel room. She knew her sister-in-law didn't approve of her, and had wanted Marcus to postpone the wedding.

When Rachel pulled open the door, the smile died on her face. "Oh, it's you, I was expecting room service."

"Sorry to disappoint you. May I come in?"

Rachel stepped aside. Marissa took in the floor to ceiling windows framing a spectacular view of the ocean, and the hand-painted armoire in the far corner of the suite. *Nothing but the best for our Rachel*, she thought as she seated herself in the overstuffed beige chair.

"Have you been able to reach B.J.?"

Rachel perched stiffly on the matching chair directly across from Marissa. "Yes. He appeared at his mother's house about noon, and she told him the news. Diane said he's very upset."

"Where has he been?"

"I don't know, and I didn't think it was any of my business, so I didn't ask."

After a brief silence Marissa said, "Shark said Marcus wanted to be cremated."

"Shark?" Rachel asked, her brow furrowed as if she were trying to remember where she had met someone named Shark.

"I mean Detective Morgan."

Rachel's upper lip curled in a sneer. "My, my. Sounds like you and Detective Morgan are getting along *very* well. Can't you even wait until Marcus's ashes are scattered before you start picking out your next man? And don't you think he's a little 'common'? But, then, I shouldn't be surprised. After all, so are you."

An icy calm descended over Marissa. She had dealt with plenty of Rachels since Hazard, Kentucky, and there was no longer any need to keep up the pretense that they would ever become friends. "You're just a sore loser, Rachel. Get over it." Marissa rose and turned toward the door. "When are the services? Like it or not, I have a right to be there."

"And don't think I wouldn't love to find a way to keep you out. Anyway, I've arranged for the Island Funeral Home to handle the cremation, and Reverend Hart will hold the memorial service on Wednesday morning at ten."

"Thank you."

"I'm not doing it for you."

Marissa squared her shoulders and stared directly at her sister-in-law. "Send the limo for me," she said over her shoulder, then closed the door softly behind her.

Chapter Four

Shark's office was typical of every small-town sheriff's department: institutional gray walls, brown metal desks, and scuffed worn linoleum. He shared the cramped workspace with his partner, Dell Hassler, who was off for the weekend attending her sister's wedding in Greenville. They were the only two officers assigned to the county death investigator's department. Already they were working on several unsolved murders that had occurred over the last few years, as well as a recent vehicular homicide. They didn't need a high-profile case like Marcus DeSilva's to add to their workload.

The number of deaths in the county had tripled in the past eleven years, in exact proportion to the increase in population in Beaufort County. And that didn't include the influx of visitors every summer, or the new Sun City Hilton Head development that would include ten thousand additional homes when it reached build out. Then there was the Parris Island Marine training base and the Beaufort Naval

Air Station. Things were changing fast in the South Carolina Lowcountry—too fast, as far as Shark was concerned.

And now this. It didn't matter if DeSilva's death was an accident or a homicide. It was his job to investigate, either way. Over the years Shark had learned to rely on his gut—and it told him this case was probably going to get ugly. Time to get at it.

He dialed the State Medical Examiner's Office, hoping the autopsy report would be ready. While he waited, on hold for what seemed like an eternity, he began making a list of people he and Dell would need to interview. Finally someone picked up and agreed to fax a copy as soon as it was off the printer. He learned that the body was being released the following morning.

After hanging up, Shark flipped through the message slips on his desk, stopping when he came to the one from Rachel Wells. B. J. DeSilva had finally turned up at his mother's house.

All right! Shark thought, grabbing his keys. *Maybe a break at last.*

A half-hour later Shark pulled up in front of a three-story gray stucco with circular drive and parking underneath. Several large palm trees and a well-manicured lawn surrounded the home. Diane DeSilva answered the door in beige cargo shorts and a blue oxford shirt. About 5'2" with short blond hair, she looked too young to have a son in college. He noted her trim legs and bare feet. Morgan had interviewed her a few years earlier when her car had been stolen, and he wondered if she would remember him.

She paused when she opened the front door, as if searching for a name.

"Detective Morgan, ma'am. I'm afraid I need to speak to B.J."

"Detective Morgan, of course. I'm sorry I didn't remember your name. Do you really have to talk to my son right now? I've just had to tell him about his father, and he's lying down."

"I promise it won't take long, but I do need to speak to him."

Reluctantly, she motioned him in. "Have a seat in the living room, I'll get him."

Morgan perched on the edge of a burgundy and white sofa and admired the large Oriental rug covering the white pine floor. A field stone fireplace took up one whole wall. He liked the look of the irregular stones. An abundance of green potted plants, all looking as if they had just come from a greenhouse, were scattered throughout the room. Nothing like his straggly cactus at home. Lots of candles on all the tables. Definitely a woman's room.

A few minutes later a tall, muscular young man slouched into the room. Dressed in a Clemson sweatshirt and blue jeans, he, too, was barefoot. B.J. looked a lot like Marcus, but had his mother's eyes and nose. He wore a heavy one-day beard, and his eyes looked bloodshot. He dropped down in one of the chairs and stared at Shark.

"I'm Detective Morgan. I'm very sorry about your father. It must have been quite a shock." Shark watched Diane DeSilva settle into a chair next to her son. "I'm sorry, ma'am, but I need to speak to B.J. privately."

"But I'm his mother."

"Please, we won't be long."

"I guess I don't have a choice," she said, as she rose stiffly and left the room.

B.J. shook his head back and forth. "I just can't believe it. I keep hoping this is a nightmare that I'll wake up from shortly."

"I wish that were the case, but it's not. You up for a few questions?"

Shark watched the boy closely, hoping to judge his truthfulness by his body language. When B.J. didn't reply he plunged ahead. "You didn't attend the wedding. Where were you?"

The boy studied the floor. "I had every intention of going. I left school yesterday morning to drive down for it."

"What happened?"

"See, I had a bet on the Georgia/Florida football game so I stopped in a bar in Columbia to get something to eat and watch the beginning of the game. I left at half time and stopped again in Walterboro to check the score. I guess I had a few beers. Before I realized it the game was over and so was the wedding. I toyed with the idea of showing up at the reception, but decided I didn't need to get into a confrontation with my father, so I just kept bar hopping and drinking. I got pretty tanked, so I pulled into a rest area when I realized I wasn't going to be able to make it home, and slept in the car. I drove on down when I woke up this morning and that's when I found out about Dad."

"Do you remember the names of any of these bars?"

"Not really. It didn't matter as long as they had beer on tap and a big-screen TV."

"You're only what, nineteen, twenty? How did you get served?" Shark asked.

B.J. chuckled. "I haven't been carded since I was sixteen."

Shark wasn't surprised considering his height and build. "I understand you and your father didn't get along very well."

"I hated him for a long time after the divorce. But things were getting a lot better lately."

"How did you feel when you found out he was getting married again?"

"Really surprised. I mean, he had a good thing going chasing a different skirt every few weeks. But after I met Marissa, I could understand. She's only a few years older than I am, and a real looker. I wouldn't mind getting a little piece of that myself."

Shark stared at the boy in the man's body, itching to take him outside and beat that cocky attitude out of him. "Do you know anyone who would want to kill your father?" he asked, reining in the personal emotions that had no place in an interrogation.

"Are you saying you don't think it was an accident?" B.J. couldn't keep the awe out of his voice. After all murder didn't happen to someone you knew, just on TV or in the movies.

"Don't know yet."

"My old man could be a hard ass sometimes, but I can't think of *anyone* who'd want to kill him."

"Okay, that's all for now, but I suggest you think real hard about the names of those bars, or what part of the city they were in. Now, ask your mother to come in for a minute so I can talk to her."

"Sure," B.J. said, as he rose and padded out of the room. A couple of minutes later Diane DeSilva entered carrying two glasses of iced tea.

"Thought you might like something to drink," she said, as she seated herself in the chair B.J. had just vacated.

"Thanks. I just have a couple of quick questions and then I'll be on my way. Do you know who handled Marcus's legal affairs?"

"Baker and Silverstein," she said without hesitation.

"I know they took care of his business stuff, but do they handle his personal things as well?"

"He used them for everything as far as I know. Unless he's changed recently."

"Where were *you* yesterday afternoon?" Shark asked abruptly.

He didn't think she could have faked the total look of shock in her wide blue eyes. "Are you implying I'm a suspect? I thought it was an accident."

"We don't know yet, so in a way, everyone is a suspect until we know exactly what happened."

"I was here, lying down, trying to get rid of a headache."

"Did anyone come by or did you talk to anyone on the phone who can verify that?"

She closed her eyes, her brows scrunched in concentration. "I don't think so. I put the answering machine on when I came home and unplugged the phone in the bedroom. I did call my mother about four o'clock, after I woke up."

"How did you feel about Marcus marrying again?"

"I was fine with it. I'm not one of those ex-wives still pining away for her husband. Marcus was very generous at the time of our divorce. In fact, we seemed to get along better afterwards than when we were still married. We spoke on the phone at least once a month, usually something about B.J. Marcus called about a week ago and asked me to encourage B.J. to come to the wedding. He really wanted him there. I told him I'd try. That's the last time we talked."

Shark drained the last swig of tea and then rose. "Thanks for your time. I think that's all for now. Don't get up. I'll find my way out. And Mrs. DeSilva?" He paused, turning to face her.

"Yes, Detective?"

"Encourage your son to be more specific about where he spent the day his father was killed. It'd be in his best interest to work on an alibi."

Chapter Five

Monday morning Shark called Dell Hassler, his partner, at a little after six o'clock. "Rise and shine, sleeping beauty."

"I'll have you know I've been up for forty-five minutes, and I almost have my face on—just doing my eyebrows now. I read about Marcus DeSilva in yesterday's paper. Figured we'd be having a busy day. What you got so far?"

Shark related what little he knew and briefly filled her in on the interviews he had done. "Meet me at the Hilton Head office once you finish putting on your face. Hey, how was the wedding?"

"About as bad as I expected. Mom and Dad barely spoke to each other, and Dad's new wife was dressed like a sixteen-year-old—all kinds of skin showing, which wasn't pretty, trust me. Of course *I* looked ravishing in my pumpkin-colored bridesmaid's dress. It really complemented my red hair."

Morgan chuckled. "You did say your sister had crappy taste."

"Speaking of which, the groom was so hung over he could barely mumble out his vows. And my sister cried through the whole ceremony—probably because she realized what everyone had been telling her for months, that her husband is an ass. But, hey, I did met a neat guy, so the weekend wasn't a total loss."

"Well, it's about time—maybe it'll improve your disposition a little. Who was the lucky guy?"

"The best man. Handsome, and actually pretty cerebral, too."

"Gonna see him again?" Shark asked as he filled a travel mug with coffee for the road.

"Maybe. He lives in Charleston. Not a doctor like my mother always hoped for, but still a professional. He's an architect."

"And is *he* an ass?"

"Depends on how we're defining the term. Actually, he is kinda cute."

"Well, I'm gonna hit it. Get a move on, girl."

"I'll be about five minutes behind you."

When Shark walked into the satellite office on Hilton Head, he wasn't surprised to find his boss, Sheriff Benjamin Grant, there before him. Six-foot three and well muscled, Grant had been the first black sheriff ever elected in Beaufort County. Immediately following the election, there had been several resignations—all from white officers. But Shark respected the man. He had a criminal justice degree from the University of South Carolina and had been in law enforcement for more than fifteen years. He commanded while rarely raising his voice and was known as a first-rate administrator.

"Morning, Shark. What's happening on the DeSilva case? The press is all over me for information."

"I'm not surprised. Just keep them off my back if you can. You know how well I get along with those vultures. This is going to be a tough one. No physical evidence at the crime scene. Killed by a bullet from a Remington thirty-

thirty, which a lot of deer hunters use. Didn't find anything in the woods, either."

"Any chance it was just an accident?" Sheriff Grant asked as he shuffled through one of several stacks of papers on Morgan's desk.

"Frankly, I don't know, but my gut tells me it was a homicide."

"Anybody have a real good reason for wanting him dead?" The sheriff chewed absently on the tip of his pen.

"There's a son who didn't show up at the wedding and doesn't have much of an alibi, an ex-wife, an ex-partner, and an ex-girlfriend for starters."

"What about the new wife?"

"Too soon to tell. We don't know yet who stands to inherit all those millions."

"Well, follow the money. Love and greed are almost always the best motives for murder. I want you to concentrate solely on *this* case since you've finished with the vehicular homicide. Keep me posted on what you find."

"Will do," Shark said with a little salute.

Dell, looking fresh and feisty after her weekend off, strode in, a large cappuccino in one hand and coffee for Shark in the other. She set the cups down and plopped into the nearest empty chair, throwing her purse and keys on the desk.

"Good morning, sir," she said nodding to the sheriff.

"When are you going to stop being so formal with me?" he asked.

"Never. My mother taught me to respect my elders, sir."

The sheriff grinned at his 5'4" deputy and shook his head. Dressed in khaki slacks, white blouse, and navy blazer, the thirty-year-old looked like someone barely out of high school. But her baby face was deceiving. She was a top-notch investigator, and a whiz on the computer. Where Shark's strength was interrogation, hers was unearthing the facts to build a case. They made a good team.

"Well, I'll let you two get at it," Grant said, walking toward his office.

Shark peeled the lid off the steaming cup of coffee, and for the next few minutes reviewed case notes with his partner.

"I'll work on the details of the will and check out the son's alibi," Dell said when he'd finished. "Who do you plan to talk to next?"

"Gene Branigan, the ex-partner."

"So, what's your impression of the new Mrs. DeSilva?" Dell asked, leaning back in her chair.

"Beautiful, talented, reacted as I would have expected in the situation. You've probably seen her on TV. She does the news on WWOJ two nights a week," Shark said, averting his eyes and putting his notebook back in his pocket.

"No! Tell me it's not the lady with the thing on her face, the one you've been carrying on about for the last month!"

"Well, actually it is. And I haven't been carrying on! I just casually mentioned a time or two that I thought she was kind of attractive."

"Bull! You've had the hots for her since the first time you saw her on TV. The man who avoids watching anything but ESPN has become a news junkie. Coincidence?"

"Can we change the subject here and get back to work?"

"By the way, speaking of your love life, did you have another date with *la femme fatale* this weekend?"

"Cute. No, she's a little too *high maintenance* for me. Wants to live in my pocket whenever we're not working. And she's too into the arts and cocktail scene for my taste. You know I hate those things. But worst of all, she doesn't like to fish!"

"Oh no, the cardinal sin! You know, a little culture wouldn't hurt you, Shark."

"Can we quit discussing my lack of couth and get back to work?" Shark reached for his notes, turning his back to Dell.

"Yes, Master," she quipped with a grin, and picked up the phone.

"Mr. Branigan, thank you for agreeing to see me this morning," Shark said, as the waitress at the Hilton Head Diner put a glass of iced tea in front of him and a cup of coffee in front of Gene Branigan.

"Just call me Gene." Marcus DeSilva's ex-partner was his exact opposite: short, balding, a former athlete, gone to seed. "I figured you'd be wanting to talk to me since Marcus and I were friends and partners for a number of years. I still can't believe he's dead."

"When did you and Marcus last speak?" Shark asked as he watched Gene fidget nervously with his spoon.

After a short silence, Gene answered, "In August. I'd tried to reach him several times recently, but he wouldn't take my calls. I guess you've heard we had a falling out. I was trying to patch things up. We'd been friends almost our whole lives, and it didn't seem right that a business disagreement should destroy that friendship."

"What kind of disagreement?"

Branigan squirmed in his seat, avoided Shark's eyes, and took a sip of coffee. "I did something really stupid. I guess I might as well tell you about it, because I'm sure you'll find out anyway."

He took a deep breath and stared out the window, as if gathering his thoughts, then turned back to Shark. "I was heavy into the stock market. Did a little day trading on the Internet, too. I bought a large amount of stock on margin, expecting it to increase dramatically in a few days. See, I had this friend who gave me this tip, said the stock would blow out its earnings report and should run up several points. Well, it did—for two days—and then there was some question about the company's accounting procedures. So, it took a nose-dive in a matter of hours, before I could get out. I had to meet my margin call. I couldn't figure out any other way to come up with the money so I *borrowed* it from the company, with the full intention of putting it back before anyone caught on. But the market went soft, and I had trouble raising the cash. I don't know how Marcus discovered it because he normally didn't pay a lot of attention to the books. Maybe the accountant questioned him about the transaction, or maybe Marcus just stumbled across it. He never said. Anyway, he stormed into my office, demanding the money. I didn't have it."

"So what happened?" Shark asked.

"We had a big blow up. I told him I would pay it back as soon as I could, but he wouldn't listen. He was like a crazy man. Said he would have trusted me with his life, stuff like that. To make a long story short, he insisted on buying out my shares in the development company, and I ended up using most of the proceeds to pay back what I'd borrowed. Marcus refused to talk to me after that. I called him several times, hoping to resume at least our friendship, but he wouldn't take my calls." Branigan was almost in tears.

Shark took a drink of his tea to give DeSilva's ex-partner time to compose himself. "Do you know anything about Marcus's will?"

"Not really. He was pretty close-mouthed about his personal affairs."

"Do you know anyone who would have a motive for murdering him?" Shark asked, looking directly into Branigan's eyes.

"Murder? I thought it was an accident," Gene said, almost dropping his coffee cup.

"We just don't know yet. We're exploring all the possibilities. So can you think of anyone who might have wanted Marcus dead?"

Gene stared off into space and after a moment said, "The guy Marissa used to date before she started seeing Marcus was in Reilly's one night, really bad-mouthing him. Said Marcus threatened him, or something."

Shark sat up a little straighter. "What's the guy's name?"

"Neil Fulton. You know, the big hotshot owner of Magnolia Realty. Always in the million dollar club, or something, every year for selling so much property. I'm sure you've seen his ads in the newspaper."

"I think I know who you mean. What did he say, exactly?"

"Something about a telephone call and Marcus threatening him. He was pretty drunk, and so was I. Sorry, that's all I remember."

"Where were you Saturday afternoon?"

Branigan's face blanched, and a light sheen of sweat broke out on his forehead. Shark didn't think it was from the cold coffee congealing in his cup. "Well, I was just running errands. You know, the grocery store, the liquor store, stuff like that." All of a sudden Shark couldn't get Branigan to make eye contact with him. "I, uh, also drove out to that new housing development going up just off the bridge, The Village at Old Towne, I think it's called. I spent some time there just going through a few of the houses that were under construction, checking out their floor plans. You know."

Shark was familiar with the development. It wasn't very far from the church where the wedding had been held. "Did anybody see you out there? Like when you were going through the models and all?" Shark took a pen out of his pocket and started making notes.

"They weren't really models. Just shells under construction. And I don't remember seeing anyone."

"What grocery store did you stop at?"

"Publix. And I went to the liquor store in Main Street."

"What time were you at the grocery store?"

"I don't know. Early afternoon. The stuff I bought wasn't perishable, so I didn't have to worry about getting it home and into the fridge."

"Did you pay with a credit card?"

"No. Cash."

"What about at the liquor store?"

"I think I was there around four or four-thirty. Something like that. I did pay with a credit card there. But surely you can't think I would kill Marcus? He was my best friend," Gene said, tears welling again in his eyes.

"It's been known to happen. Especially when best friends have a falling out. I think that's all for now, Mr. Branigan. But I may need to talk to you again. Thanks for agreeing to meet with me. I'll be in touch," Shark said as he stood, picked up the check, and headed to the cashier.

He swung out into traffic and headed straight to the supermarket. Something about Branigan didn't fit right. He appeared genuinely upset by Marcus's death, but he had seemed damned uncomfortable when asked about his activities on Saturday afternoon.

Shark parked in the crowded Publix lot, walked inside, and asked to speak to the manager. With the surprised man's permission he spoke briefly with the cashiers on duty who had also been on the Saturday afternoon shift. None of them seemed to recognize Branigan's name. He realized he needed a picture. He took down the addresses and phone numbers of the two who were off.

Next, Shark swung by Main Street Liquors, practically across the street. The clerk, Randy Paulsen, said he knew who Gene was. "He usually comes in a couple of times a month. Likes the fancy wines. Even buys a case occasionally. I was kinda surprised when he only bought a bottle of Glenfiddich Saturday. Figured maybe it was a gift, or something, because I don't ever remember selling him scotch before." He dug out a copy of the credit card receipt for Saturday. Gene Branigan's total came to $45.38, and the time on the receipt said 4:59 P.M.

Plenty of time to shoot Marcus and get back here, Shark thought. "Anything else you can tell me?" he asked.

"Just that I thought Gene seemed kinda upset about something," Randy Paulsen replied. "He usually wants to know what new wine we've gotten in, and he reads all the labels and takes forever picking something out. But Saturday he went straight for the scotch and didn't even ask me about wine at all. And he was pale and kinda sweaty. I even asked him if he was sick."

Shark filed these impressions away, along with all the other information he'd gathered in this second full day of an investigation that still had more questions than answers.

Chapter Six

Shark hurried to the office to share with Dell what he had learned and to see what she had found out about the will. She was just hanging up the phone as he plopped down in front of her desk.

"Maybe we have our first viable suspect," Shark said excitedly. He repeated what he had learned from Gene Branigan and his conversation with the liquor store clerk. "I stopped at Publix, but no one recognized his name. Pull Gene's picture from the Department of Motor Vehicles so we can take it over to Publix and see if anyone remembers his face. Two of the cashiers who worked Saturday were off today, but I got their addresses and phone numbers. The bit about being at that development, The Village at Old Towne, puts him in the vicinity. I think we need to check that out, too. Maybe some of the workmen out there can pin the time down for us. Oh, and Gene said Marissa dated a guy by the name of Neil Fulton before she started seeing Marcus, and Gene overheard him in a bar one night saying that Marcus had threatened him."

"Did she mention Neil Fulton to you when you questioned her?"

"No. But she had just seen her husband murdered, and I was throwing a lot of questions at her. I'll ask her about him, don't worry."

"I'll run out to the development and follow up on the Publix thing," Dell said, making a note to herself.

"What did you find out about the will?"

"Maybe we can add to your suspect list. Marcus changed his will just ten days ago. He left seventy-five thousand dollars to his housekeeper, Mrs. Rosa Gonzales, a hundred thousand to the Self Family Arts Center, and the same amount to the Access Network, which is a service organization for HIV patients, and fifty thousand to the Beaufort County Library. His sister, Rachel, gets five hundred grand."

"What about B.J.?"

"He gets a cool two million outright and one-half the proceeds from the sale of the business, if he decides not to take it over, and the remainder of the estate goes to his spouse. If Marissa is deceased, her share of the estate goes to the son, and if B.J. dies, then his proceeds go to Marissa. The new Mrs. DeSilva inherits a fortune—which sounds like a pretty good motive for murder to me."

"What about the previous will?"

"It left the same for the housekeeper and the charitable donations, but the sister got one million and B.J. got the rest."

Shark paused. "What if B.J. didn't know his father had changed his will and wanted to bump him off before he had a chance to include Marissa? That would be a pretty good motive as well, don't you think?"

"Or maybe Rachel had someone get rid of her brother, not knowing he had already changed it. Maybe she thought he would take her out of the will completely, once he got married."

"See if you can find out if she has any financial problems. Maybe her business is in trouble," Shark said, jotting down notes.

"Will do. I think we need to dig a lot deeper into all of them, as well as Gene Branigan."

"Anyway, Marissa implied her previous husband left her pretty well off when he died, so I'm not sure she would need Marcus's money."

Dell raised her eyebrows. "She had another husband who died? Tell me more about that. Are we dealing with a *black widow* here?"

The burger Shark had wolfed down in thirty seconds flat for lunch was turning to a cold lump in the pit of his stomach. "Her last husband fell off a horse. He owned some kind of fancy stable. That's about all I know."

"People who own horses are usually pretty skilled riders. And he just happens to fall off his horse? Doesn't that sound a little suspicious to you?"

As much as Shark hated to admit it, he said, "Well, maybe. But it could have just been an accident. They do happen, you know."

"I'll see what I can dig up," Dell said with a glint in her eye.

"Let me give Marissa a call and see about picking up a key to Marcus's office."

She answered on the first ring. "Marissa, this is Detective Morgan. My partner and I need to go through Marcus's office. Do you have a key?"

"Yes, there's an extra one in the desk drawer."

"Good. We'll be by in a few minutes to pick it up."

A short time later Shark rang the bell as Dell looked around and whispered softly, "Wow, I'm impressed."

Marissa answered the door in blue jeans and a white turtleneck. She smiled at Shark and then sobered when she saw Dell standing behind him. Shark made the introductions, watching as they checked each other out, the way women do.

Shark was right, she is beautiful, Dell thought.

After a short silence Marissa invited them into the foyer and handed Shark the key.

"Does anyone else have a key to the office?" he asked.

"Just the cleaning lady and Marcus's accountant. Tim Silvers always goes to Marcus's office to do his work since Marcus complained about having to carry everything over to Tim's."

"Do you know if Gene Branigan still has a key?" Dell asked.

"No. Marcus changed the locks when Gene left."

"I'll drop this off after we're finished." Dell preceded him out the door, and Shark turned back to ask, "Do you know if B.J. has a key?"

"I have no idea."

Marcus's office was in the Courtyard Building at the south end of the island near the entrance to Sea Pines Plantation. The decor was much more spartan than they'd expected. Topographic surveys and a model of a development, covered a half-dozen tables scattered around the big, open room. In one corner stood a large mahogany desk and a high-backed black leather chair with two smaller matching chairs in front. Six filing cabinets were banked against the left wall. The desk was clean, no papers marring its smooth surface. The computer stood silent. About what you'd expect when someone planned to be away for an extended period. Shark was drawn to a picture of Marissa in a long black dress, split to mid-thigh, a choker of diamonds at her throat.

"You want the desk or the filing cabinets?" Shark asked Dell, already knowing what her answer would be.

"I'll start with the desk. I'm afraid you won't be able to keep your eyes off that picture of the widow woman, and you might miss something. Anyway I'll get a lot farther with the computer than you will."

Shark gave her a dirty look and pulled out the top drawer of the first filing cabinet. "This could take days."

"You're right about that," Dell said, as she settled in and pulled open the center desk drawer.

Four hours later, they were sprawled in the two chairs in front of Marcus's desk. "The only thing of significance I found was this file on Coastal Development. They've been after Marcus to sell them a large parcel of land he owns out on Highway 278 that adjoins theirs, where they plan to build a shopping center and housing development. But it looks like Marcus planned a project of his own out there. Coastal kept increasing their offer, and even said they'd be willing to buy his whole damn company, if it would cement the deal. We're talking major bucks here," Shark said, as he propped his feet up on the corner of Marcus's desk. "What about you?"

"Looks like cash flow wasn't a problem. The business checking account balance is seven hundred forty-nine thousand. His latest development, Tall Pines, is almost completed. That's the model over on the table. He owns multiple tracts of land on Highway two seventy-eight. There are several rough drafts for two more developments he planned as well. Nothing raised any red flags."

Shark was silent for a couple of minutes, then asked, "So do you think the development guys want his land so bad they would knock him off and hope to buy it from the grieving widow?"

"Hard to say. I've certainly heard of stranger things. I'll start stroking the computer keys when we get back to the office and see what I can come up with."

"I'll drop you off, then return the key to Marissa, see how she reacts to the contents of the will," Shark said, as he reluctantly removed his feet from the desk and stretched.

"Are you *sure* you don't want me to go with you? I don't think you can be very objective when it comes to the mole that needs to be kissed lady," Dell teased.

"I'll be just fine, thank you. I'm not the one who falls into bed with someone she's just met."

"You're just jealous I got laid last weekend, and you didn't. I know a willing coroner whose number I can give you."

"Enough about Anna! Let's hit a drive-thru and pick up a sandwich. I'm starved."

Forty-five minutes later Shark stood in front of Marissa's door, his finger on the bell. When he didn't get an answer, he tried again. Still nothing. As he turned and started down the steps, the door suddenly opened. He turned to find Marissa in a white terrycloth robe, a white towel wrapped around her head.

"Sorry, I was in the shower. Please, come in."

Shark retraced his steps. "I wanted to drop off the key and talk to you for a few minutes."

Clutching the front of her robe, Marissa said, "Just give me a minute to get dressed. Make yourself comfortable."

Ten minutes later Marissa returned fully clothed, her hair dry and pulled back in a ponytail. She looked like a college girl. She had on the same tight jeans as the last time he'd seen her, but with a red silk blouse now. It contrasted well with her dark hair.

"Sorry to keep you waiting. I just got back from a walk on the beach. Windy out there today. I felt as if I had sand everywhere."

"Not a problem," he said, amazed and frightened at the same time at the effect she had on him.

"Would you like something to drink? I was about to have a glass of iced tea."

"That sounds great. Do you need any help?"

"No thanks. Let's sit on the porch. It's such a beautiful day, and this house seems so empty without Mrs. Gonzales and Marcus. I keep expecting him to come racing in the door." Her lips trembled and she looked quickly down at the floor, before escaping to the kitchen.

When she returned a few minutes later, she was back in control. "Did you find anything at the office?" Marissa asked, handing him a glass.

"Frankly, not much. Just a couple of things to check out. But I do want to ask you about something else."

"What's that?"

"Prior to hooking up with Marcus, did you go out with anyone else here on the island?"

"I had a half dozen dates with a guy named Neil Fulton, a realtor."

"Tell me about that."

"Not much to tell really. I met him one day when I was walking on South Beach, right after I moved to Sea Pines. We exchanged a few words and kept running into each other on the beach, which wasn't surprising since he owned an oceanfront home there. He was recently divorced, and we went out to dinner a few times. That's about it."

"How did he react, when you started seeing Marcus?"

"Actually, he was pretty pissed. You would have thought he owned me or something."

"Why do you say that?"

"He kept calling and leaving messages on my answering machine for weeks after I stopped seeing him."

"When did you last hear from him?"

"About a week after I moved in with Marcus. He called and left another message. When Marcus and I came in from the theater and he heard Neil's message, he was furious. He called and read him the riot act, and I haven't heard from Neil since. Do you think he had something to do with this?"

"I don't know, but apparently he was overheard in a bar saying Marcus had threatened to kill him. Did you hear Marcus say anything like that?"

"No. I had gone upstairs to change my clothes when he called Neil."

Shark took a sip of his tea, then took a deep breath and studied her face as he revealed the contents of the will. Her shock seemed totally genuine.

"I can't believe it. I thought he would have left everything to B.J. He never said anything to me about changing his will. Like I said before, I didn't know for certain that he had one. Now people will think I killed him for his money!"

"Not necessarily."

"Oh, I know how people gossip. It was awful after Eric died. I could hear his friends whispering about the money, speculating. I can't go through that again, the pointing and the silent accusations. I wish he had left everything to B.J.," she wailed.

Shark rose quickly, and laid a comforting hand on her trembling shoulder. "Take it easy. Just because you stand to inherit the bulk of Marcus's fortune doesn't make you a murderer in everyone's eyes."

"And what about in your eyes? Doesn't it make *you* suspicious of me?" she asked, looking up at him imploringly.

He wished he could reassure her. She looked so damn vulnerable. He wanted to take her in his arms and protect her. But honesty was another of his annoying habits. "Me, I'm suspicious of everyone. It goes with the job."

It was not the answer Marissa was hoping for. She quickly looked away, as Shark resumed his seat. "Well, I'm glad he left something to Mrs. Gonzales," she said. "She's a nice lady and has been with him for many years. The money will make her life a lot easier. Does she know yet? About Marcus?"

"I doubt it. But we do need to contact her as soon as possible. Do you have an address for her in Uruguay?"

"She writes to a sister there. I think I can find the information in her room. Excuse me. I'll go look."

Marissa returned a few minutes later and handed him a piece of paper with an address and phone number on it. "Thanks," he said as he slipped it in his pocket.

"By the way, while you were going through the office did you find anything relating to a company called Coastal Development?"

Shark's head jerked up. "As a matter of fact I did. Why?"

"A man named Daniel Lawrence called this afternoon, and said Marcus had agreed to sell him some land out on Highway two seventy-eight. He also told me they were in negotiations to buy the business as well. He said he was sorry to hear about Marcus's accident, but that the offer still stood, and he would like to come by and discuss it with me in a week or two. I told him I couldn't even think about anything like that right now."

"That's real interesting. According to the information in the file we found, Marcus had refused to sell them either the land or the business."

"Do you think it means anything?" Marissa asked.

"I don't know, but it looked like big bucks were involved. Dell and I'll get right on it." Shark paused in the foyer and turned to face her. "So how are *you* doing?"

"As well as can be expected, I guess. I thought Marcus and I would spend the rest of our lives together. Instead we had just a few months. I felt my life was finally on track. Now I have to start thinking again about where I want to go and what I'm going to do."

"Do you think you'll stay here?"

"I don't really know. All I can think about now is getting through the next few days. I keep thinking about Marcus being cremated tomorrow, and it's almost more than I can bear. I dread the memorial service on Wednesday and then having to spread his ashes at sea. Will you be there?"

"Yes. Dell and I'll both be at the memorial service. Now I've got to go. I'll talk to you soon. And remember you can call me *anytime*."

Shark stopped by the office and handed Dell the phone number and address of Mrs. Gonzales. "I think you should be the one to call her. She may be more comfortable talking to a woman."

"Okay. I'll try and get through right now. I have no idea what time it is down there, do you?"

"Not a clue."

Dell dialed all fifteen numbers, expecting there to be a delay, and was surprised when the phone started ringing almost immediately.

"*Hola*," a female voice said.

"Rosa Gonzales, *por favor*," Dell replied in her best high-school Spanish.

"*Un momento.*"

Dell could hear rapid Spanish being spoken in the background.

"*Hola,*" another female voice said.

"Rosa Gonzales?"

"*Si.*"

"*Habla inglas?*" Dell prayed.

"Yes. Who is this, please?" Mrs. Gonzales asked hesitantly.

"I'm Deputy Hassler with the Beaufort County Sheriff's Department."

"Why you call Rosa?"

"I have some bad news for you. Your employer, Marcus DeSilva, died on the day of his wedding."

"Oh no! *Señor* DeSilva dead? Accident?"

"We don't know. He was shot on the steps of the church. It could have been an accident from deer hunters in the woods across the road from the church, or it could have been murder. That's what we're trying to find out."

"*Señor* DeSilva shot? *Santa Maria, Madre de Dios*," she said.

"Mrs. Gonzales, I'm really sorry, but I need to ask you some questions."

"Anything to help *Señor* DeSilva," she said, composing herself a little.

"Do you know anyone who might possibly want to hurt Mr. DeSilva?"

"No, no hurt. Good man."

"You've worked for him for a long time."

"*Si*, many years. He good to Rosa."

"Mr. DeSilva's previous business partner, Gene Branigan, what can you tell me about him?"

"*Mucho* good friends, like brothers for a long time. Then big fight. *Señor* Gene no longer come."

"I understand that Mr. Branigan called recently to speak to Mr. DeSilva."

"*Si*, three or four times, but *Señor* DeSilva would no talk."

"Did that upset Mr. Branigan?"

"*Si, mucho* mad, say bad words, so Rosa hang up."

"Did Mr. Branigan ever come to the house and try to see Mr. DeSilva after the fight?"

"*Señor* Gene no come after fight."

"Okay. What about Rachel, Mr. DeSilva's sister? Did she and her brother get along very well?"

"Talk on phone and computer. No see very often. She come few months ago and ask for *mucho dinero*."

Dell sat up straighter in her chair. "She asked Mr. DeSilva for money?"

"*Si*. Could hear loud talk in living room last time she come."

"What did Mr. DeSilva say?"

"He say give little money, no big."

"Then what happened?"

"She cry and go in car. No see after that."

Changing focus, Dell asked, "How did B.J. and his father get along?"

"Bad boy. Mean to papa."

"How was he mean?"

"Talk bad words to papa for long time. Not so much lately."

"Did he ever ask his father for money?"

"Rosa not know. *Señor* DeSilva *mucho* love B.J. Want him to come work in business after school."

"What can you tell me about Mrs. DeSilva?"

"Bad woman. No like."

"Why?"

"She no nice to Rosa."

"How was she not nice?"

"Throw clothes on floor. Make big messes for Rosa to clean up. Nice to Rosa when *Señor* around but not when he gone. Rosa tell *Señor* DeSilva, woman no good for him."

"What did he say?"

"He just laugh. Say *mucho amor.*"

"Did you ever hear them talking about money or a will?"

Rosa paused for a minute. "No hear talk about *dinero.*"

"Mrs. Gonzales, Mr. DeSilva left you some money in his will. I'll give his attorney your phone number, and I'm sure he'll contact you soon."

"*Muchas gracias.* Help Rosa?"

"If I can."

"Ask *Señora* DeSilva to send Rosa's things."

"Sure. Is there anything else you can tell me that might help our investigation?"

There was a long pause. Dell began to wonder if the connection had been broken. Then Mrs. Gonzales said, "*Señor* DeSilva mucho mad on phone when man call for *Señora.* Talk bad and shout. Say kill him."

"Do you know who this man was?" Dell asked.

"No, but man talk to *Señora* when *Señora* not home."

"He didn't give you a name when he called?"

"No, no name."

"Well thanks for answering my questions. I'm really sorry about Mr. DeSilva."

Dell hung up the phone and looked down at the notes she had made. So Rachel had asked Marcus for money, B.J. and his dad didn't get along, and another man had been calling Marissa. And Marcus had threatened to kill him. *Wow! That was one long-distance call that had been worth the money.* She couldn't wait to fill Shark in.

Chapter Seven

Tuesday morning Shark arrived at the Hilton Head office and found Dell already at the computer. They reviewed what she had learned from Mrs. Gonzales.

"Sounds like I need to have a conversation with Neil Fulton. I'll be back in a little while."

Shark walked into Magnolia Realty and Business Brokers and flashed his badge at the petite redhead at the reception desk. "I need to speak to Neil Fulton."

"Mr. Fulton is with a client right now. He should be finished shortly. Please have a seat, and I'll let him know you're here, as soon as he's free."

Shark sank into the soft floral sofa and looked around. The cream-colored walls were covered with several paintings that looked expensive. He knew that Fulton was a high flier. Hilton Head Island seemed to be full of people who tripped over more money in a year than he would probably make in a lifetime. He had seen Fulton's ads in the newspaper and knew he specialized in selling oceanfront homes, and he had recently become a business broker as well. *Let's* *see, a 7% commission on a two million–dollar house, and that's cheap for oceanfront these days, is a cool $140,0000. You didn't have to sell many of those before you're rolling in the dough.*

"God, I should have gone into real estate," Shark muttered softly.

"Mr. Fulton can see you now. Go down this hall, and it's the last door on the right."

Shark knocked and walked in. Neil Fulton rose behind the desk. He was tall with an athletic build, and was impeccably dressed. Handsome as a male model, his voice carried the smooth tones of a professional salesman. "Officer, how can I help you?"

"I'm Detective Morgan, and I need to talk to you about Marcus DeSilva." Shark watched the color drain from Fulton's face.

"Have a seat," he said, dropping back into his chair. "That was a terrible tragedy, but I'm not sure how I can help you."

"I understand you were dating Marissa DeSilva before she started seeing Marcus."

"Yeah, we had a few casual dinners, that's all," he said, looking down at the desk.

"How did you feel when she started seeing Marcus?"

Neil Fulton paused before answering. "Frankly I was disappointed. I thought perhaps, given more time, that Marissa and I would have gotten closer. She is a beautiful woman, as I'm sure you've noticed."

"Were you in love with her?"

"I was very fond of her, but I'm not sure I'd call it love."

"But you *did* call it love on the messages you left on her answering machine," Shark said, throwing it out, not really knowing if it was true.

Neil Fulton's head jerked up. "Well, you know how it is. Women like to hear the *L* word. I might have exaggerated my feelings a little bit. I thought she was making a mistake hooking up with a guy like DeSilva. I'm sure you know his reputation as a womanizer. I just didn't want to see Marissa get hurt." Fulton continued to avoid eye contact with Shark, fiddling nervously with things on his desk.

"Tell me about the last conversation you and Marcus had."

"Oh, he was pissed. Threatened to beat the hell out of me, and other schoolyard bully crap like that, if I ever tried to see Marissa or contact her again."

"Did he threaten to kill you?"

Neil Fulton squirmed in his chair, rearranging the perfect crease in his black worsted trousers. "I think he may have mentioned that in the conversation."

"Did you take him seriously?"

"Let's just say I decided she wasn't worth the hassle."

"Where were you last Saturday afternoon?" Shark asked abruptly.

"Why, am I a suspect?" he asked, finally looking directly at Shark.

"Everyone is, at the moment."

"Then I guess I'm in trouble. I was here at the office, alone, catching up on some stuff."

"Can anyone verify that?"

"Not unless you can figure out a way to get a statement from Rufus, my dog."

Shark waited to see if Fulton would fill the silence. Finally he asked, "Did you talk to anyone on the phone?"

Shark watched the look of confidence return to Neil's face. "Yes, I did make a couple of calls to clients."

"About what time?"

"I don't know for sure, but I can give you their names and phone numbers."

Shark took down the information, thanked Fulton for his time, and headed back to the office. He found Dell still sitting in front of the computer. She listened with interest as he gave her a quick synopsis of the interview. "So check his office phone records and see when the calls were made."

"That should be easy enough to do. I'll take care of that today. By the way, I pulled pictures of B.J. and Gene Branigan off the DMV records. I figured you'd need one of the kid to check out his alibi in Columbia and Walterboro. I'll take the one of Branigan over to Publix later."

"Good."

"I've already found a little information on Coastal Development. CEO is Daniel Lawrence, and they're a major player in shopping center and housing developments all over the country. Their last yearly report seemed to be in order, and it appears they have a sufficient amount of operating capital. The company is privately held, and they've been around for about fifteen years. I'll see what else I can find out. By the way, do you know Marissa's last name before she married DeSilva? I want to start checking out the death of her last husband."

"Langford was what she used on TV, but I don't know if that was her last husband's or her maiden name. Once you get as much info as you can on Coastal Development, we'll give Lawrence a call. He contacted Marissa yesterday and told her that, before Marcus died, he had agreed to sell them his business. Told her they would still like to do the deal."

"So Lawrence already contacted the widow. Interesting."

"Yeah, I thought so too."

"You said you wanted to talk to Reverend Hart this morning. Need me to go along?"

"Sure, if you like. Maybe you'll pick up something I don't. I'll give him a call and see what time is good for him."

At eleven o'clock Shark and Dell walked in the side entrance of the church and made their way to Reverend Hart's office. When they entered, they were surprised to find a woman, probably in her early thirties, leaning over the minister, both of them apparently engrossed in the papers spread out on the desk. Their eyes were drawn immediately to her black eye and the ace wrap on her right wrist.

Reverend Hart introduced her as Jo Parker, and explained that she was a church volunteer who did office work for him. "Detective Morgan, I don't believe I've met your partner."

Dell offered her hand to the pastor. Jo quickly excused herself and almost ran from the room.

"Reverend, we just need to ask you a few questions. I assume you've had an opportunity to replay the events of Saturday over in your mind. Did you think of anything else that might be helpful?" Shark asked.

"You're right. I've gone over it a hundred times in my head, but I haven't come up with anything."

"What can you tell us about Marcus? Has he been a member of your congregation for a long time?" Dell asked.

"About eight years." Reverend Hart absently fanned the pages of a well-worn bible.

"Would you say the two of you were close?"

"If you're asking, did he discuss private matters with me, the answer is no. He was always very generous with his monetary contributions, and even paid for half of the new roof last year, but he wasn't involved as a deacon or with church committees. And I never did any counseling with him. I *was* rather surprised when he told me he was getting married again."

"Why is that?" Shark asked.

"Oh, nothing in particular. He just had a certain reputation. I met with him and Marissa a few times to discuss the wedding details. Other than that he was only at church a few times a year, like on Easter and Christmas."

"What about Mrs. DeSilva? Would you share any impressions of her you got during the meetings?" Dell asked.

"Marissa seemed bright and friendly, but I sensed a certain loneliness in her. She said her parents were deceased, and there were no siblings. She briefly mentioned the loss of her last husband. I don't think she had any real close friends."

"What gave you that impression?" Shark asked.

"She said there might be a few people from her work at the ceremony, but that almost all the guests would be family and friends of Marcus."

"What about the two of them, together?" Dell asked.

"It was obvious that Marcus was deeply in love with her. He rarely took his eyes off her and was always holding her hand—touching her arm, as we talked. He seemed happier than I've seen him in years. I don't know what else I can tell you."

"Well, I appreciate your taking the time to talk to us. If you think of anything else, please give me a call," Shark said, as he handed Reverend Hart his business card.

They walked out of the office and found Jo Parker busily typing at a computer workstation crammed into the tiny reception area. She didn't look up. "Excuse me. Could you show me where the ladies' room is?" Dell asked with a reassuring smile. "I get so turned around in here."

"I'll wait for you in the car," Shark said, in response to the almost imperceptible nod of Dell's head. He knew she'd gone to the can right before they left the office, and she had iron kidneys. She always outlasted him on a stake out. He knew she was up to something.

When the two women had walked far enough down the hall to be out of earshot of the Reverend's office, Dell put her hand gently on Jo's. "I really don't need the ladies' room. I just wanted to talk to you in private. Who beat you up?"

Jo's hand went automatically to her swollen left eye. "I . . . I fell off a bicycle," she stammered.

"I don't think so. Hurt your wrist maybe, but you don't get a shiner like that falling off a bike," Dell said softly. "You get injuries like that from someone using you as a punching bag." Jo twisted the cheap gold band on her third finger. "If your husband, or anyone else in your family, is abusing you, I can help. All you have to do is *ask*. I can get you into a shelter. Here's my card. I'm going to write my home phone number on the back. You can call me night or day. No one deserves to be treated like this, and it's *not* your fault. Please call me and let me help you."

Jo shrank back against the wall as Dell pushed the business card into her hand. "Really, it's not what you think."

"Just keep the card and remember you can call me. There are shelters where you'll be safe." She left Jo Parker huddled in a corner, a position she was probably all too familiar with.

Dell threw herself into the front seat and slammed the door behind her.

"What was that all about?" Shark asked, putting the unmarked car into gear.

Dell exhaled deeply. "Let's just say, I don't think she got that black eye falling off a bicycle as she claims. I gave her my card, but I'm not holding my breath she'll call. Whoever is beating her, has her intimidated."

Shark glanced at his partner with admiration. He knew Dell's father had smacked her mother around, and that Dell's antennae were always tuned into domestic abuse. He hadn't even thought to ask Mrs. Parker about it.

They were both silent, lost in thought, as they made their way down the county road to Highway 278. Suddenly Dell said, "What if Marcus wasn't the target?"

"What do you mean?"

"Just go with me here. There were three people standing on that step. We assumed Marcus was the target, since he's the one who died. What if Marissa was the one they were after?"

"Who's *they*? And why would anyone want to kill Marissa?"

"Maybe B.J. knew his father had already changed the will, and he would inherit her part of the estate if she was dead. No, wait. That won't work because Marcus would have to be dead too. Okay, maybe it was a crazy fan who had a thing for her and was upset she was getting married."

"Don't you think you're heading off into left field a little here? We've already got a list of suspects that reads like the Beaufort County phone book. You really want to open up another whole can of worms?"

"Well, we can at least ask her if anyone has been sending her threatening letters, can't we?"

"Okay, I'll talk to her."

"And don't forget Reverend Hart," Dell added.

"That's really reaching, don't you think?"

"Ministers have been known to indulge in sins of the flesh with members of their congregation. They're only human, you know."

"I'll let you be the one to ask the good Reverend if he's playing hanky panky with the Deacon's wife," Shark said sarcastically.

He dropped his partner off at the office, so she could glean what she could from the computer and he called Marissa to tell her he would be right over.

A few minutes later, they sat comfortably on her patio, sipping Red Zinger iced tea and watching the tall sea oats sway in a light breeze. "So how are you doing?" he asked.

"I don't know. I can't seem to quit crying, and I'm still shocked about Marcus's will. I was certain he would leave everything to B.J."

"Obviously he wanted you to have part of his estate as well." Shark sat his glass on the table and leaned forward, his elbows resting on his knees.

"Marissa, you know we have to explore all possibilities in an investigation like this, no matter how far-fetched they might seem. Is there any chance *you* could have been the target, instead of Marcus?"

Marissa jerked upright in her chair. "Me? But who would want to kill me?"

"Take it easy," Shark said, as he laid a hand on her arm. "Just think about it. I don't want to frighten you. But has anyone been sending you threatening letters at work, or have you received a lot of mail from a particular fan?"

Marissa sat back, relaxing a little under his touch. "I've gotten an occasional fan letter, but nothing threatening. This isn't *Sixty Minutes*, you know. Just a dinky local station. I'm not exactly a star," she added almost wistfully.

"Just because you didn't get any letters, doesn't mean there's not a lot of crazies out there. I'm really concerned about you being here alone, is there anyone who could stay with you for a few days?"

"I'm not going to ask anyone to put themselves at risk by staying here," Marissa said emphatically. "Although, Jason McCalvey, the general manager at the station, did offer to stay with me the day Marcus died. But he has a son he needs to take care of. And anyway, I didn't think that would be a very good idea, since he sort of has a thing for me."

"Tell me more about that," Shark said, his pulse quickening a little.

"Not much to tell really. He invited me out several times before I started seeing Marcus. I never went though. He's my boss, and not really my type anyway. After Marcus and I started dating, Jason kept telling me Marcus was a big playboy, and I should beware. He did get pretty upset when I told him I was quitting, and he offered me my job back after Marcus died. You don't think he has anything to do with this, do you?"

"I haven't ruled anyone out yet. I'll have a talk with him," Shark said, as he stood and began to pace. "I know you and Rachel don't get along very well, but what about inviting her to stay with you for a few days?"

Marissa chuckled. "That's about as likely as hell freezing over this afternoon."

"I just don't think you should be alone. What about checking into a hotel?"

Marissa shook her head emphatically. "I'm staying right here. I've got a good security system. And there are guards at the gate, and even some patrolling at night, so unless someone has a pass, they can't get into the plantation. I'm probably safer here than anywhere else."

Shark sighed. What he would really like to do was just take her home with him where he could keep her safe himself. But that was crazy, and he knew it. "Maybe you're right. I'll stop and have a chat with the Security Chief on the way out and ask him to instruct his men to be doubly careful monitoring your house and visitors." Reluctantly, he rose. "I'd better go. I'll see you at the memorial service in the morning. In the meantime, I want you to think seriously about anyone who might want you out of the way."

When Shark returned to the office, he repeated the gist of the conversation to Dell. He gathered the picture of B.J. and the few details he'd provided about the bars he frequented on the day Marcus died, and hit the road.

Shark mulled things over, as he made his way up Interstate 95 toward Columbia. His list of suspects grew, the longer he thought about it: B.J., Gene Branigan, and Neil Fulton. The developer guy, Lawrence. Maybe even Marcus's sister, if she was in a financial crunch. And then there was Jason McCalvey. He had invited Marissa out several times, was against her marriage, and felt Marcus was the reason she was leaving the station. If DeSilva were out of the picture, Jason might have figured Marissa would go back to work, and he could have another chance with her.

And of course there was Marissa herself.

As Shark approached the city limits of Columbia he tried to ignore Dell's favorite scenario—Marissa as a black widow. *She's gotta be way off base*, he told himself.

Shark drove to the west side of Columbia and got off at the first exit B.J. would have come to. *I'll start here and work my way back.*

There were only two bars right off that exit, The Dew Drop Inn and The Oasis. In both he asked the bartenders if they had been on duty Saturday afternoon. They had, but neither recognized B.J.'s picture. Shark returned to his car.

The next exit consisted primarily of gas stations, convenience stores, and fast-food places. He drove for three miles, but found no bars.

Just before he reached the next off ramp, he noticed a sign for the University of South Carolina and a sea of signs advertising restaurants, hotels, and gas stations. *Maybe the university sign had attracted B.J.'s attention.*

Shark pulled into the parking lot of the first bar he came to, just a block off the interstate. He pushed through the door of O'Shaunessey's, into a dimly lit interior, and chuckled as he approached an Asian kid wiping the top of the bar with a dirty towel. *Definitely not Mr. O'Shaunessey.* Shark lowered himself onto a stool and ordered a beer.

"Bud okay?"

"Whatever you've got on tap," Shark replied. He knew he wouldn't be drinking much of it anyway.

When the kid had carefully set the beer down in front of him, Shark asked, "Were you working Saturday afternoon?"

"Why do you want to know?"

"Because a friend of mine was driving my car and someone hit it in your parking lot. At least that's the story he's telling me."

"Yeah, I was working, but I didn't see anything like that."

"Let me show you a picture of my buddy, see if you recognize him." Shark whipped it out of his pocket and pushed it across the bar.

"No, I don't think he was in here. At least not while I was working."

"Is this where most of the college kids hang out?" Shark asked, standing up.

"No, we don't get too many of them in here. Mostly Jude's Sports Bar or The Watering Hole."

"Is either one of them close by?"

"The Watering Hole is a few blocks down on the left, and Jude's is about a mile farther, on the other side of the street."

"Thanks," Shark said, as he threw a five-dollar bill on the bar.

The Watering Hole was much larger and even had a small dance floor. The bartender looked busy so Shark just pointed to the tab for a draft beer. The guy nodded his head and continued throwing ice in the blender. Shark guessed by the amount of tequila going in, that he was mixing margaritas.

Shark grabbed the stool just being vacated by a kid that didn't look old enough to drive, let alone drink. *Or maybe I'm just getting old.*

A few minutes later the bartender slid a beer onto a napkin in front of him. The nametag on his red polo shirt read "Jeff." "Got a minute?" Shark asked.

"About that."

"A buddy of mine was in here Saturday afternoon, said the bartender was real friendly. That you by any chance?"

"Yeah, I was working Saturday afternoon. What's your buddy's name?"

"Just happen to have a picture of him with me," Shark said, reaching into his pocket. He pushed B.J.'s DMV photo across the bar.

Jeff glanced at it, then looked up. "You a cop or something?"

"Yeah," Shark answered and discreetly flashed his badge.

"So what did the guy do?"

"Probably nothing. I'm just trying to confirm he was where he said he was."

Jeff picked up the picture and studied it carefully. "Lots of guys come through here on a weekend. I can't say I remember him, but that doesn't mean he wasn't here."

"Well, thanks. Maybe I was mistaken about the name of the bar." Shark took a couple of sips of his beer and reached for a cigarette—momentarily forgetting he didn't have any. Times like this he really missed them.

The parking lot at Jude's Sports Bar was full, and Shark had to circle a couple of times before a space opened up.

He pushed open the door and just looked around for a minute. Three big-screen TVs were tuned to a variety of sporting events. There were no empty stools at the bar, so Shark elbowed his way in at the end and caught the bartender's eye.

The man who approached was way too old for the scraggly gray ponytail hanging down his back. His large red-veined nose told Shark he probably drank up a good share of the profits. The black letters scrawled across his greasy white shirt announced that Jude himself was behind the bar.

"Heineken," Shark yelled over the noise of the TVs.

Jude returned with the bottle and a frosted glass. "I need to ask you something," Shark said, reaching into his pocket.

"What's that?"

"Were you working Saturday afternoon?"

"Yeah, I'm always working. Why?"

"Happen to see this kid?" Shark handed him the picture of B.J.

"Why do you wanna know?" he asked looking at Shark more closely.

With people yelling drink orders at the guy, right and left, Shark knew he didn't have much time. He pushed his wallet across the bar. Jude opened it, then snapped it closed and slid it back to Shark.

"What kinda trouble is he in?"

"Probably not much. Just need to know if he was where he said he was," Shark said, pouring the Heineken into the glass.

"Yeah, I remember him. He was here for quite a while. Kept saying he should get on the road, had a wedding or something to go to. But he just kept drinking and watching the football game. Said he had a lot of dough riding on it. Sounded real upset when Georgia was behind at half time."

"Do you remember what time he left?"

"Not really. We were pretty busy that afternoon, with the game and all. But he wasn't here when it was over. I'm sure about that."

"Thanks," Shark said and handed him a ten-dollar bill. "Keep the change." He took a quick gulp of his beer and headed to the men's room.

Shark pulled out of the parking lot and back toward Interstate 26. At least it was a start. But if B.J. had left at half time and put the pedal to the metal he could still have been at the church in time to shoot Marcus. According to his statement, B.J.'s next stop had been in Walterboro, a little over an hour away. It wasn't a big town, so it shouldn't be too hard to verify that. Maybe he could at least eliminate one suspect by the end of the evening.

Shark got off at the Walterboro exit and pulled into the parking lot of the first bar he came to, Marvin's Hole in the Wall, which was a pretty apt description. The bartender who had worked Saturday afternoon wasn't there.

It was the same story at the next two places. At his last stop, Rita's Roadhouse, he struck out again. Rita didn't recognize B.J.'s picture, but she knew how to grill a mean steak. The home fries were Cajun hot, just the way he liked them. And he allowed himself to finish a beer, since he knew his day was finally over. He would have to come back, or send Dell, to track down the bartenders who had been off. So B.J., no longer at the top of the suspect list, still couldn't be ruled out.

Chapter Eight

Wednesday morning, cars overflowed the parking lot and were jammed along both sides of the road as far as Shark could see as he sought refuge from the sun under an oak tree, dripping Spanish moss. Dell was inside the church amongst the standing room only crowd. Shark noted several familiar faces, movers and shakers in the community. Even Mayor Victor Thornton had put in an appearance. Shark decided to circulate among the small groups that remained outside to see if he could hear any snippets of interesting conversation. He had caught only a quick glimpse of Marissa as she, Rachel, and B.J. entered the church.

Ten minutes later, he heard the swell of the organ and knew the service was underway. The church steps overflowed with people who couldn't fit in the sanctuary.

The service seemed to go on forever, but finally mourners began to make their way slowly to their cars. Marissa and Rachel, followed by B.J. and Reverend Alan Hart, walked quickly to the black limousine. Marissa carried a small elaborate urn in her arms. Shark knew they were planning to scatter Marcus's ashes at sea, right after the service.

Dell climbed into the unmarked car. As Shark pulled out, he asked, "So what did you get?"

"Not much. Several people referred to the *tragic accident*, and a few were whispering they heard it was *murder*. The consensus of opinion seemed to be that the widow was properly attired and appeared sufficiently upset, although they were disappointed she didn't faint. Several men were speculating on what would happen to Marcus's company, whether Marissa would sell it or try to run it herself. What about you, get anything?"

"Nothing useful. Some people were wondering if Gene Branigan would try and buy the business. A couple of guys betting on how soon the *rich widow* would be back in the dating game. That's about it. No one carrying a deer rifle."

Back at the office, Dell gathered a sheaf of printouts and settled in to share the information with Shark. "First of all, the phone records confirm that someone was in Neil Fulton's office making calls at the time Marcus died. I spoke with the receptionist there, and she said she wasn't aware of anyone else being in the office on Saturday. She stated that Neil had left several files on her desk, so she knew he'd been there sometime over the weekend. So I think we can put him on the back burner for now."

"Maybe, but he did have a good motive. He wanted Marissa, and Marcus had threatened him."

"Well, I didn't say cross him off the suspect list completely. Just move him down a few slots."

"Okay. What else you got?"

"Jason McCalvey is divorced with one son, age nine. He's been station manager for five years. He lives on Lady's Island in Beaufort, and his house is carrying a mortgage of a hundred and ten thousand dollars. He's had a couple of late payments and he can't seem to get his credit cards below eighteen grand. His credit report showed a salary of fifty-five thousand and about four thousand in income from investments. He appears to be living way beyond his means. Nothing else of any significance."

"Add that to the fact that he invited Marissa out on several dates, and I guess I'd better have a conversation with him. What else?"

"Langford was Marissa's maiden name which she resumed after her divorce from her first husband, Devon Phillips, and again after her second husband, Eric Meier, died. Her parents were working-class folks. You're not going to believe this, but the night of her high-school graduation, they died in a fire. It was ruled arson."

"Arson?" Shark asked, his stomach beginning to burn.

"Yeah, arson. Seems Marissa was the prime suspect for a while. It was widely known she didn't get along well with her parents. She wanted to go to college, and they said they couldn't afford it. But after the fire she inherited ten thousand dollars in life insurance and about the same amount from the coverage on the house and contents. Just about enough to get through the state college. Don't you think that's convenient?"

"So why didn't they arrest her?" Shark reached in his desk drawer and shook three Tums into his hand.

"Because she had an iron-clad alibi. She was at an all-night graduation party. And no one remembered seeing her leave."

"Did they ever arrest anyone?"

"No, it's still an open case. Anyway, her junior year in college she married this Devon Phillips guy. He was from an upper middle–class family—father a lawyer, mother an optometrist. They were married about a year and divorced around the time of graduation. Phillips now lives in San Francisco and is still single. Then Marissa took a job at a TV station in Lexington. She met Eric Meier at some kind of town meeting she was covering, and they married a few months later. About a year after that he dies from a fall off his horse. Are we beginning to see a pattern here?"

"Any sign of foul play?"

"He was riding alone, and the police couldn't find any evidence that it wasn't just an accident. I talked to the lead investigator, Drew Solomon, and he said he felt in his gut it was homicide, but he had nothing to prove it. His body was discovered when the horse returned to the barn without him. Solomon said he suspected Marissa had a hand in the death somehow, since she was the sole beneficiary of a large insurance policy, as well as heir to the horse farm and all the other assets. But she was at a luncheon at the country club, in full view of a hundred people, when it happened."

"So obviously she couldn't have done it!"

"Maybe not directly, but she could have had an accomplice. Solomon tried to find evidence of a lover who could have been her partner in the crime, but he came up empty. Said she came out squeaky clean. A few months later she sold everything, collected the insurance, and moved to Hilton Head."

Shark didn't like the feeling he was getting in his gut. He knew Dell still saw Marissa as a black widow—the spider that devours its mate. But he just couldn't see her as a predator. He had to admit, though, that the arson did bother him a lot, especially coupled with the accidental death of her previous husband. "So spit out what you're thinking," he said to Dell.

"We have a poor girl who wants to go to college, but her parents can't afford it. They die in a suspicious fire, and suddenly the money's available. She marries into a higher-class family. It doesn't work out, for whatever reason, and she gets divorced. She then marries a guy with a lot more money, and he accidentally dies, leaving her wealthy. She moves to Hilton Head and almost immediately becomes involved with someone who's a lot older, but filthy rich, who gets shot on their wedding day and leaves her a multi-millionaire. It does smell a little rotten, don't you think?"

"Let's say all your suspicions are correct. Why didn't she kill the first husband?"

"Maybe he didn't have enough insurance money to make it worth taking the risk. I know you want to get in Marissa's pants, so I really don't think you can look at her objectively as a possible suspect."

"You get me some facts, instead of empty suppositions, and I'll do my job," Shark snapped. "And we still haven't ruled out the possibility that *she* was the target. And what about the minister? Have you checked him out yet?"

"As a matter of fact, I did. He's been married twenty-eight years to the same woman, good credit report, and according to the church deacons I talked with, there's never been any hint of inappropriate behavior on his part with parishioners or anyone else."

"Anything new on Coastal Development?" Shark asked, as he fiddled with a pencil on the desk.

"I'm expecting some more reports on them this afternoon. And by the way, no one at Publix remembered Gene Branigan's being there Saturday afternoon. I also drove out to that housing development, while you were in Columbia, but none of them worked on Saturday. At least, that's what I think they said. Most of them are Hispanic, and their English isn't very good."

"That's what I suspected. I didn't think he was telling me the truth. So he has no alibi until he showed up at the liquor store about five o'clock. I need to talk to him again. But I think I'll let him stew for a day or two first."

Shark stood up and grabbed his sport coat off the back of his chair. "If you're still going to Waterboro this afternoon to finish checking on B.J.'s alibi, I'll go talk to Jason McCalvey. I've got a couple of other things I want to follow up on too. I probably won't be back in the office today, so reach me on my cell phone if you need me."

Dell just shook her head in exasperation as she watched Shark storm from the office.

His dark mood didn't improve as he fought the traffic to the Beaufort offices of WWOJ. And it didn't help that he was desperately craving a nicotine hit.

Shark identified himself to a busty blond who escorted him to Jason McCalvey's office. Someone who knew what he was doing had obviously tailored McCalvey's pinstriped suit.

How does a guy living on the edge buy suits that cost more than I make in a month?

"Thank you for agreeing to see me," Shark said, pulling out one of the chairs in front of Jason McCalvey's desk.

"I certainly want to help in any way I can, but I'm not sure what I can tell you."

"Well, for starters, how did Mrs. DeSilva get along with her coworkers?" Shark asked.

"Fine I guess, just the normal jealousy and bickering between female reporters. Nothing out of the ordinary."

"Mrs. DeSilva indicated to me she hadn't been receiving any threatening letters or unusual amounts of fan mail. Would you agree with that?"

"That's correct. Our viewership did increase dramatically after Marissa came aboard, and I was certainly disappointed when she told me she was quitting. I hope now that her circumstances have changed, she'll consider returning."

"I understand that you had asked Mrs. DeSilva out on several dates."

"That was before she started seeing Marcus. And she never accepted my offer. She said she didn't feel it would be appropriate, since I was her boss." Jason shifted nervously in his chair. "After all, she's a very attractive woman."

"So, to the best of your knowledge, no one had threatened Mrs. DeSilva or hassled her in any way," Shark summed up.

"That's right. Why are you asking these questions about Marissa? Do you think someone murdered Marcus because she was marrying him?"

"I'm the one asking the questions. And why do you say *murdered*? We haven't ruled out an accidental shooting."

"Just the scuttlebutt around."

"And what exactly have you heard?" Shark asked, studying McCalvey's face intently.

"Just that your list of suspects goes on and on, and you haven't been able to zero in on anyone in particular yet. That Marissa is the most likely suspect since she has the most to gain, which I find absurd. Anyone who knows Marissa must realize she's not capable of doing something like that. And your biggest fear is that you may never have enough evidence to arrest anyone," Jason added. His initial nervousness seemed to have been replaced by a cockiness that grated on Shark.

Shark rose to leave. "Thanks for your time. Keep yourself available, I may have more questions."

He forced himself to close the door quietly behind him. *Boy, I really don't like this guy. But I just can't see him dirtying those well-manicured hands to commit murder.*

Shark walked out to McCalvey's secretary, Jenny, according to the nameplate on her desk. He figured, in most places, secretaries knew more than anyone else about what was going on. Shark put on his best smile and perched on the corner of her desk.

"Hi!"

"Hi yourself."

"I wonder if you can help me. I'm investigating the death of Marcus DeSilva, and I have a few questions about Marissa."

Jenny's smile faded, then she reached up and began to twirl a piece of her long brown hair around her index finger. "It was *so* awful. *Poor* Marissa," she said, glancing up at him coyly.

"Were you and Marissa close?"

Jenny chuckled. "Not hardly. She barely gave me the time of day. It was beneath her to mix with us common folk."

"Did she have any close friends here I can talk to?"

"She has *no* friends here. All the other girls hate her."

"Why?"

"Because she acted like a big shot from day one. Said she'd been on some big station up in Lexington. We may be just a local station, but we do a good job. She acted like she was doing us this big favor by filling in here a couple of days a week. And once she started dating Marcus, her head would hardly fit through the door. He was always calling here and sending her huge bouquets of flowers."

"Do you open the mail?"

"Yeah, that's part of my job."

"Did Marissa receive any threatening letters or a lot of mail from a particular fan?"

"Well, I wouldn't exactly call them fan mail. But she did receive some downright nasty ones, after her engagement was in the newspaper."

"Do you still have them?"

"No. I gave them to Jayce, uh, I mean Mr. McCalvey."

"Thanks for the info."

Shark marched back down the hall and opened Jason McCalvey's door without bothering to knock. "I thought you said Marissa didn't get any threatening letters. Jenny just told me she did."

"I wouldn't really call them threatening. Crude maybe, but not threatening."

"So let's see them."

"I don't have them anymore, I destroyed them."

"Did you show them to Marissa?"

"No, of course not."

"What did they say?"

"They referred to Marcus as an old man, said how much better they could take care of her. A couple of them were pretty graphic about what they'd like to do to her."

"Do you remember anything about the envelopes or post-marks?"

"No. I just figured they were creeps, and tossed everything."

"That was an incredibly stupid thing to do." Shark's fists clenched with the effort to control his temper.

"How the hell did I know DeSilva would get himself shot and you would want to see them?"

Shark slammed out of the office and it didn't help his mood any to know that McCalvey was right. He spent the next hour interviewing the other employees of the station, but didn't learn anything useful.

Back in his car, he realized it was too late to return to Hilton Head. Frustrated he couldn't seem to get a handle on this case, he decided a "boat fix" would give him the perfect opportunity to think things through.

When Shark got home, he changed into his fishing clothes, fixed a cooler of beer and sandwiches, and grabbed some frozen bait from the freezer. He attached his old red pickup to the boat trailer, and pointed it in the direction of Port Royal landing.

As he traveled the familiar road, his mind returned to Marissa. He knew that the spreading of the ashes had to have been a difficult experience for her, and he wondered how she was holding up. His fingers settled briefly on the buttons of the cell phone until he heard Dell's voice in his head. *Not smart, Morgan.*

The hell with you, partner, this feels right.

"Hello," a subdued voice answered.

"Hi, it's Shark. How're you doing?"

"Not so hot. I've been sitting here crying, and now I feel like the walls are closing in on me. If I don't get out of here, I'm just going to scream!"

Shark spoke without thinking. "Well then how about some shark fishing? I'm on my way to the dock as we speak."

Marissa hesitated. "Are you sure it's okay? I mean . . ."

"Just meet me at Saw Mill Creek boat landing."

"Where's that?"

"Get on Highway two seventy-eight and after you cross the bridge turn right on the road to Waddell Mariculture Center. There's a boat landing at the end of the road. I'll pick you up there in thirty minutes. Bring a flashlight. There're no lights at the boat landing and it'll probably be dark by the time we get back."

"I'll be there."

Shark could hear Dell cursing him, if she ever found out. He'd just have to make sure she didn't.

It was four o'clock when Shark cut the engine and glided his boat expertly to the dock. He saw Marissa hurrying down the ramp. "Have any trouble finding it?" he asked, as she stepped unsteadily onto the floating dock.

"Not really," she answered, surveying the small fishing boat. *Sure a lot different from Marcus's yacht*, she thought, as Shark took her hand and helped her aboard.

As soon as she was seated, Shark restarted the outboard and roared away. "This is the Colleton River. We're going up to where it meets the Chechesse. There's a shark hole close to Daw's Island," he yelled over at her. Marissa just nodded, since the noise of the engine made it difficult to talk.

Although there wasn't a lot of chop on the river, at thirty miles an hour, Marissa felt every jarring bounce from her docksiders up through her spine. The wind whipped her unbound hair, slapping it against her face as the boat screamed along.

Through dry, itching eyes, she watched the riverfront mansions whizz by. A few minutes later, Shark cut the engine and they anchored off the small island. The mournful cries of seagulls pierced the sudden silence.

"Let me get a couple of lines in the water, and then we can talk," Shark said. Marissa cringed, as he ran the large silver hook through the eyes of the dead fish, and cast it far out into the water, then repeated the whole process with the second line. "Fresh bait is really better, but we don't have a lot of time to waste trying to catch some. I had these poagies in the freezer," he said, slipping the poles into rod holders on the back of the boat.

"Yuck," Marissa said, at the thought of the slimy dead fish nestled against a carton of ice cream in Shark's refrigerator.

"Look!" Shark yelled, pointing to three dolphins that had just broken the surface of the water not far from the boat.

"They're beautiful. I've never seen any up this close before. On Marcus's boat we were so much farther away from the water."

"You used to be able to feed them, and they'd come right up to the boat and take the fish out of your hand. There were even dolphin feeding cruises out of Shelter Cove Marina. But a few years ago they made it illegal."

"Why?" Marissa asked.

"Because the dolphins would follow the boats and beg for food. The wildlife people were afraid it was interfering with their normal feeding habits, and tourists feed them all kinds of crazy things like hot-dogs and marshmallows."

Marissa slipped on her jacket as the wind began to pick up a little, and the sun started its daily march to the horizon. "Do you catch shark at night?" she asked.

"Dusk and early evening are the best times," Shark said, settling himself on the seat opposite her. "Would you like a beer? Sorry, but that's all I brought. I didn't know I would be entertaining a lady, or I'd have stuck in some fancy wine."

"A beer's fine," Marissa said, leaning back into the rocking motion of the boat. Shark popped the tab and handed her a Coors.

"Tell me about your boat," Marissa said.

"It's a Sea Pro. I've had her about three years. I have plastic windows that zip in around the canopy here so I can use her year-round. Nothing fancy, but ideal for fishing and shrimping. Probably looks like a toy compared to Marcus's boat."

Marissa took a sip of beer and set the can down on the dashboard. "Does your boat have a name?"

"*Tiburon*. That's Spanish for shark."

The lines drifted farther and farther on an outgoing tide. Off to the right, a small fish leapt out of the water. Marissa caught a brief glimpse of silvery scales. "So do you keep what you catch or throw them back?"

"Depends on their size. Have you ever eaten shark?"

"No!"

"It's good. A very mild fish with no bones. It's great on the grill with butter, lemon juice and a little garlic. Or you can deep-fry it. You'll have to let me fix some for you sometime."

"If you say so," Marissa said, unconvinced. They fell silent, both of them drawn to the deeping pinks and purples of the approaching sunset spreading out across the water.

"So, how did things go today?" Shark asked softly.

"The memorial service is kind of a blur in my mind. All these people I didn't know, offering their condolences. Rachel was as cold as ever. And the spreading of the ashes was the worst. It was strange to think that handful of gray powder used to be lively, joking Marcus. I don't even have a grave to take flowers to." Marissa stared off to the horizon.

"It's been a difficult day for you," Shark said, as he reached over and touched her knee. Marissa started shaking, and before he knew it he had pulled her out of her seat and into his arms. He liked the feel of her there.

"It's okay to cry. After the ordeal you've been through the last few days, you're entitled. Just let it go," he whispered to her. And though she clung to him, her face buried in the collar of his soft denim shirt, he felt no tears.

In too short a time for Shark, Marissa regained her composure. Gently she extricated herself from his arms and sat back down. "I'm sorry," she said pulling a tissue from her pocket and wiping at her eyes. "It's just all so overwhelming."

"You have nothing to feel sorry about," Shark said quietly.

"It's just that I don't have anyone to talk to about all that's been happening."

"Don't you have any close women friends?"

"Not really. I had hoped to make some life-long friendships when I went away to college, but it didn't happen. I guess I get along better with men than women. Believe me, I wish I had the shoulder of a 'best girlfriend' to cry on."

"I told you, just pick up the phone and call me, anytime you want,"

"I know. But I feel awkward talking to you, when you're the one investigating Marcus's death. Is anything happening with the case?"

Shark filled her in on his trip to Columbia to check out B.J.'s alibi and his conversation with Jason McCalvey, but avoided telling her about the letters. Shark knew he needed, for his own peace of mind, as well as the investigation, to ask her some hard questions. He decided just to get it over with.

"As part of our work, we do background checks on all the major players. I need to ask you a couple of things about your past."

"If you have to," she said, avoiding his eyes and squaring her shoulders. "I'll answer anything if it'll help."

"Tell me about the night your parents died."

"What do my parents have to do with all this?" Marissa hugged her arms around her body, as if she was suddenly cold. "Is that why you invited me to join you here tonight? To interrogate me?"

"No. You're the one who said you needed to get out of the house, remember? I'd need to ask you these things sometime anyway, so it might as well be now."

"What do you want to know?" she asked curtly.

"Just tell me about that night, in your own words."

Marissa paused to pull the collar of her jacket up around her neck and gazed out over the water. "It was the night of my high-school graduation. I had gone to a party after the ceremony, and about four o'clock in the morning, a policeman showed up and told me there had been a fire at my house. By the time I got there, the house was leveled, and my parents had already been taken away. I was devastated, especially after they said it was arson. I couldn't believe it. My dad worked in a hardware store and my mom in a dry cleaners. Who would want to kill them?"

"Did the police question you?"

"Yes, several times. They wanted to know if someone had a grudge against my parents or me. The only person I could think of was my ex-boyfriend, Tom Jarrett. We had dated for two years, and I'd just broken up with him about ten days before. He wanted to get married right after graduation, and I was determined to go to college, one way or another."

"So how'd did you plan to pay for it?"

"I had applied for financial aid and intended to get a job while I was going to school. My parents thought I was silly and should just marry Tom. But I didn't want to spend the rest of my life married to a garage mechanic in Hazard, Kentucky. A few days after the funeral I left there, and I've never been back."

"Did you leave the party at all that night?"

"No! You can't possibly believe *I* killed my parents. My God, what kind of a person do you think I am?"

"Did the police interview your ex-boyfriend?" Shark asked, avoiding a direct answer to her question.

"Yes, I think they might have suspected him, but didn't have enough evidence to arrest him. I've often wondered if Tom had something to do with it. He was really angry about the breakup, and my car was parked in front of the house that night. I had ridden to the party with a girlfriend. I know Tom was at the party at some point, but I couldn't remember if he was there all night."

Shark wanted to believe her, wasn't sure if really did, but decided to move on. "Now, tell me about your second husband's death."

"Why? Do you think I killed my parents, Eric, *and* Marcus? Is that what this is all about?" she screamed at him.

Shark leaned back and ran his hands through his short graying hair, as much to calm himself as Marissa. He didn't like it when she was upset with him. "Look, it just seems a lot of people you have been closely involved with have died."

"And you think I killed *all* of them? Just tell me the truth!"

Shark looked away briefly, then met her eyes. "No, I don't."

"What about your partner? Does she think I'm a mass murderer?"

"I don't know what Dell thinks. I do know she deals with *facts*, what she can pull off a computer or from reports. Several investigators involved with those cases have had suspicions that you may have somehow been involved. You were the sole heir, and you didn't get along well with your parents, plus the fact that you inherited a lot of money when Eric died. Those things tend to make people suspicious. Me, I go on my gut. I watch people's body language, how they react to my questions, and other subtle things when I interview them. I don't know what else to tell you."

"Well, who else would my parents make beneficiary? I was the only child. Granted, we didn't get along very well at times, but that's certainly not unusual. They didn't want me to leave Hazard, and I was determined to go. But I *didn't* kill them," Marissa said emphatically. "And it's not like I inherited much money when they died."

Zzzzzzzzzzzzzzzzz. The line screamed on the pole closest to Marissa as the end bent over sharply toward the water. Shark raced to grab it out of the rod holder. "Here, take this and reel in the fish!" he said, pushing the pole toward her.

"No, you do it! I don't know what to do. I'll do something wrong and the fish will get away," she said backing up.

"Come here. I want you to reel in this fish. You'll do just fine. Just pull back gently and reel in slowly, like this. Then let the fish have a little line so he can run, then reel in gently again."

Marissa reluctantly took the pole and tried to do exactly what Shark told her. Suddenly she found the rhythm, and Shark watched as she pitted herself against the fish. From the look of determination on her face, he knew the fish didn't have a chance. When she finally brought it alongside, Shark leaned over, lifted the line and displayed her trophy.

"It's a sand shark. Just right for eating. Now, I'll show you how we clean them, since you have to do it right away."

Marissa cringed as Shark gutted the fish, then cut off the head and fins. He sliced the gray, nearly boneless meat into filets. "Do you want to take these home and try them on your grill?" Shark asked.

"No thanks. I'll pass. Why do you leave the skin on?"

"Helps to hold it together on the grill when you're cooking it. You don't know what you're missing. Are you sure?"

"I'm sure."

Shark rebaited the pole. "How about another beer?" he asked.

Marissa nodded as she sank back down on the boat cushion. "Well, that was pretty exciting," Marissa said. She pulled her feet up under her, sipping on her beer as darkness fell and the nighttime silence settled around them.

Shark could have sat like that forever, the beautiful woman he dreamed about only a few feet away, his boat rocking gently on the peaceful river. But he was a cop. First, last, and always. "I'm sorry, but we need to finish our conversation about Eric."

Marissa took a deep breath. "What do you want me to say. Eric was a great guy and I was happier than I'd ever been. At first I was afraid around the horses, but I got over that as soon as Eric taught me how to ride. We loved to go out together at sunrise and I wanted to learn to jump."

"What about the day he died?"

"I was at a luncheon. To this day I can't imagine what made him fall. He was a skilled rider. I often wonder if it would have made any difference if I had been with him. I don't know what else to tell you."

"Did the police question you after his death?"

"Yes, several times. Even though a hundred people saw me at that luncheon, they still tried to imply I was involved. They accused me of having a lover, terrible things like that. It was awful. The detective that questioned me kept harping on the fact that I was the sole heir. Eric didn't have any siblings, and his mother was well off. So who else would he leave everything to? I *was* his wife after all."

Shark believed her—about everything.

It was completely dark now, and Shark's stomach was reminding him he hadn't eaten lunch. They shared the tuna-fish sandwiches. Over the next hour they avoided talking any more about the investigation and caught two more fish—a stingray and a little shark they threw back. The temperature was dropping fast.

"I think I better get you back to the boat landing before it gets any colder. I'll pull the anchor and we can head out." Fifteen minutes later Shark pulled up and tied off the boat to the floating dock. "Let me walk you to your car. It's pretty deserted out here at night."

Marissa handed him her flashlight, and they made their way to the parking lot. "Thanks for getting me out of the house for a little while. I think it helped," Marissa said, as she pulled out her car keys.

"My pleasure. I might turn you into a fisherman yet. Take it easy on this road. There are lots of really bad curves, and there's practically no moon tonight. I'll probably talk to you tomorrow," Shark said as he closed her car door. His eyes followed her taillights until she pulled out onto Saw Mill Creek Road, and then he headed back to his boat.

As Marissa made her way down the winding road, she worried about all the questions Shark had asked her about her parents and Eric. She thought she had answered them well, and he seemed to believe her.

Marissa braked for the first ninety-degree turn and felt the brakes go a little mushy. "Guess I better get that checked out tomorrow," she muttered, accelerating as a straight patch of road opened up. Her thoughts returned to the conversation with Shark. She wanted him to trust her enough to share what was going on with the investigation.

Marissa slowed and braked for another curve, but her foot went right to the floor. Her hands gripped the steering wheel, as she fought to hold the car on the road. She pumped the brakes furiously. "Nooooooo!" she screamed, as the tall pine trees raced toward her. "I can't die like this, not now!"

Chapter Nine

"**O**h God, not tonight," Shark muttered, as Anna Connors reparked her car in front of his house so he could back the boat into the driveway. She carried a bottle of wine in one hand, as she approached his truck.

"Hey, I thought you might help me drink this," she said, reaching up to give him a quick kiss on the cheek. "You didn't call me all weekend," she whined, as Shark unlocked the front door and flipped on the lights. "You're not ignoring me, are you?" She trailed Shark into the kitchen where he set the cooler and his keys on the counter.

"Look, I've been real busy on the DeSilva investigation."

Anna leaned into him, pinning him against the counter. She waited for him to hug her close, but he just stood there. She reached up and placed her hand behind his neck to pull his mouth down to hers.

"God, Anna, give me a break," he said, jerking away. "I've been working twenty-four seven on this, and I'm exhausted. You know how the press has been crucifying us."

Anna pulled two glasses out of the cupboard and skillfully uncorked the bottle of Chardonnay. "Not too tired to go out on that blasted boat of yours, I see," she said, as she handed him a glass.

"I needed to do some thinking," he said, as he headed toward the living room. He sank down on the couch and raised his glass.

"I know something that'll take your mind off the case," Anna said as she sat down on his lap.

"I don't think this is a good idea," he said as he moved her off his lap and stood up. "I'm sorry, Anna, but I've got to get some sleep. Let's make it another time."

Anna looked up at Shark's expression, decided she wasn't going to get what she'd come for, and sighed. "Okay, I can take a hint. Anything happening on the case?" She stood up and drained her glass of wine in one long swallow.

"Nothing. That's the problem." Shark walked over and opened the front door.

Anna followed him and stopped on the threshold. "Okay. I'll take a raincheck. I'll leave the wine, and maybe we can finish it next time." She reached up and gave him a quick kiss. "Get some rest," she whispered in his ear, then walked down the drive.

"Thank God," Shark muttered as he made his way to the bathroom. He left his clothes where they dropped, showered off the salt water and the smell of fish guts, and fell into bed. Sleep came instantly, his last conscious thought, a vision of Marissa, her face turned up to his, inviting his slow, deep kiss.

Shark groaned as the insistent ringing finally penetrated. He rolled over, groping for the phone in the dark. The bedside clock read 3:10. "Yeah," he grumbled into the receiver.

"Detective Morgan? Sorry to bother you in the middle of the night, sir. This is Deputy Pickford."

Shark sighed as he pictured another one of the new deputies on the force. *This better be good,* he thought.

"I was called out on an auto accident, and the lady involved is Marissa DeSilva." Shark, instantly alert, threw off the covers and sat stiffly on the side of the bed. "I know you're investigating the death of her husband, so I thought maybe I should let you know."

"Is she hurt?"

"Doc said she has a concussion and is in shock. She hasn't regained consciousness yet. They're working on her as we speak."

"What happened?" Shark asked, quickly working his legs into a pair of bluejeans.

"She crashed into some trees on Saw Mill Creek Road. Must have been there for quite awhile. A guy going home through the back gate of Colleton River Plantation found her."

"Impound her car and don't let anyone touch it. It may not have been an accident. And don't let anyone near her, but the doctors and nurses. I'll be right there."

Shark hurriedly finished dressing, grabbed his car keys, and sprinted out the door. He hit the speed dial for Dell and had the Mustang up to eighty, before she picked up. He told her what little he knew and asked her to meet him at the hospital. He tossed the mobile phone onto the seat and reached for his pack of cigarettes, then realized he had none. *Damn!*

Dell was already questioning Deputy Pickford when Shark strode into the emergency room. Pickford's uniform hung loosely on his tall, thin frame and his face was covered with freckles, matching his short red hair. He was closing his notebook and putting it back in his pocket when Shark walked up. "We'll take it from here, Deputy," Dell said.

"Yes ma'am," he answered, then nodded at Shark. "Sir." His back was as straight as a new marine recruit as he marched through the door.

"How is she?" Shark tried for a professional tone, but couldn't keep the concern out of his voice.

"She still hasn't regained consciousness. They've got her up in X-ray, doing a CAT scan to see how severe her head injury is. I can't figure out what the hell she was doing on Saw Mill Creek Road this time of night."

Shark cleared his throat and studied his shoes. "I know the answer to that," he said softly.

"You asinine fool," Dell snapped, after he'd related his fishing story. "I should have the Sheriff bounce you right off this case."

"It's not what you think. She needed to get out of the house, and I used the opportunity to question her about the death of her parents and her second husband," Shark said defensively.

"Well, you better have gotten enough information to make it worth putting your job at risk. I hope to hell you didn't give her any booze."

"We had a couple beers, okay? But there's more to this than a simple DUI."

"What's that supposed to mean?"

"I think someone may have tampered with her car, while it was parked at the boat landing."

"So are you back to thinking they were after her all along?"

"Maybe. Anyway, I want a team to go over that car with a magnifying glass. God, this investigation is getting more complicated all the time. We don't even know who the damn *target* is!"

"Well, we can rule out B.J. for doing Marcus. I went to Walterboro this afternoon, and his alibi checked out. But that doesn't mean he couldn't have tried to bump off Marissa last night to get a larger share of the inheritance."

A tall gray-haired doctor in surgical scrubs pushed through the door to the waiting room.

"Is either of you a member of the DeSilva family?"

"No family here, but we're the investigating officers," Dell replied.

"Is she going to be all right?" Shark asked.

"She has a pretty severe concussion, a sprained wrist and multiple cuts and abrasions. And she suffered mild hypothermia. Fortunately, there doesn't appear to be any intracranial bleeding. The CAT scan was negative. So, barring complications, she should make a full recovery."

Shark finally let out a deep breath. "Is she awake yet? We really need to talk to her as soon as possible."

"No, and it may be awhile."

"When do you think she'll come around?" Dell asked.

"Hard to say. It will depend on how much bruising of the brain is involved. Hopefully, within the next twenty-four hours."

"Can we see her?" Shark asked. "Not officially, no questions, it's just that she doesn't have anyone else," he added quickly.

"Sure. They just took her up to room two-twelve. All the ICU beds are full. Tell them I said it was okay."

"Dr. Lockhart, please report to ER," a voice on the intercom announced.

"Got to go." He nodded before briskly walking away.

Dell and Shark rode a silent elevator to the second floor. Shark's breath caught as they walked into Marissa's room. She was lying there, still as death. Both eyes were already black, her left wrist was in a brace, and an IV ran in her right arm. Several small bandages dotted her forehead and neck. Her black eyelashes rested against cheeks totally bleached of color.

Shark picked up her right hand and said, "Marissa, it's Shark. You've been in an auto accident, and you're in Hilton Head Hospital. If you can hear me, squeeze my hand." He waited, but there was no response.

"I think we should station an officer outside her door until we figure out what's going on," Dell whispered.

"*I'll* stay with her for now. You go on home and get some sleep. We can't do anything until the team comes in and goes over her car," Shark said emphatically.

"I don't think you should be the one to stay," Dell argued.

"That's not up for discussion. By the time I drove to Beaufort, it would be time to get up and come back over here. You only live ten miles away. No use in both of us losing any more sleep. So go!"

Dell could see arguing would get her nowhere. "I'll go take a shower and meet you back at the office later."

Shark was relieved to be alone, finally, with Marissa. With Dell gone he could put aside his cop persona for awhile. He pulled a chair close to the bed and took Marissa's hand again in his. "I'll just stay with you, Sleeping Beauty, until you decide to wake up." Try as he might, he couldn't keep his eyes from straying to that beguiling imperfection next to her inviting mouth. He fought it as long as he could. Then, looking around to make sure he was unobserved, he leaned over and softly kissed it. The reality exceeded the fantasy. Then he quickly brushed her lips with his. "Hope you don't mind, but I just had to do that," he whispered. Marissa lay motionless.

A few minutes later, when a nurse came in to check Marissa's vital signs, Shark was once again the detached cop. "Stable," she muttered, then quickly replaced the blood pressure cuff in the metal holder above the bed and hurried from the room.

Shark sat in the silent room, his mind churning. Had they been wrong all along? Was Marissa really the target? Could B.J. have tried to kill her? Was he good with cars? Did Marissa have a will? If so, who was the beneficiary? Too many questions, and not enough answers.

Every half-hour the nurse came back in and went through the same routine. Each time Shark asked if there was any change and always got the same negative response.

At 6:30, Dr. Lockhart stuck his head in the door to check on Marissa, before he went off duty. Shark had fallen asleep in the chair next to the bed, still holding her hand. Dr. Lockhart approached and called her name loudly. Shark was instantly awake.

"Sorry, didn't mean to scare you. But you have to talk loudly to patients who are in a coma. Have you gotten any response from her?" Dr. Lockhart asked.

"None." Shark gently eased his hand away from Marissa's.

The doctor shined a light into both of Marissa's eyes, to check her pupils. "At least they're equal and reacting well to light, which is a good sign," he said, as he pulled out a pin and stuck it in her arms, then her legs and feet. "No response to painful stimuli, so she may be out for quite a while yet. If she doesn't come around today, we'll do another CAT scan and make sure there is still no evidence of an intracranial bleed. She's one lucky lady. I understand the car she was driving is practically made of plastic, and her air bag didn't open. Things would have been a lot worse if she was driving faster."

"Doctor, we're not sure if this was an accident or an attempted homicide. Her husband died recently under mysterious circumstances. I want to restrict her visitors and station a guard outside the door, until we determine the cause of the crash."

The doctor looked up, surprised. "I read in the newspaper about her husband getting shot. It does seem like quite a coincidence. I'll write an order for no visitors, unless they are cleared by you."

"Thanks for your cooperation."

A little after seven Deputy Sayles rapped twice on Marissa's door and entered. "Dell said I should relieve you and guard Mrs. DeSilva. She said she'd meet you at the office."

Shark stood up stiffly and stretched. "Okay. The doctor has ordered no visitors unless cleared by us. If anyone shows up, I want you to call me right away. And don't let anyone but hospital staff in this room. I want you present at all times."

"Yes, sir. You can count on me," he whispered. "Do you think someone tried to kill her?"

"I don't know. And until we can rule it out, I don't want her out of your sight."

As Shark walked down the hall toward the elevator, he felt as if he had left a part of himself in Marissa's room. He wanted to be there when she woke up, but he also needed to get a look at her car. Inspecting it might lead his investigation in a whole new direction.

Chapter Ten

On the way to the office, Shark hit McDonald's drive-thru and ordered two Egg McMuffins and large coffees.

His breakfast sandwich was gone by the time he pulled into the parking lot. He was so hungry, he thought about eating Dell's too, but fought the urge and instead placed the sack in front of her, slumping into the chair by her desk. Sheriff Grant looked up from the computer printout he'd been studying and turned to Shark.

"You look beat. Why don't you go on home and catch some shut-eye."

"No thanks, I'm all right."

"Any change in Mrs. DeSilva's condition?" he asked Shark.

"No. She's still unconscious."

"I told the team to examine her car first thing and call us right away when they're finished. So what do you think is going on, Shark? Accident or foul play?"

Shark took a sip of his coffee to stall. "Until the team goes over her car, your guess is as good as mine. If it's been tampered with, B.J. would have the most to gain if she died."

"See if he has an alibi for last night. Keep me informed. The reporters are already speculating that there's a connection to Marcus's death, and hounding me for a statement. I can't put them off for too long."

Sheriff Grant lumbered back to his office, and Shark glanced over at Dell. "Well?" he asked with a knot in his stomach.

Dell let him squirm for a minute then said, "No, I didn't say anything to him about why Marissa was on that deserted road, but I *should* have. If you pull another stunt like that, so help me, I will. I've never seen you act so stupid. What is it, love?"

The sense of relief was apparent on Shark's face. "No, of course not. All I know is she's the first person in a long time who makes me feel like I'm sixteen again."

"Spare me," Dell said rolling her eyes. "At least I hope you found out something useful from her. What did she say about the deaths of her parents and her previous husband?"

Shark related his conversation with Marissa.

"Don't you think it's a little strange that she agrees to go *fishing* with you on the very day that she spreads her dead husband's ashes?"

"I don't know what to think about any of this. She just said she was going nuts and needed to get out of the house."

"Well, it still sounds odd to me. I think I need to do a little more digging into her background. But right now we better find out if the kid's got an alibi for last night."

Diane DeSilva was a lot less cooperative than the last time they had spoken. All she would say was that B.J. had left to go back to school about 3:30 the previous afternoon. Dell had to persuade her to give up his phone number at school.

"Three-thirty, huh? That's about the time Marissa was driving out to meet me. B.J. could have seen her car, followed her, and tampered with it while it was parked at the boat landing. He could have been back on the road to Clemson before we ever got back," Shark said excitedly.

"I'll check with his roommate and see what time he got there," Dell said.

"Also, let's find out more about B.J. Remember how I told you one of the bartenders said he remembered B.J. because he had a big bet on the Georgia/Florida game the day Marcus died? A lot of college kids are heavy into sports gambling. Maybe that's one of B.J.'s vices," Shark said, as he drummed the pencil against the telephone.

"Good idea."

"And what's the skinny on Daniel Lawrence, at Coastal Development?"

"I've talked to his secretary several times. Apparently he's out of town and should be back today or tomorrow. I'll try and set up an appointment, as soon as he returns."

"The sooner, the better." Shark stood up. "I'm going to go over to Beaufort and have a look at Marissa's car myself."

"What do you think you're going to find that the team won't?"

"I don't know. It's just something I have to do," Shark said, grabbing his coffee and heading towards the door.

"Yeah, I hear you," Dell said shaking her head.

"Call me if there's any change in Marissa's condition."

"Sure." Dell reached for the phone and dialed B.J.'s number.

Traffic moved slowly, as Shark made his way toward Beaufort. It didn't matter how much of a hurry you were in, it was impossible to make good time. Called the Killing Road, SC 170 had the dubious distinction of being the deadliest stretch in all of South Carolina. After a while, you didn't even notice all the crosses that lined the shoulder. As often as Shark traveled this road, he worried that he would become a statistic himself one day.

Finally, after what seemed like an eternity, he pulled into the lot where the team was going over Marissa's car. He stopped dead in his tracks when he saw it. The tiny Miata's whole front end was jammed into the front seat. He was amazed that Marissa had survived.

He approached Phil Weiss, the head of the three-man team, examining the mangled wreck.

"What can you tell me, Phil?"

"And good morning to you too, Shark. Yes, I'm having a fine day, and you?"

"Cut the crap, Phil. Just tell me what you've found."

"God, someone kick you out of the wrong side of the bed this morning, or what? Only a hole in the brake hose, so far. All the fluid leaked out. No brakes, equals crash."

"Someone put it there?"

"Anything's possible, but it doesn't look like it. The hole isn't perfectly symmetrical like you'd get if someone deliberately punctured the line."

"Are you sure? Maybe it was done with a jagged instrument."

"Look, Shark, it appears to be from normal wear and tear on the hose. Possibly a rock caused the final puncture, but the hose appeared in pretty bad shape. I would guess it was just an accident, but there's always a slim chance it may have been tampered with."

"Guessing isn't good enough, Phil. Someone's life may be at stake here."

The head of the team bristled. "I know you're investigating Marcus DeSilva's death. I understand that if someone tampered with his wife's car, that it would be significant in your investigation. I'm telling you, no one did. In my professional opinion, it was just an accident. And that's what I intend to report to the Sheriff."

"I want to see the hose," Shark said.

"Suit yourself." Calling to one of his men, Phil yelled, "Hey Tim. Put the car back on the lift so the hot-shot detective here can here can have a look-see for himself." He turned on his heel and walked away.

After careful inspection, Shark had to agree the whole hose looked in pretty bad shape. As hard as he tried, he could find nothing that seemed suspicious. On one hand, he felt relief that maybe Marissa wasn't the target, but on the other, he was frustrated to be back to square one on the investigation. He had to be overlooking something, he thought, but what?

Walking to the back of the garage, he found Phil again. "Sorry about that pal. I have to agree with you. It doesn't look like it's been tampered with, but I'm not one hundred percent sure either."

Shark could tell his attempt at an apology wasn't cutting any ice. "Well, I'm thrilled you agree. Look, I don't tell you how to do your job, so don't tell me how to do mine. You know damned well we're never one hundred percent certain, but this is as close as it gets. I'll see you around."

Frustrated he had pissed off a good man, Shark slumped in his car and punched buttons on his cell phone. "Any change in Marissa's condition?" he asked as soon as Dell answered.

"No. What did you find out about the car?"

Shark relayed Phil's conclusion, but added there was a slim chance it could have been tampered with. "Did you get hold of B.J.?"

"No, but I did talk to his roommate, Jeff Blakely. He said he wasn't sure what time B.J. got back last night. He didn't get in himself until around two this morning, and he said B.J. was already asleep when he got home."

"Did you ask Blakely about the gambling?"

"Yeah. He got real quiet when I brought that up. Stammered around a little and said he really didn't know. That the two of them were roommates, but didn't hang with the same crowd."

"I know a guy who may have a line on the bookies in that area. I'll follow up on it when I get back to the office. I'm headed your way now."

"Okay. See you in a little while. I'll work on B.J.'s finances in the meantime."

Two hours of sleep in a hard plastic chair and the run-in with Phil Weiss, had left Shark with a screaming headache. On the way out of town, he swung by his house and washed down three extra-strength Tylenol with the last swig of milk that was three days past the expiration date, and tasting a little funky. He changed out of his fishing jeans, which had been closest at hand when he'd raced out this morning, and into more appropriate attire for the office. He would have liked to take time for a shower. Even in clean clothes he felt as if he still smelled like bait. Instead he made a quick bologna and cheese sandwich and grabbed a Coke for the road.

Back at the office he watched Dell work her magic with the computer keys, trying to get as much information as possible on B.J. DeSilva's financial picture. They were surprised to find he had been arrested for passing bad checks. They hadn't thought to run a sheet to see if he had a criminal record.

A little before five, they received a call from the hospital that Marissa had regained consciousness. Shark jumped up immediately and headed for the door.

"Want me to go with you?" Dell called after him.

"No need. I just thought I would stop by and see her for a few minutes, since she doesn't have any family or close friends here. Why don't you come by my place around seven-thirty tomorrow, and we'll drive up to Clemson, see what we can come up with."

"Sure thing. And Shark, remember Marissa is still a suspect in Marcus's death."

"I'm not sure if anyone is really a suspect at this point, but I hear what you're saying."

Shark made a quick stop at the Harris Teeter grocery store. Arms loaded with his purchases, he paused at the door to her room. After receiving Phil Weiss's report, the Sheriff had removed the officer on guard duty. Shark knocked tentatively, feeling like a nervous teenager on a first date, and then stuck his head in the door.

"Can I come in?" he asked, then stopped. Jason Mc-Calvey, impeccable in another perfectly tailored suit, sat next to Marissa's bed.

"Of course," Marissa answered with a smile on her face.

A huge bouquet, in a cut crystal vase, nearly covered the bedside table next to her. Shark laid the cellophane-wrapped white carnations, interspersed with three red roses, on her tray table. He sat the small Whitman's Sampler next to them.

"Thank you so much. How thoughtful."

"My mother always said chocolate could cure anything that ails you." Shark could almost feel the smirk on Jason McCalvey's face and knew, instinctively, that he had been the bearer of the funeral arrangement of lilies and orchids.

"Well, I guess I'll go and let you get some rest. Remember, you promised you'd call if there's anything you need," Jason said, rising.

"Thanks for coming. And for the lovely flowers."

Shark watched the door close behind him, then turned to Marissa. "How are you feeling?"

"A little woozy. I guess I'd better learn not to tangle with big trees," she said with a half smile.

"Do you remember anything about what happened?" Shark asked.

"Not really. Actually, I don't remember much about the last couple of days. Just flashes here and there. Do you know what caused the accident?"

"Your brake hose had a hole in it, and you lost all the fluid which made your brakes fail. The whole thing was pretty worn. Looked like a rock might have punctured it. Do you have any memory of us being out in my boat last night?"

"I sort of recall being on a boat, but I'm not sure if that was to spread Marcus's ashes or something else. Everything is all kind of jumbled together."

"That's pretty normal, after a blow to the head like you had. Things will get clearer with time. Can I bring you anything?"

Marissa paused. "I'd love to have some of my own things to wear, since the doctor says I have to stay here for a couple of days. And maybe my brush and comb. And a toothbrush. I mean, if you have the time and wouldn't mind getting them from home. I hate to impose on you, but I don't know who else to ask. My keys are in my purse in the top drawer."

Shark was pleased that there was finally something he could do for her. "I'll be glad to go by your place and pick up your things. What else? Something to read?"

"There's a book on the nightstand and a hand-held CD player I use when I walk on the beach. That would be nice." Marissa attempted to stifle a yawn.

"Why don't you rest, and I'll go get your stuff right now. By the time you wake up, I'll be back with your things."

Marissa reached over and squeezed his hand. "Thank you, Shark."

He retrieved her housekey and closed the door quietly, whistling tunelessly as he walked down the hall.

Shark opened Marissa's front door and turned off the security system. The house was so quiet, he could hear the ticking of a clock somewhere.

He climbed the stairs, opening several doors, before he found the master suite. It looked like something out of a magazine. A king-sized bed with four tall posters and some kind of gauzy material over the top dominated the room. Two large bookcases and a desk stood opposite a bank of windows. Shark could see a sliver of moon lighting up the beach, just a few yards away.

But what really drew his attention was the large pedestal, about waist-high, supporting a dolphin sculpture he immediately knew was a Wyland. Shark had been to the Wyland gallery on Hilton Head and loved his murals of whales and sea life. He was the only artist Shark knew anything about, probably because all his stuff had to do with fish or the ocean, Shark's two greatest loves. One day he vowed to make the trip out to Long Beach and see the three-acre mural called Whaling Wall 33. Like most people, Shark considered Wyland to be the best marine sculptor in the world. He stood admiring the curve of the dolphin's tail rising in the air, knowing he would never be able to afford to own one, not on a cop's salary.

Finally tearing himself away, he gathered the book, CD player and a few disks from the nightstand. He made his way down a narrow hall toward a bathroom with huge walk-in closets on each side. Marissa's was as large as his living room. Built-in drawers lined one wall and several racks of clothes hung impeccably in order by color. He shook his head at the row after row of shoes. A man only needed two pair of dress shoes—one brown, one black, and a couple pair of sneakers. He had never been able to understand why women needed so many different colors. He used to ask his wife, but she'd say he wouldn't understand. And she was right. He didn't.

Shark spotted a medium-size suitcase, drew it out and opened it on the chair. He opened the top drawer, and the scent of roses immediately filled the room. Shark just stood and stared for a moment, then ran his rough hands gently over the silky surface of the sheerest, most delicate underwear he had ever seen. Guiltily, he slammed the drawer closed. He felt like an intruder. He remembered the time when he was thirteen, and he and his buddy Sammy had gone through Sammy's sixteen-year-old sister's underwear drawer. And now he arrested perverts for doing much the same thing.

In the next few he found socks and stockings, but no gowns. Then he looked over at the clothes rack and spotted several silky peignoirs. As he inspected these sexy gowns, he envisioned Marissa floating in his arms. He wasn't sure how long the fantasy lasted, but when he snapped out of it, the shame sent him dashing from the closet empty handed.

Chapter Eleven

As Shark was filling a thermos with coffee for their road trip to Clemson, Dell strode into the kitchen waving a bag from Chesapeake Bagel. "Fuel," she muttered, as she dropped into a chair at the kitchen table.

"And good morning to you, too," Shark said, with a smile. Knowing Dell was not a morning person, he set a cup of coffee in front of her. Dressed in jeans, a red turtleneck and navy blazer, she looked like a college kid herself.

"I hate it when you're so cheerful at this time of the morning," she said, lowering her eyes and taking a sip of her coffee.

"Two sugars and a touch of cream, just the way you like it," Shark said, tightening the lid on the thermos. "Ready to get started?"

"Give me a minute here, okay?" Shark leaned against the counter and looked pointedly at his watch. "Okay, okay, I can take a hint. Your car or mine?" She unwound her body slowly, stood up, and stretched.

"Mine. I don't think you're awake enough to drive," Shark said, picking up the thermos and his keys.

"Good. Then I can sleep a little more." Dell yawned and started toward the front door.

Thirty minutes and two cups of coffee later, Dell began to revive. "So besides talking to B.J. and his roommate, what else do you have planned for today?"

"I want to go by the station and talk to Glen Zook. He's the most knowledgeable guy about the betting scene in the area. I spoke with him briefly yesterday and told him we'd be stopping by today. What's the latest on Daniel Lawrence at Coastal Development?"

"We have an appointment with him at ten on Monday. That's the first day he's back in the office. So, how was Marissa last night?"

"As well as can be expected I guess. Things are kind of jumbled up in her memory. Doesn't remember a lot about the twenty-four hours before the accident." Before Dell could probe any deeper and he'd be forced to admit he'd gone through Marissa's underwear drawer last night, he changed the subject. "So, heard anything from the dude in Charleston you met at the wedding?"

"Funny you should ask. He called last night, and we've got a date tomorrow. And his name is Joshua."

"Where are you going?"

"I think I'll take him to the Oyster Factory for dinner. Oh, I almost forgot. Your favorite female coroner called right after you left yesterday. Said to remind you not to forget you promised to go with her to the exhibit at the Whiteside Gallery tomorrow night. What kind of exhibit?"

Shark groaned. "Some sculptor from New York I never heard of. I've got to figure out a way to get out of it. Any ideas?"

"Frankly, I think you should go. It might help get your mind off the Black Widow."

"Damn it, Dell! You have no right to call her that. There's not one scrap of evidence to support that statement."

"Yeah, well, just call it woman's intuition. Look, you've got this poor little girl from Hazard, Kentucky who gets filthy rich in a few short years on the backs of two dead husbands. If you would use the head on your shoulders, instead of the one in your pants you'd be suspicious, too. Honestly, Shark, what's really with you and this broad? Granted, you've been in an emotional and physical vacuum since Laura died. I was thrilled when you and Anna finally started dating. Then along comes Miss Newscaster, and you immediately drop Anna. What gives? Do you really think a woman like Marissa would be interested in a guy who buys his shirts at Walmart? Once a woman develops a taste for champagne, she rarely goes back to beer for long. Guilty or innocent, she's still expensive."

Shark's eyes narrowed as he glanced over at Dell. His heart was beating so loudly he was sure she could hear it. He took a deep breath and reined in his anger. "I don't know. There's just something about her. It's not just her beauty, although you must admit she is easy on the eyes. It's her vulnerability."

Dell snorted and scrunched farther down in the seat.

"What if you're wrong? What if her husbands' deaths were both tragic accidents? If she really was a black widow, why didn't she kill her first husband, Devon Phillips? That doesn't fit your precious pattern."

"Look, let's not argue about this. I just don't want to see you screw up your career and maybe get hurt on top of that."

"Well, I'm a big boy. And remember, we have *no evidence* that even makes her a suspect."

They rode the next twenty miles in silence. Under different circumstances, Dell would have been thrilled to see Shark interested in someone. Three years was long enough to mourn Laura. She knew he wanted to have kids someday, but she just didn't see Marissa as the *mommy type*.

By mid-morning, they had been lulled almost to sleep by the monotonous scenery along the interstate. They were just a few miles from the campus, when Dell broke the uncomfortable silence. "I used to date a guy from Clemson when I was in college. Did you know the campus was once the Fort Hill Plantation of John C. Calhoun? The university was founded by Calhoun's son-in-law, Thomas Green Clemson, as an agricultural college. It was an all-male military school until 1955."

Shark smiled over at Dell. "That pretty head of yours is just filled with amazing and useless facts. I've lived in South Carolina all my life, and I didn't know that."

As they drove onto campus, Dell whipped some papers out of her purse, including a map she had pulled off the Internet that would take them straight to B. J's dorm. "Turn right here and then at the second street, take a left. Should be about a mile then to Calhoun Hall."

"The miracle of the Web. Me, I was just planning to stop and ask directions," Shark muttered.

"Yeah, sure. Men never stop. At least this way we won't have to drive around for an hour, pretending we know where we're going."

"Sometimes you can be too organized. Takes all the fun out of it," he shot back at her.

"You're just pissed you didn't think of it."

A few minutes later they flashed their badges at the front desk of the dorm and were directed to the third floor. They had purposely not alerted B.J. they were coming.

They knocked on 312, but got no answer. Shark pounded again, louder. "Go away," a faint voice muttered from inside.

"Open up. Police," Shark said gruffly.

A couple minutes later B.J. stuck his tousled head around the door. "What the hell?" he asked when he recognized Shark.

"Open up, B.J. We want to talk to you." The boy glanced over at Dell, moved away from the door, and flopped down on the bed. The detectives edged into the cramped room.

"What's it now? I told you everything before."

"Where's your roommate?" Dell asked.

B.J. looked up, suddenly alert. "What's he got to do with anything?"

"Just answer the question, kid," Shark snapped.

"What time is it?" he asked.

"Ten forty-five," Shark answered.

"He's in calculus class till eleven. Then he usually goes to the library till his next class at twelve."

"Is this him?" Dell asked, picking up a picture off the desk of a couple in formal attire.

"Yeah, that's him. But why do you want to talk to Jeff? Is he in some kind of trouble?"

Dell put the picture in her purse and left the room without replying. Shark sat down on the rumpled bed facing B.J.'s and surveyed the room. It was a mess. Two large pizza boxes and several empty beer cans only added to the general clutter. Piles of dirty jeans and socks made it smell like a locker room. A stack of books on the desk by the computer apparently hadn't been touched in a while, evidenced by the cobweb running from the top of the pile to the pencil sharpener.

"Why aren't you in class?" Shark asked casually.

"What business is it of yours anyway? And why should I bother going to class? As soon as I get my money, I'm out of here."

"Think that's what your Dad would want?"

"Who cares? He's not around to tell me what to do anymore."

"So, you're just going to drop out. Then what are you going to do?"

"I'm not sure yet. Maybe kick around Europe for a while. When I was a kid I wanted to paint. Maybe I'll take some art classes. The old man always said art was okay for a hobby, but not a career. It was his bright idea for me to get an MBA so I could join him in his business. It sure as hell wasn't mine."

"Once you pay off all your gambling debts, doesn't look like you'll have a lot left."

B.J.'s head snapped up. "I don't know what you're talking about."

"Cut the crap, B.J. I know you've been arrested for passing bad checks. We've gone over your financial records and talked to some people."

"But I can explain about the checks. It was all the bank's fault."

"Can it, B.J. I've heard that song before. It always starts out with a small bet on just one game, doesn't it? But then it gets out of control fast. You're a couple bucks shy of being completely wiped out. How much did you lose on the Georgia/Florida game? I heard you had a lot riding on that one. My guess is you dropped several grand."

"Don't tell me you've never bet on a ball game before," the boy challenged.

Shark didn't reply, just let the silence lengthen. It wasn't long before B.J. felt the need to fill the void.

"So, I got a little behind. It's no big deal."

"More than a little, I think. Your father's timely death gets you out of the hole, at least temporarily. Makes for a pretty good motive for murder, if you ask me."

"Look! I told you. I had nothing to do with my dad's death. And I resent you implying that I would kill my own father to pay off a gambling debt," he shouted.

"That why you're going to skip out to Europe for a while? Figure out of sight, out of mind? Well, let me tell you, son, bookies have long memories, and they aren't the forgiving type. I've dealt with enough dead bodies to know that for a fact. Especially when they find out about your inheritance. That may at least save you from some broken knee caps, or worse."

B.J. ran both of his hands through his already greasy hair. "Okay. So I got in a little over my head. I'll have enough to pay them off and still go to Europe for awhile. Especially after the business is sold."

Shark grilled B.J. for another half-hour, concentrating on establishing his whereabouts during the time Marissa's car was accessible at the boat landing. He seemed to have no more or no less knowledge about cars than the average teenage boy. Shark decided, if in fact the Miata had been tampered with, B.J. was as likely a candidate as any other. When he figured he had wrung everything he could out of the kid, he returned to the car to wait on Dell.

Thirty minutes later she climbed into the passenger seat. "Well?" Shark asked.

"Pulling teeth from a donkey must be easier than getting roommates to talk about each other. But, finally, due to my superb interrogation skills, I got the scoop. Seems B.J.'s into his bookie for about a hundred grand."

Shark whistled. "Jesus!"

"Tell me about it. He's been getting some nasty phone calls about paying up. Ten days ago two very intimidating guys showed up at their door to have a little friendly chat with B.J. Jeff didn't stick around to hear the conversation, but said that B.J. seemed really scared when he came back to the room later. Said something about trying to get a loan from his mom or dad. Jeff's the nerdy type, and I'm inclined to believe him."

"Any chance he might have bumped off Marcus to help out his roomie?"

"None. He almost wet his pants talking to me. I don't think he has the nerve. Oh, by the way, their bookie's name is Axel."

Shark told her what little he'd learned from B.J. as they headed off campus and looked for a place to have lunch. They spent the next hour wolfing down bacon cheeseburgers at Wendy's and comparing notes. "Let's go by the station and talk to Glen Zook, and see what we can find out about the bookie," Shark said, dumping the few scraps left on their tray into the overflowing trash receptacle.

Thirty minutes later, they were seated in Zook's office reporting what little they knew. The overweight, balding detective had twenty years on the force and every one of them was stamped on his face.

"What can you tell us about this guy, Axel?" Shark asked.

"Major player. Controls almost all the betting on campus and a large part of what goes on in the rest of the area. Word is he's connected to Vegas, probably the mob. Keeps extending these kids credit until they get in way over their heads, then doesn't have a lot of patience when they don't pay up. Periodically, he makes an example of someone to keep the others in line. I don't think they've killed anyone around here, at least not that we know of. But they've come close. One kid I know of is paralyzed from the waist down. Sounds like B.J. was in deep shit if they paid him a personal visit."

"Any chance you can keep an eye on our boy and see if anyone else makes contact?" Dell asked.

"Get serious, honey. I don't have the time or the manpower to babysit one kid. I've got sixteen thousand of them up there to worry about."

Shark dragged Dell out of the station, before she had a chance to pull a gun on the obnoxious Detective Zook.

She spent most of the drive home, muttering "pig" under her breath. When they finally pulled into Shark's driveway, Dell rummaged in her purse, pulled out her keys, and headed straight for her car.

"Hey, want to come in for a beer before you go?" Shark called after her.

"I think I'll pass."

"Well, don't be pissed at me, I didn't call you *honey*."

"I know. Sorry. It's been a long day."

"Have a good time on your date tomorrow night."

"Thanks, you too. Hope the exhibit isn't too boring."

"Trust me. I'll never know."

"What a rat you are! At least call Anna tonight so she has enough time to line someone else up to go with her."

"I'll do that right now. See you Monday at the office, if not before."

As soon as Shark had opened a beer, he picked up the phone and dialed Anna's number. The gods were smiling—he got her answering machine. He made his excuses and hung up quickly, then immediately dialed Marissa's room number at the hospital.

"Hello," she answered on the first ring.

"It's Shark. How're you feeling?"

Marissa sighed. "Bored to tears. But the doctor said I can go home tomorrow."

"That's great news!"

"Thanks for dropping my stuff off last night. Sorry I was asleep when you came back. You should have wakened me. By the way, what's with the granny gown? I don't think you found that in *my* closet."

Shark paused, embarrassed. "Well, I didn't want to rifle through your things. I saw several practically see-through gowns hanging in your closet that looked more appropriate for a bedroom than a hospital room. So I just stopped and picked up a gown like my mother used to wear."

Marissa laughed. "Well, I'm surprised she ever had any kids."

Shark loved to hear her laugh. He wished she would do it more often. He wanted to see her—no, he *needed* to see her. "So, you feel up to company?" he asked casually.

"Sure. Come on by. Are you on the island?"

"No, I'm at home. I can be there in about an hour."

"I'll look forward to it."

Shark hung up the phone, thrilled at the sound of those words. He changed quickly into jeans and a red Polo turtleneck. It took him a little digging in the back of the hall closet to locate the small trunk he hadn't opened in years. He smiled to himself as he stuffed everything into a brown paper bag and headed out.

An hour and a half later Shark walked into Marissa's room with the sack in one hand and two large plastic cups in the other.

"Hi!" he said, unloading everything on the bedside tray. With a flourish he lifted one of the lids. "A chocolate shake for madam?"

"Great! How did you know I was craving one of these?"

"ESP. It's from Ice Cream Sensations on Main Street. They make shakes to die for."

"*Ummmm*. This is wonderful. What's in the sack?"

"Entertainment, my dear, entertainment." Shark spread a deck of cards and a Scrabble game out on the tray.

Marissa laughed and shook her head. "Oh no, I'm terrible at Scrabble."

"What a relief! Me, too. I'm much better at cards."

"I haven't handled a deck of cards since I was a kid. My dad used to play crazy eights with me if I pestered him long enough."

"Crazy eights or gin rummy. Name your game," Shark said, wiggling his eyebrows in a bad Groucho Marx imitation.

"Something tells me I'm in trouble, no matter what I choose."

Shark pulled up a chair, lowered the bedside table and shuffled the cards. Marissa swung her legs over the side of the bed and draped the sheet modestly around her. She was wearing the flannel gown he had brought the night before. It was pink and white checked with a high neckline. She had pushed the long sleeves up to her elbows. He had to admit, it did look a little silly on her. He couldn't help remembering all those sexy see-though things in her closet. *Maybe someday . . .*

For the next two hours they played rummy and sipped milkshakes. He tried to avoid answering any specific questions about how he'd spent his day.

"I give up," Shark finally said as he threw down his cards after Marissa went out again. She'd already won two games of rummy and three of crazy eights. "I think you keep extra eights up those long sleeves of yours. Now, if we were playing poker, I'd put you to shame."

"Oh what a sorry loser you are. The next time, we can play poker, and maybe I'll have to let you win, so you don't take your cards and go home."

"Speaking of going home, I'd better hit the road and let you get some rest. What time are you being discharged tomorrow?" he asked as he straightened the deck and put it back in the box.

"Dr. Lockhart said he would be by first thing in the morning. If everything looks okay he'll let me go then."

"Okay, I'll come by about ten and take you home when you're ready."

"Are you sure? I can take a cab. You've done so much for me already. I hate to impose on you again."

Shark stared into Marissa's eyes and said softly, "It's not an imposition, I want to do it. Not another word."

Marissa reached up, put her hand on the back of his neck, and pulled his face close to hers. Gently she kissed his cheek. "Thank you Shark. For everything. I don't know how I'll ever repay you for your kindness."

"You just did."

Shark whistled all the way down the hall to the elevator.

Chapter Twelve

The next morning Shark arrived at the hospital five minutes before ten, but it was almost noon before they completed the checkout process and were headed toward Marissa's.

"Feel like getting some lunch on the way home?" Shark asked, glancing over at her. He was glad he had tossed in the red velour warm-up suit when he'd packed her bag. He liked her in red. With her dark hair she looked scrumptious, almost good enough to eat. *Get your mind out of the gutter,* he ordered himself.

"That would be great. I'm not sure what's left in the refrigerator."

There weren't many restaurants between the hospital and Palmetto Dunes, so he pulled into the Cracker Barrel. "This okay?" he asked.

"Great! I haven't eaten here in years."

Shark asked the hostess if they could sit out on the screened porch, since it was a beautiful sunny day. Over lunch they chatted about inconsequential things.

By the time they arrived at Marissa's, Shark could tell she was getting tired. "I'll go, so you can take a nap?"

Marissa paused. "I am tired, but that doesn't mean you have to leave, unless you have someplace you need to be?"

"Not really. I can just tell you're worn out."

"Then I have a proposition for you. Why don't I get a couple of steaks out of the freezer to thaw for dinner? I'll go rest for an hour or so, and when I get up we can take a short walk on the beach. The least I can do is fix dinner for you, after all you've done for me. And if you're real good, maybe I'll let you win a game of cards afterwards. What do you say?"

Shark was thrilled. There was no place else he'd rather be. "That would be lovely, but only if you promise not to throw the card game."

Marissa laughed. "It's a deal. Will you be too bored while I lie down?"

"No. I'll just sit out on the deck and enjoy the ocean. You go rest now."

Shark plopped down on a chaise and, after a few minutes, dozed off to the sound of the surf. An hour and a half later he woke up, thirsty. He made his way into the kitchen and poured himself a glass of ice water. He decided he should check on Marissa.

He made his way quietly up the stairs and stopped at the open door of her room. He crept over to her bedside. Covered with a beige afghan, she was still asleep, her hair splayed out on the pillow. His breath caught in his chest. He wasn't sure how long he stood there, captivated by the child-like vulnerability of her sleeping face. When she stirred, he quietly hurried out of the room. When she came downstairs a few minutes later, he was sitting on the couch studying a book of Wyland's sculptures.

"Do you like Wyland?" she asked sitting down next to him.

She smelled like soap and toothpaste and some exotic fragrance he couldn't put a name to. "I love his work," he said forcing his attention back to the photographs. "I noticed one of his sculptures in your bedroom, when I picked up your things."

"Yes. Marcus always said anyone who loved the ocean would have to love Wyland."

"I've always dreamed of going out to the Long Beach Convention Center and seeing the Whaling Wall."

Marissa shook her head. "What is it about men, whales and dolphins? Don't get me wrong. I like his work, but men seem to mention his name with such reverence."

"Don't ask me. I'm one of those guys who doesn't know squat about art, except I know what I like. Ready for that walk on the beach?"

They cut short their beach walk. The temperature was dropping rapidly, and they were both shivering by the time they got back. "Would you start a fire in the fireplace?" Marissa asked. "I feel chilled to the bone."

"That sounds good. Just point me to the firewood."

Shark made two trips downstairs to the garage, and a few minutes later had a decent fire going. Marissa came in balancing a small tray precariously in her good hand.

"How about a glass of Merlot? Or I have beer if you would prefer."

"Wine is great." Shark pulled a couple of cushions off the couch and placed them on the floor in front of the roaring fire. "Come over here and sit by the fire and get warm." Shark took the tray and set it between the two of them on the hearth. Both seemed absorbed in the flickering of the flames, but the silence was comfortable.

Marissa, still staring into the fire, asked, "You told me right after Marcus died that you had lost someone close to you. Would I be prying, if I asked who?"

Shark didn't respond immediately. When he did, it was in a voice Marissa had never heard before. "My wife, Laura, died three years ago."

"I'm sorry. Was it an accident?"

"No," he said softly. "She had this little mole on her back. It had been there ever since I had known her. Gradually it started growing, just a little, and she complained of it itching. Then one day she went in for her regular checkup and asked the doctor to take a look at it. He told her it was probably nothing, but referred her to a dermatologist to have it removed. It turned out to be malignant melanoma. It had already metastasized to her spine at that point and six months later it invaded her brain and she died."

"I'm so sorry." Marissa reached over and put her hand on his arm. "That must have been so difficult for you. Do you have any children?"

"No. We were trying to start a family when she was diagnosed."

"How did you handle it? I thought I wouldn't survive after Eric's death, and now with Marcus dying too, I don't know how to go on."

"I didn't handle it very well for a long time. I started drinking and smoking too much. I tried to work all the time so I didn't have to go home to an empty house. Then about a year ago I stopped all the self-destructive behavior, except the cigarettes, which I finally gave up a couple of weeks ago. I decided Laura wouldn't like the person I had become. So now, I try to go out in my boat and enjoy the ocean and this beautiful earth that God created and not think about Laura so much. But it takes time. The healing doesn't happen overnight."

"Do you ever think about getting married again?" Marissa asked softly.

"Right after Laura died, I couldn't even entertain that thought. I was afraid to care about anyone because I knew I couldn't go through that again. But, I would like to have kids someday and that usually requires a wife. How about you?"

"After all this, I just don't know. I feel like I must be a jinx or something. Everyone I've ever loved has died. But, like you, I've always wanted a family. I got pregnant once, right after Eric and I were married. But I had a miscarriage when I was just a few weeks along. We were desperately hoping for a child and doing all the temperature and ovulation charts when he died. Afterwards, I often thought a baby might have helped to ease some of the pain and loneliness. I knew Marcus didn't want any more kids, but I loved him so much it didn't seem important at the time. And, in the back of my mind, I always thought he would come around after we were married."

"So are you telling me that you're never going to marry again?"

"I don't think I should, do you? I feel like I have this curse when it comes to husbands."

"Enough of this gloomy talk," Shark said, pulling a deck of cards out of his pocket. "Got a jar of pennies somewhere we can use for poker chips, unless you want to play strip poker."

Marissa laughed. "Detective, I'm shocked. I think we better stick to seven-card stud. I'll go get the pennies. And by the way, I always play deuces and one-eyed jacks are wild."

Shark rolled his eyes. "Typical female. Got to have wild cards."

Two hours later Marissa had a healthy pile of pennies in front of her, and Shark was down to his last five. "If I don't win this hand I may have to ask for a loan."

"In your dreams," Marissa said, as she slapped down three kings—one of which was a wild card—beating Shark's pair of aces.

"Damn! If we weren't playing with wild cards, I would have won."

"Quit whining! Just think, if we had been playing strip poker you would be naked now."

"Maybe I should start the steaks." The blush on his face had nothing to do with the heat from the fire.

"Good plan," Marissa laughed. "I'll try and make us a salad, although this brace on my wrist is a pain."

The steaks were grilled to perfection, and they lingered a long time over the meal. "It's so nice to have someone to share dinner with," Marissa said, as she played with the rim of her wineglass.

"I know what you mean. I hate eating alone, and cooking for one is the pits."

They stacked their plates in the dishwasher and settled again in front of the fireplace. Shark added a few more logs while Marissa refilled their wineglasses. They were working on their second bottle. "What kind of music do you like?" Marissa asked.

"Got any Buffett?"

Marissa grinned. "As a matter of fact I do. Marcus hated him, but I've been a Parrothead since I was a teenager."

As soon as "Margaritaville" blared from the speaker, Shark started singing along. There wasn't a Buffett tune he didn't know all the words to. By the time "Cheeseburger in Paradise" came on, he was standing in front of the fire using his wineglass as a microphone and singing at the top of his lungs. Marissa was laughing so hard tears ran down her cheeks. When the song ended, Shark collapsed onto the pillows. "I could never marry a woman who doesn't like Buffett."

"So what other qualifications does your potential mate have to have?"

Shark answered, without hesitation, "She has to like fishing and love the ocean." Then he reached over and gently moved a soft strand of black hair away from her cheek. "And being as beautiful as you are, certainly wouldn't hurt."

"Thank you." She placed an index finger softly on his face and slowly traced the ragged path of the scar. "Tell me about this," she whispered. Shark reached up and ran a hand down the thin line that extended down the left side of his face and heard the faint rasp of the day's stubble. He captured her hand and carried it to his chest.

"Nothing much to tell really. Several years ago I answered a domestic abuse call. As I was cuffing the husband, his twelve-year-old son came from out of nowhere and cut me with a steak knife. End of story."

"It must have taken a lot of stitches."

"A hundred and sixty-eight, but who counted?"

"Did you ever get shot?"

Wanting to change the subject, Shark said, "You know, I have a confession to make. I used to watch you on TV and fantasize about kissing this spot right here." He rubbed his thumb gently across the small imperfection next to her mouth.

A flush of color stained her cheeks and her eyes widened, the pupils dilating as she stared up at him. From the wine, he told himself.

"And do you ever act out your fantasies?" Marissa whispered, her face now just inches from his.

They were caught in a magnetic field that held them a scant inch apart. He tried to tell himself to back off, but he couldn't. Or maybe wouldn't was a better word. Something more powerful than common sense pulled him toward her. His eyes were drawn to her mouth, ripe and red and made for a man to kiss. He'd wanted a taste of it since the first moment he'd laid eyes on her in the church, and now he pushed away all the reasons he shouldn't take a taste of it.

Her lips parted slightly, and Shark took the action as a silent invitation. He cupped her cheek, catching his thumb beneath her chin and tilting her face to a better angle, then lowered his mouth to hers before she could tell him to stop.

Soft, sweet, tasting of wine. He kept the kiss light, but he never wanted it to end. If he could stop time, he would do it right now. It was all he had imagined, and more than he had bargained for.

A warning bell sounded somewhere in the back of his mind. She was trouble. Tangled up in the murder investigation, and he hated the idea of his professional life and his personal life crossing paths that way. He'd never crossed that line before, and he couldn't now.

Reluctantly, Shark broke off the kiss. His hands stroked her hair. "That was even better than I imagined," he said breathlessly.

"You should learn to act on your impulses more often. Any other fantasizes I can fulfill for you?"

Shark chuckled. "I'm afraid they're X-rated. I don't think I can share them with you. I'd better add a couple more logs to the fire." He stood on shaky legs, crossed the room and opened the door to the stairs that descended to the garage. He was grateful for the brisk temperature that helped cool his passion and clear his head.

I knew he wanted me. It was only a matter of time. Marissa plumped up the pillows in front of the fireplace and arranged herself seductively.

Shark returned loaded down with several oak logs. He added two to the fire and stacked the others on the hearth. He avoided Marissa's eyes when he turned to her and said, "I guess I'd better hit the road, let you get some rest."

Marissa smiled and stared up at him. "Why don't you fix us a cognac before you go?"

Shark gazed down at her hair splayed across the pillow. The pop and crackle of the logs as they caught was the only sound in the room, except for the roaring of his heartbeat in his head. With the cast on her arm and the dark circles under her eyes, she looked so vulnerable.

Without uttering a word he crossed to the bar and filled one brandy snifter with Remy Martin. The reality of where he was and what he had done washed over him like an icy shower. He had broken all his professional and personal rules about never getting involved with a suspect.

As he approached, she sat up. "Where's your drink?" she asked as she took the snifter out of his hand.

"I can't drink anymore since I'm driving home. Wouldn't look good for me to get stopped for a DUI."

Marissa didn't reply. She locked eyes with him for a moment, then rose and made her way over to the bar. In a matter of seconds she returned with another snifter half full of the amber liquid. She held it out to Shark. "Then don't drive. Stay here with me tonight."

"I can't do that."

"Please, Shark. I don't want to be alone. I haven't slept in days. I'm exhausted. We can sleep right there, in front of the fire, fully clothed. You don't even have to touch me. You can even sleep on the couch if you want," she pleaded.

Shark turned his head and stared down at the floor.

"I can't do that, Marissa."

"Why?"

"You know why."

"Because you suspect me of murdering my husband?" she asked, the anger apparent in her voice.

"I didn't say that."

"No, but that's what you're thinking. If you walk out that door then I'll know it's because you really believe that I had something to do with Marcus's death." Tears filled her eyes as she gazed up at him.

Shark knew what it was like to feel alone. He'd been alone too long. To need someone's comfort, someone's strength. Just the touch of another human being, their arms around you. He knew he shouldn't, but he couldn't walk away from her. He reached out, took the glass, and felt the warmth of the cognac on the back of his throat.

Marissa smiled, took his hand and led him back to the fireplace. She knew he might regret this in the morning, but at least tonight, she wouldn't be alone.

After Shark fell asleep, Marissa lay next to him, still awake. She stared into the flames, her mind drifting back to graduation night, to that *other fire*. She could still smell the smoke and feel the heat parching her skin. She remembered standing next to the policeman, dazed, staring at the pile of smoldering rubble that had been her house, praying no one would discover her thoughts. She remembered crying, not for her father, but for Mama, old before her time and as much a victim of his drunken rages as Marissa herself had been. They thought she wept with grief, with fear of being left alone in the world. Only she knew they were tears of relief, both she and Mama finally free of his tyranny. True, she had become an orphan, but nothing could be worse than the hell she had been living in.

Shark mumbled in his sleep and shifted his arm where it lay across her shoulder. With a sigh, Marissa pulled her gaze away from the fire. Turning back into his arm, she nestled her head against his chest. A hint of a smile played across her lips. She had vowed that night long ago, that never again would someone else use her, unless it was for *her* gain.

Chapter Thirteen

Driving home Sunday morning, Shark had mixed feelings. Guilty and concerned about putting his career on the line, he cringed at the thought of Dell ever finding out what he had done. But the image of Marissa was uppermost in his mind. He had never desired a woman as much as he did Marissa. He replayed the night over and over in his mind, as he drove.

Shark walked into his bedroom and, peeling off his shirt to jump in the shower, he suddenly stopped dead in his tracks. His pager lay on his nightstand. In his hurry to change clothes and get to the hospital, he had forgotten it. He grabbed it up and breathed a big sigh of relief when he saw there were no messages. As he turned toward the bathroom, it went off. Quickly he clicked it on and recognized Dell's mobile number. He perched on the edge of the bed and called her.

"What's up?"

When Dell answered it was her no-nonsense professional voice. "Probable murder/suicide in Port Royal. Meet me at thirteen Walker Street. I'm about ten miles from the Broad Creek Bridge."

Shark rebuttoned his shirt, grabbed his gun and badge, and raced to his car.

Eight minutes later he pulled up at the address Dell had given him. Several police cars and the coroner's wagon were already there. He ducked under the yellow police tape and met Deputy Sayles at the front door. "Who's the Primary?" he asked.

"Pickford. He's in the back."

Shark made his way to the blood-spattered bedroom, where Anna Connors crouched over a middle-aged female half on and half off the bed. The second body, male, was sprawled across the rumpled sheets, with an apparent gunshot wound to the head.

"What we got, Anna?"

"Looks like he strangled his wife and then shot himself."

"Identity?"

"Jacob and Mary Prestcott. Pickford says he's been arrested a couple of times for domestic abuse. I understand she filed for divorce and a restraining order on Friday. Lotta good it did her."

"Nasty, nasty," Dell said from the doorway. Shark repeated what little he knew, and they began to work the crime scene.

At 7:15 the next morning Shark picked up the phone to call Marissa. He had intended to touch base with her the night before, but exhaustion and the late hour had sent him straight to bed. He had dialed only the first three digits before he abruptly hung up. She probably wasn't an early riser, and Dell was on her way for their appointment in Charleston with Daniel Lawrence. He would wait and call later.

Shark had just walked away from the phone when Dell paraded in, dressed in a navy skirt, white turtleneck, and matching jacket. "Wow! What's the occasion? I can see your legs."

"I don't know. Maybe I'm just feeling real female this morning."

"Ah, so the date went well with Joshua."

"Better than well—fantastic!"

Shark raised his eyebrows. "My, my. Is he destined to be the father of your children?"

Dell picked up the dishtowel off the counter and threw it at him.

"Peace offering," Shark said, as he handed her a cup of coffee and a blueberry muffin.

By mid-morning, they were seated in the reception room at Coastal Development. They had been waiting impatiently for fifteen minutes. "This is a bunch of bullshit," Shark said, irritably. "Who does this guy think he is to keep us hanging like this?"

The phone buzzed on the receptionist's desk and she looked up, smiling. "Mr. Lawrence will see you now. Down the hall, the first office on the right."

Daniel Lawrence met them at the door. "Come in. Sorry to keep you waiting, but I was on a long-distance call. First day back in the office is always a bear. Please, sit down." He motioned them toward the gray leather sofa, then took a seat in a chair across the glass-topped coffee table.

"Would you like some coffee, or a soda?" he asked. They both declined.

Daniel Lawrence wasn't what Shark had expected. Short and almost bald, he had to be in his sixties. His glasses kept slipping down his nose. His suit appeared rumpled, as if he had slept in it. Shark had envisioned a tall, impeccably dressed, younger man.

"What can I do for you?" he asked, pushing his glasses back up on his nose.

Shark spoke first. "It came to our attention, while investigating Marcus DeSilva's death, that you had some dealings with him. Would you mind telling us about that."

"Of course not. I was sorry to hear about DeSilva's death, but our relationship was strictly business. He owned a tract of land that adjoins some we own on Highway two seventy-eight. We plan to build a shopping center there. With the development of Sun City, we think it's a prime location."

"And you needed DeSilva's land, to make the deal?" Shark asked.

"Several large stores have expressed an interest in the shopping center. To fully develop it to its potential, we need more space for parking. We offered to buy DeSilva's tract, but he refused. As an extra incentive, I told him I would buy out his company as well, but again he refused. Said he'd like to buy our property instead." Lawrence smiled and shook his head. "Of course, that wasn't an option."

"Mrs. DeSilva said you called and told *her*, that in fact, her husband had agreed to sell you his company," Dell said coolly.

Surprised, Daniel Lawrence looked from Dell to Shark. "I don't understand. I've never spoken with Mrs. DeSilva. I do plan to renew the offer I made to him, but I would never do that, until a decent amount of time had passed. I am not an insensitive man."

Dell glanced over at her partner. They both knew someone was lying—and Shark was afraid it wasn't Daniel Lawrence. But why would Marissa say he called? Surely she knew it was something they could easily check. And how would she even know about Coastal Development, unless Marcus had mentioned it to her?"

"It seems to me that Mr. DeSilva's death was very timely and increases your chance of getting your hands on his land. That sounds like a pretty good motive for murder to me," Shark said.

Daniel Lawrence threw up his hands. "Wait, wait just a minute. You think Marcus DeSilva was *murdered*? I understood it was an accident."

"We're exploring all possibilities. We haven't ruled out anything yet."

"Detective Morgan, stop right there. I run a legitimate business. We develop properties all over the country. There's not a piece of land on God's green earth that's worth murdering someone over. If one project doesn't work out, I just move on to the next one. I had absolutely nothing to do with Marcus's death."

"Where were you on the day he was shot?" Dell asked.

"I was home packing for my trip to California."

"Is there anyone who can confirm that?"

"No, I'm a bachelor."

"Do you know if anyone else was interested in buying that tract of land?"

Daniel Lawrence paused. "I honestly don't know the answer to that. But there's so much development going on in that area, I wouldn't be surprised. That whole corridor is going to be a gold mine, especially after the University of South Carolina builds their four-year campus extension. Land values have already skyrocketed since two seventy-eight was completed out to Interstate ninety-five, and they're only going to continue to appreciate in value."

"Is there anything else you can tell us that might shed any light on our investigation?" Shark asked, fairly certain they had already gotten everything Daniel Lawrence had to offer.

"I don't believe so, but I'll certainly call if anything occurs to me."

He accepted Shark's card, and Dell thanked him for his cooperation.

Back in the car, they both agreed that Daniel Lawrence seemed totally legit. "I'll check and make sure he really was in California, but I think we can scratch him off the list," Dell said.

Just outside of Charleston, traffic came to a complete standstill. Ahead of them they could see a solid line of vehicles, backed up for miles. "Damn, wouldn't you know it. Hope we're not stuck here too long. I'm starving," Dell said disgustedly.

An hour later, they had moved not an inch. People had gotten out of their cars, some tossing Frisbees, others chatting, to pass the time. They learned a gasoline truck had overturned, caught fire, and that there were several fatalities. Numerous ambulances, fire trucks, and policemen were now on the scene.

Shark desperately wanted a cigarette. Trying to ignore his craving, he scrunched down in his seat and closed his eyes. "Wake me when traffic starts to move."

"Damn you, Shark. I wish I could fall asleep, on command, like that." Dell opened the passenger door, and yelled to the car in back of her. "Got a magazine, newspaper, or anything I can read?"

Finally, at two forty-five, Dell poked Shark awake, as the cars in front of them began to creep forward. "Hold on a second, while I return this *Field and Stream* back to my buddy in the Jeep back there."

"*Field and Stream*?" Shark said, as she leaped back into her seat. "You must have really been desperate."

"It was better than listening to you snore. Anyway, stop at the first filling station you come to. I'm starved and I have to pee. Otherwise we'll be swimming in here, before we get back to Beaufort."

It was four-thirty by the time Dell slumped down on Shark's couch and kicked off her pumps. "What a wasted day."

"I'll say. You got all dressed up for nothing. I think your legs were wasted on Mr. Lawrence," Shark said, handing her a beer.

"So, how was the exhibit Saturday night?" Dell took a long pull of the cold brew.

"Fine, I imagine. I didn't go. Tell me more about Joshua," he said, trying to change the subject. It didn't work.

"I bet Anna was pissed. What did she say, when you canceled?"

"She wasn't home when I called. I left a message on her answering machine."

"No wonder she was a little frosty to you Sunday morning at the crime scene. I thought maybe you two had a spat or something. So what did you do Saturday night?"

Shark hesitated. He didn't want to lie to his partner. He never had, and he didn't want to start now. "Listened to a little music and drank a lot of wine."

Shark thanked the gods, she left it there.

Chapter Fourteen

Shark was five minutes from the office Tuesday morning, when he got the call that there had been a fatal accident on Highway 278. He made a U-turn, and headed back in the direction of Moss Creek Plantation. He told the dispatcher he was responding, and the dispatcher in turn relayed that Dell was headed out the door.

Traffic was at a standstill, forcing Shark to drive on the right-hand shoulder. He finally had to park in front of Gold's Gym and hoof it the rest of the way. He found a maroon Oldsmobile that had been impacted by a cement truck on the entire left side. It appeared the driver of the car had exited Moss Creek Plantation and attempted to cross two lanes of traffic to make a left-hand turn.

"He just pulled right out in front of me and then seemed to stop," the operator of the truck was telling Deputy Sayles as Shark walked up. "I tried to brake, but there wasn't enough time," he babbled, tears streaming down his cheeks.

Shark hated these kinds of accidents where it was just bad timing, and someone ended up dead. He looked up to see Dell trotting across the intersection, her face pink with exertion. "Little out of shape are we?" Shark teased.

"Go to hell. What have we got?"

Shark told her what little he knew. "Deceased was an eighty-two-year-old male, named Harold Swiecke. Appears he pulled out in front of the cement truck and stopped in the middle of the road. Cement truck couldn't stop. Mr. Swiecke knocks on the pearly gates. End of story."

"Was the truck speeding?" Dell asked.

"Going about sixty, it appears. Only five miles over the speed limit."

"Sometimes, that's all it takes."

Shark and Dell worked the scene for another two hours and spent the rest of the day dealing with the paperwork. At four-thirty, Dell pulled the last report off the printer and slipped it into the case file. "I've had it for today. I'm heading out. How about you?"

"I have an appointment at five o'clock to talk to Tim Silvers, Marcus's accountant," Shark said, as he leaned on the corner of her desk.

"Want me to go with you?"

"No, I can handle it. Why don't you go on home."

"If you're sure." Dell turned off the computer and retrieved her purse from the bottom desk drawer. "I'll see you in the morning then."

As soon as Dell walked out the door Shark picked up the phone and dialed Marissa's number. He let it ring until the answering machine clicked on, then hung up without leaving a message.

Shark pulled into the parking lot of the Water's Edge complex at two minutes till five. Inside he located the number for Silver's office. The middle-aged receptionist looked up as he pushed open the door.

"Detective Morgan?" she asked with a pleasant smile.

"Yes ma'am."

"Mr. Silvers is expecting you." As she rose to lead him back toward the accountant's office, she said over her shoulder, "It was so tragic about Mr. DeSilva."

"Sure was."

Tim Silver's hair was more salt than pepper. He removed his wire framed reading glasses, and stood to shake hands with the detective. "Have a seat. I'm not sure how I can help you, but I'll do anything I can. I still can't believe Marcus is gone."

"Had you been his accountant for a long time?"

"About eight years. He was my first major client, after I moved to the island. Once he came aboard, he referred several more good clients to me."

"I understand you went to his place to do his books. Isn't that unusual?"

"Actually, no. Over half my clients' work is done in their offices. That's what sets me apart from other accountants. I just take my laptop, set it up on site, and if I need additional information about something, it's right there."

"What can you tell me about DeSilva's financial situation?"

"Marcus was a very wealthy man, as you probably already know. He had a thriving development business and had a real knack for stocks and REITS."

"REITS?"

"I'm sorry, that stands for Real Estate Investments Trusts. He also owned several large parcels of land on Highway two seventy-eight, which have appreciated unbelievably in value over the past two years."

"What do you know about Coastal Development?"

"Not much really. I know they made Marcus an offer to buy one of his tracts of land, and even his entire business."

"How did DeSilva feel about that?"

"He said there was no way he would consider selling, so we never discussed it any further."

"Were you aware of the problem he had with Gene Branigan's taking money from the business?"

"Sure, although I was really surprised when that happened. Gene and Marcus had been friends and partners for years. I was shocked, when I discovered several checks that

Gene had made out to cash. It came to almost ninety-three thousand dollars over a period of a couple of weeks. There was no explanation of what they were for, so of course I asked Marcus. I needed to know what category to post them under on the spreadsheet."

"How did Marcus react?"

"At first he didn't seem overly concerned, just said he would find out. The next thing I knew, Marcus called and said Gene was out. Not only had he terminated the partnership, he also told me Gene was no longer an employee. Marcus closed out all the checking accounts, and transferred all the money into new ones. He asked me to go back over disbursements and see if there were any other checks made out for cash. I went back three years and didn't find any. That's really all I know."

"Can you think of anything else that may be helpful in our investigation?"

Tim Silvers paused for a minute. "Really, I can't."

"Well, thank you for your time," Shark said, shaking hands with the accountant.

He hadn't expected much from this interview, and he had gotten even less.

That evening Shark lay in bed, flipping through the TV channels and shelling pistachio nuts to keep his hands busy. God he wanted a cigarette. He had already gained five pounds. The doctors were right—everything did taste better since he'd quit. He wasn't sure which was worse, the smoking or the softness beginning to accumulate around his middle.

He was restless, having not had his daily fix of Marissa in three days. He had tried several times since he had gotten home, but she hadn't answered. He picked up the phone and dialed again. This time she answered on the second ring.

"Hi. It's me. How are you?"

"Fine," she answered coolly.

"I started to call you Sunday night when I got in, but was afraid it was too late. And again early the next morning, but I didn't know if you would be up yet. And tonight I tried several times, but there was no answer." He knew it sounded like excuses but he didn't want her to think he had any regrets about Saturday night.

"I was at the grocery. I picked up a few things hoping you would come by for dinner. Did you really think of calling those other times?"

"Absolutely. I wouldn't lie. I am a policeman, after all. I got a call as soon as I got home Sunday morning, and then there was a fatal accident today."

"I heard about the wreck on the car radio. Did you also investigate that murder in Port Royal I read about in the paper?"

"Yes. I didn't get home until late that night."

"What a terrible tragedy." There was a pause, and then Marissa said hesitantly, "I want you to know I'm not sorry about inviting you to stay with me Saturday night."

"I'm not either, but you have to understand it can't happen again until Marcus's case is closed."

He waited for what seemed like an eternity before Marissa answered. "I do understand, I guess. But that doesn't mean I like it."

Shark chuckled. "I'm not crazy about the idea either. Every time I'm around you it's all I can do to keep my hands to myself."

"When will I see you?"

"I don't know. I'm up to my ears in work right now."

"Can you at least come for dinner tomorrow night?"

Shark hesitated. He knew what would happen if he did. "I don't think I can make any firm plans right now. Why don't I call you in a couple of days."

"I understand. It's just so lonely here by myself all the time. A person can only read and walk on the beach so much."

"You should try and get out more. Sitting around that empty house isn't good for you. Go shopping."

"Why do men think shopping always makes women feel better?"

"Well it couldn't make you feel worse."

When Shark hung up the phone, he settled back into the pillows, feeling some of the day's tension drain away.

For the next few days, Shark and Dell were busy working their open cases. He spoke to Marissa briefly a couple of times on the phone, but did not see her.

Saturday evening, about ten minutes after he got home, Anna Connors rang his doorbell. Surprised, he invited her in.

"I think we need to talk," Anna said as she walked past him and sat down on the edge of the couch.

"Would you like something to drink?"

"No thanks. What's going on, Shark? Have I pissed you off or something?"

"No," he said, looking quickly away. "I've been really busy at work."

"You and I are always busy at work. That's not going to change until people quit dying, which isn't likely. But we always found time before. I don't get it."

Shark paused, not sure how to phrase what needed to be said. "I just don't think I'm the guy you're looking for, Anna. We don't have the same interests. You deserve someone much better than me."

Before Anna could reply, the doorbell rang. Relieved, Shark scrambled off the couch. He opened the door, shocked to find Marissa standing on his porch.

"You've got company. Sorry, I should have called first. Here, I baked you a peach pie," she said, thrusting it into his hands.

Flabbergasted, he said the first thing that popped into his head. "How did you know where I live?"

Marissa smiled. "I looked you up in the phone book. It didn't exactly take a detective."

Behind him, Shark felt Anna move into the open doorway. "My, my, if it isn't Mrs. DeSilva. You're right, Shark, I deserve better." She brushed past him and, ignoring Marissa, flung herself into the car.

Embarrassed, Marissa began backing off the porch. "I'm so sorry. I'll just go now."

"No, wait. Why don't you come in as long as you're here? That was just the coroner."

Marissa looked at him skeptically. "Something tells me this wasn't a professional call." She stepped into the tiny foyer and stood stiffly just inside the door.

"Thank you for the pie. How did you know peach was my favorite?"

"I didn't. I had some peaches in the freezer, and I was so bored I just started baking."

"Sit down, and let me put this in the kitchen."

When Shark returned, he handed Marissa a glass of red wine. "I don't have any Merlot, but it's not a bad Cabernet."

"Thanks. So, are you and the coroner an item?"

"No. We had a few dates. She came by because I've canceled the last few and haven't called her. She wanted to know what was up. I told her I wasn't the guy she's looking for."

Relief was visible on Marissa's face. "I'm glad I wasn't the cause of spoiling your evening. I know I should have called first. I was just so lonely."

"I know. Have you had dinner yet?" Shark asked.

"No. I haven't had much of an appetite since Marcus died."

"Why don't I defrost some shark filets and throw them on the grill? You said you've never tasted it before."

"Really, you don't have to do that. I should just go," Marissa said, without much conviction.

Shark reached over and took her hand. "Please stay. I don't want you to go."

Marissa looked up into his eyes, then wrapped her arms around his waist. He could feel the dampness of her tears through the thin fabric of his shirt. "I feel so alone. I knew you'd understand—because of Laura."

Shark held her for a moment, stroking her back. "You're gonna be okay. It just takes a long time. Now, dry those tears and let me go get dinner out of the freezer."

They lingered over their pie and coffee, neither wanting the evening to end. Shark worked hard at keeping their conversation light, and his hands off Marissa. What he really wanted to do was take her in his arms and hold her close, but he wouldn't allow himself that luxury.

At ten-thirty, Marissa stood up. "It's getting late. I'd better head home."

Shark didn't say anything to dissuade her. "Thanks for the delicious pie and great company."

"You're right, the shark was really good." Marissa paused at the door, giving him every opportunity to ask her to stay. When he didn't, she reached up to give him a quick hug and a brief kiss.

It took everything he had to let her walk down the driveway.

Chapter Fifteen

Ever since the murder/suicide in Port Royal, Dell couldn't get Jo Parker off her mind. As she drove to work Monday morning, she decided to call her as soon as she got to the office.

Dell poured a cup of coffee and dialed Reverend Hart's number. Expecting Jo to pick up, she was surprised when the minister himself answered.

"Reverend Hart, this is Deputy Dell Hassler. Detective Morgan and I spoke with you about Marcus DeSilva."

"Of course. As a matter of fact I've been trying to decide, for the past couple of days, whether or not I should call you."

"Really? Did you recall something significant?"

"Well, I don't know if it means anything or not, but I did think it was a little odd."

"What's that?"

"I remembered that there was a man, seated in the very last row of the church, who stood up and left just as the ceremony started."

"Do you know who it was?" Dell tried to keep the excitement out of her voice.

"Yes. It was Gene Branigan, Marcus's partner."

Dell almost dropped her coffee cup. "Did you see him after that?"

"Not that I recall. Do you think it's important?"

Dell flipped back through her notes, stopping to jab the point of her pencil at the place in Shark's interview where Branigan denied being anywhere near the church. "Possibly. I appreciate your letting us know."

"Now, what was it you wanted to speak to me about?"

"Actually I was calling for your assistant, Jo Parker. Is she there?"

"No, I'm sorry, she only comes in one day a week. Do you want me to give her a message the next time she's here?"

"Please just tell her I called."

"I'll do that."

Shark walked in just as Dell hung up the phone. "You're not going to believe this—Gene Branigan was at the wedding."

"What? How did you find that out?"

"From Reverend Hart. I called to speak to his assistant, Jo Parker. You remember, the one with the shiner. I couldn't get her off my mind since that case in Port Royal. I don't want her to end up the same way. Anyway, she wasn't there. Reverend Hart answered the phone and said he'd been trying to decide whether to tell us that he remembered Gene sitting in the back row and leaving just as the ceremony started. And he never saw him after that."

"Son of a bitch. Do you think that would have given him enough time to get positioned over in the woods?"

"I don't know. I think it would be close, it would depend on how far into the woods he went."

"I think it's time to have another conversation with Gene," Shark said, pulling out his notebook to find the number. Shark picked up the phone.

"Hello," a woman answered, and it suddenly occurred to Shark that he didn't know if Branigan was married or not.

"I need to speak to Gene, please."

"Hold on a second." Shark cleaned his fingernails, while he waited on Branigan to come to the phone.

"Yeah," Gene said.

"This is Detective Morgan. I need to speak to you right away. Don't leave the house. I'll be there in just a few minutes."

"No, wait! You can't—Why don't we meet where we met before? That's about halfway for both of us," Gene said hurriedly.

"Okay, but be there in fifteen minutes," Shark ordered.

Shark turned to Dell. "Come on. We're going to meet him at the Hilton Head Diner."

Dell grabbed her purse and raced to catch up with him.

They were already on their second cup of coffee when Gene slid into the booth opposite them. Shark didn't even bother to introduce Dell, just jabbed an accusing finger in the direction of Branigan's face. "You lied to me."

"What do you mean?" Gene tried for a look of righteous indignation, but the effort fell short.

"Cut the crap, Branigan. You were at the church."

Gene closed his eyes momentarily and Shark was surprised to see what almost looked like relief flood over his face. "I'm sorry, I know it was stupid of me to lie to you. I knew how it would look. But you have to believe me, I didn't kill him."

"So why were you there? Don't tell me you got an invitation."

"No, of course not. But Marcus was still my best friend. I had planned just to sit in the car and catch a glimpse of him after the ceremony. Instead, when so many people showed up, I thought I could slip into the church unnoticed and leave before the ceremony was over. I knew Marcus didn't want me there, but I had to go."

"Then why did you leave just as the service started?" Dell asked.

"Because, when Marcus turned to face the back of the church, waiting for Marissa to come down the aisle, I could tell he was searching the crowd for someone. I was afraid he might have seen me. So as soon as the ceremony started, I returned to my car and waited there until it was over. I watched Marissa throw her bouquet, and Marcus remove her garter. He looked so happy. Then I heard a shot, and Marcus slumped down on the steps."

"What did you do then?" Shark asked.

"I jumped out of the car, to go to him. But when I saw there were people already working on him, I stopped. And then I just panicked. All I could think about was just getting the hell out of there. So I did."

"I think that's a bunch of crap. I think you stood in the back of that church thinking that all your life you'd played second fiddle to Marcus DeSilva, and all you got for your trouble was thrown out on your ass. And I think you decided it was time for Gene Branigan to settle the score."

"No, I swear to you, I had nothing to do with it."

"Do you own a rifle?" Dell asked.

"No, I hate guns. Please, you have to believe me."

"Is there anyone who can confirm you were in your car when the shot was fired?" Shark asked.

"I saw several people I knew, but I don't know if they saw me."

"Give me the names," Dell said as she pulled a notebook out of her purse.

"All I can say is, you better hope to hell that one of them can confirm you were visible when the shot was fired," Shark said quietly. He nodded to Dell, and they stood up to leave. "And don't even think about leaving the island."

Back in the car, Shark asked, "So what do you think?"

"I don't know. He sounded sincere, and his only motive would be maybe to buy the business back after Marcus died. But if he couldn't even raise enough cash to meet his margin call, where would he get the money?"

"See what you can find out about his current financial affairs. Maybe he made a killing in the market and now has the funds."

"I'll get on it as soon as I contact these people he said may be able to alibi him."

When they returned to the office, Dell began checking her notes on the interviews that they had conducted with the wedding guests. Two hours later she leaned on the edge of Shark's desk to report. "Out of the four names Gene gave me, three of the people don't remember seeing him there. We have no record of any interview with the fourth guy, Hank Miller."

"Maybe he left before we arrived."

"Possibly. I called his house, and his wife said he's at work on a construction job in Port Royal Plantation, on Outpost Lane. Do you want to go with me to talk to him?"

"Yeah. Let's go."

A few minutes later, they located the job site and asked the first workman they encountered to point out Hank Miller. They found him working inside, on the interior trim of the huge house.

"I'm Detective Morgan, and this is my partner, Deputy Hassler. We need a couple minutes of your time."

"Sure. I'm always looking for an excuse to take a break. What can I do for you?"

"Were you at Marcus DeSilva's wedding?" Shark asked.

Hank Miller looked away for a moment, then stared down at the floor. "Yeah. I was there. I knew I probably shouldn't have left before you guys arrived, but I was concerned about my wife's safety. She's seven months pregnant."

"We can understand your concern. Tell us, did you see Gene Branigan at the church around the time the shot was fired in the woods?" Dell asked.

Hank Miller thought for a minute. "Now that you mention it, I did see Gene standing by his car when I was hurrying Mary down the road to the van. He must have left too, because I think his car was gone when we drove by."

Dell and Shark exchanged raised eyebrows.

"Well, thanks for your time. That's really the only question we had."

"Did you see anything that day that might help us in our investigation?" Dell asked.

"No. I'm sorry."

"Well, next time, don't leave before the police get there. Okay?" Shark said.

Miller nodded sheepishly.

Back in the car Dell sighed. "I guess we can scratch Branigan off the suspect list."

"Looks like we're right back where we started," Shark said disgustedly. "With nothing."

Jo Parker stood in the steamy shower and let the hot water ease the muscles in her neck and shoulders. It had been a long day. She wished she could just stay there all night—it was safer. Her husband, Bubba, had started drinking as soon as he got home from work. He was more upset than normal, because he'd had another run-in with his supervisor at the Ford dealership, where he worked in the service department. Jo prayed he wouldn't get fired from this job, like he had the last two. She also hoped he would drink enough to pass out on the couch, so she could get a good night's sleep.

Suddenly the shower curtain was ripped back, and cold air invaded her space. She'd seen that look on Bubba's face too often not to know what it meant. She backed into the corner of the shower, trying to become a smaller target, unsure of what he was waving in his hand.

"You been flapping your mouth to the police!" he screamed, pulling Jo out of the shower by her hair. "Who's Hassler? And what the hell's his card doing in your purse.

What did you tell him?" Before Jo could answer, he back-handed her across the face.

"Nothing, I swear. I can explain. Please don't hit me again," she pleaded, as she sank down onto her knees and tried to protect her face. "It was just some woman from the police department who came to talk to Reverend Hart about Marcus DeSilva. She gave both of us one of her cards before she left. That's all. I swear!"

"Lies! That's all I ever get from you. Lies about not spreading your legs for the good reverend. Lies about everything!" The kick caught Jo in the ribs and sent her sprawling face down on the floor. Bubba tore Dell's card into little pieces and let them drift onto his wife's back like snowflakes. "If I ever find out you been talking to the police about me, I'll kill you. You hear me? Now get in the bed!"

Jo rose slowly to her feet, her breath coming in short, labored gasps. She was growing increasingly afraid of Bubba. It certainly wasn't the first time he had hit her, but it was the first time he had threatened to kill her. And with a whole closet full of guns and rifles, he could make her fear a reality in a heartbeat.

Chapter Sixteen

Early Thursday morning the phone woke Shark from a deep sleep. "Yeah," he muttered, fumbling the receiver to his ear.

"This is Deputy Sheila Long. Sorry to bother you so early, but we just received a call from Clemson that a vehicle, registered to B. J. DeSilva, crashed and burned. They're asking us to notify next of kin and request dental records. I know you're handling the DeSilva case, and I thought that maybe you'd want to be the one to contact his mother. If not, I'll take care of it."

Shark was suddenly wide awake. "What happened?"

"I don't know much. Apparently the car ran off the road into a deep ravine and burst into flames. There isn't much left of the body to make a positive ID. That's why they need the dental records."

"I'll take care of the notification. Thanks for calling me."

Shark immediately dialed Dell's number, then hurriedly dressed. The phone rang several times before Dell finally answered. He quickly relayed what had happened and told her he would pick her up in just a few minutes.

Shark raced down the highway, his mind churning. Had the same person who shot Marcus, killed B.J. as well? Had his gambling debts finally caught up with him? Did he receive his inheritance and then fake his own death? Couldn't anything be easy in this case?

Dell handed him a strong cup of coffee, as she climbed into the passenger seat. "My, my, doesn't this make things more interesting. If I remember correctly, darling Marissa inherits B.J.'s portion of the estate if he's deceased. Makes her a prime suspect in my book."

"There you go jumping to conclusions. We don't even know yet if it was anything more than an accident. Maybe B.J. was drunk or something. Let's just take it one step at a time and look at the facts, before you start measuring people for handcuffs."

At the office Shark put in a call to the primary officer on the scene of the accident, in Clemson. There wasn't much left, period. They had run the license tag and recovered a Hilton Head Prep class ring from the body. That pretty much cinched it for Shark. While it could have been someone else driving B.J.'s car, it was a pretty sure bet that Marcus DeSilva, with all his millions, had sent his son to the elite private school on the island.

He hung up the phone and just shook his head. "Shit! Body and car burned to a crisp. How do you explain something like that to a mother? I hate this part of the job."

Shark and Dell were surprised to see lights already on when they pulled up. Diane DeSilva answered the door in a white terry bathrobe. "What the hell are you doing here this time of the morning?" she demanded.

"We need to talk to you, Mrs. DeSilva. May we come in?" Dell asked softly.

Noting the look on their faces, she began to back away from the door, her hands held out in front of her as if to ward off the words she couldn't bear to hear. "No, no, no," she repeated over and over again like a litany. Shark grasped her upper arm and tried to guide her to a chair. "Please Diane. You have to sit down."

"My son is dead, isn't he."

Gently Shark told her as much as they knew. Dell crossed to the minibar and poured out a good measure of brandy, then carried it back to Diane.

"I had this dream last night. B.J. was calling for me, and I couldn't find him."

"We won't know, until they compare the dental records, that it was definitely him. But I'm afraid it looks that way. We'll need the name of his dentist."

"She killed him."

"Who?"

"I spoke with him late yesterday afternoon. He said she called and invited him to dinner last night. She killed him, I know she did! Oh my God, what am I going to do?"

"Who called him, Diane?" Dell asked, afraid to look at Shark.

"Her—Marissa."

As Shark started the car, Dell turned to him and said, "I think it's time to arouse Sleeping Beauty." Shark remained silent, just headed the car in that direction.

They pulled into Marissa's driveway at 6:45 A.M. Despite ringing the doorbell of the darkened house several times, they got no response. "Doesn't look like the princess is home. Do you know what kind of car she's driving since her accident?" Dell asked.

"Marcus's black Porsche."

"Why am I not surprised. Let's go back to the office, run the tag, and put out an APB." Dell led the way back down the steps. "You handle that, and I'll contact the dentist and arrange to pick up B.J.'s records when the office opens." Shark just nodded and didn't say anything. He wasn't sure he could.

"When we find Marissa, I don't want you interrogating her alone. Maybe it would be best if you weren't there at all. I'm not sure you can be objective," Dell said sharply.

Shark shook his head. "No, we'll talk to her *together*," he said slowly, emphasizing each word.

"Fine, you are the boss, after all."

After a short silence, Shark asked. "When are the funds from the estate supposed to be disbursed?"

"I don't know for sure. I'll find out when we get back." They rode the rest of the way without speaking, each lost in their own thoughts.

At the station, they found Sheriff Grant waiting for them. "I heard. What have you got?"

"Find Marissa DeSilva *now*," he said emphatically, when he listened to Dell recount the facts.

Shark and Dell retreated to their separate desks and began working the phones. Shark put out the APB and contacted the Clemson Police Department. He spoke with the officer he'd been in contact with earlier, who referred him to the detective assigned to the case, John Longfellow. Shark relayed the information about the car he felt Marissa was probably driving and asked that Longfellow have his officers canvas the parking lots of the upscale hotels in the area. If they found her car, he asked to be notified immediately.

"I'll keep you informed as a courtesy, but remember, this is *our* case," Detective Longfellow replied coolly.

Dell made arrangements with the dental office, then contacted one of the partners of Baker and Silverstein law firm. She hung up after a brief conversation. "Checks were to be disbursed next Monday on the life settlement of the estate," she announced, without looking up from her notes. "Under the circumstances, I asked him to put a hold on that until he heard from us."

Shark just nodded and kept his back turned.

At 8:15, Dell left to pick up the dental records and arrange for a courier to take them to Clemson.

With Dell gone, the tension level dropped a couple of notches. Shark was just heading back to his desk with a fresh cup of coffee when his phone rang. Longfellow informed Shark that they had confirmed with B.J.'s roommate that B.J. was meeting his stepmother for dinner the previous night. And they had located Marissa DeSilva at the Ramada Inn and were bringing her in for questioning. He promised to call Shark when they finished.

Shark made his way to Sheriff Grant's office and gave him the gist of the Clemson detective's call. "If they don't hold her and she returns to the island, I want you to talk to her as soon as possible. We need to determine if there's a connection between these two deaths. Did you fill them in on the whole picture?"

"Yes sir, I did."

"Let me know immediately what you find out. I'm going to have to give the press some kind of statement."

"Yes, sir," Shark said, and quickly returned to his desk.

When Dell returned a short time later, Shark was relieved to find both of them ready to get back to business. "Damn, I was hoping we could get to her first," Dell said after hearing Marissa had been located. "Now her defenses will be up."

Shark tried to concentrate, but couldn't shake the image of Marissa, surrounded by hostile cops, all firing questions at her. It wasn't until after one, as Shark was choking down cold french fries, at Dell's insistence, that his phone finally rang.

"We're releasing Marissa DeSilva to return home, but I warned her not to leave the state until further notice. There were no grounds to hold her." Longfellow didn't sound as if the news made him very happy, but Shark's tense shoulders dropped with relief. "She was cooperative and appeared genuinely distressed when we told her about her stepson. She confirmed they met for dinner at The Oasis, and they both left the restaurant at approximately ten-thirty last night. She stated the kid had a lot to drink at dinner.

Their bill confirmed this, and their waiter said he was slurring his words some when he left. The parking lot attendant said he saw the deceased grab Mrs. DeSilva and kiss her, as she was getting into her car. She slapped him, and hurriedly drove away. The kid laughed, and got in his car."

"Did he follow her?" Shark asked.

"Not that we know of. Mrs. DeSilva stated she then returned to her hotel room and had no further contact with her stepson. At approximately twelve forty-five A.M. she contacted the front desk about a problem with the heat in her room, and they offered to move her. She changed rooms at one A.M. The accident occurred at approximately one forty-five."

"So she's got an alibi." Shark wondered why Longfellow hadn't said so in the first place.

"We haven't been able to determine where the deceased went after he left the restaurant. We'll continue to canvas all the bars and local hangouts. If he continued drinking, the odds are we're just dealing with an accident. Although it is rather suspicious, in view of his father's recent death. I'll follow up on the gambling angle and keep you informed."

"Thanks, I really appreciate that. We'll be interviewing Mrs. DeSilva, as well. If I learn anything that might help your investigation, I'll be sure to pass it along. My partner sent the dental records by courier this morning, so you should be receiving them shortly."

"Thanks. I appreciate your promptness. Let's stay in touch."

Shark couldn't keep the relief out of his voice, as he relayed the conversation to Dell.

"I don't like the sound of this room-switching thing. Sounds to me like she was trying to establish an alibi."

"Let's just talk to her first, before you start jumping to conclusions again."

"She should be back by six. I think we should be there waiting for her, if that meets with your approval, sir," Dell said, turning away and rifling through a stack of computer printouts.

Dell had watched as Shark shuffled case files from one side of his desk to the other all afternoon, accomplishing absolutely nothing. Every five minutes or so, his eyes had strayed to the clock. She wondered again how deep a relationship had developed between her partner and Marissa. But she still had the utmost faith in his professionalism. Despite his feelings for the widow, she was sure he wouldn't do anything to compromise the case.

At exactly five o'clock, Shark rose from his desk. "Let's go," he said, heading for the door. Dell had to trot to catch up with him. She didn't see how Marissa could be back yet, but then she remembered that Sleeping Beauty was driving the Porsche.

A few minutes later, they pulled into Marissa's driveway. "I'll go ring the bell, just in case she's already here," Dell said, opening the car door.

A couple of minutes later, she was back. "No sign of anyone." She slipped off her loafers and slouched down in the seat. "We could have a long wait, if she doesn't come directly home."

"Where else is she going to go? She doesn't have any friends here."

A long hour later, Dell looked over at Shark. "So much for your theory about coming right home."

"She'll be here shortly. Just be patient." But Shark was beginning to wonder himself. Maybe she'd been too upset to drive and decided to stay another night in Clemson. If she didn't show up soon, he'd call the Ramada and make sure she'd checked out.

At seven o'clock, Dell muttered, "God I'm hungry. Wanna go get a sandwich?"

"No," was all Shark said.

The words were hardly out of his mouth when the garage door suddenly started to rise. They watched the black Porsche roar into the garage and skid to a stop. Shark was at the driver's door as Marissa opened it.

"Oh, Shark, thank God you're here." She flung herself at him, her arms wrapped around his waist. "It's so awful about B.J. And the police questioned me for hours. When is this nightmare ever going to end?"

Shark quickly extricated himself from her arms and stepped back. "We need to talk to you, Marissa."

Marissa stopped when she saw Dell standing just inside the garage. She squared her shoulders before turning back to Shark. "So this is an official visit then. I'm sorry. I thought you were here as a friend. I've already told the police in Clemson everything I know."

"We still need to talk to you. Can we go inside?"

Without answering, Marissa climbed the stairs to the house. Shark and Dell followed silently.

"Excuse me for just a moment," Marissa said calmly, as she glided up the steps to the second floor.

"Is there a bathroom down here? I need to go, too," Dell said. Shark motioned towards a powder room off the foyer.

When Marissa returned a few minutes later, Dell was seated on the sofa, and Shark was pacing. "Can we just get this over with? I've had about enough police grilling for one day." Marissa lowered herself onto the couch, as far away from Dell as she could get, and ignored Shark completely.

"We're not here to grill you, Marissa. We just need you to tell us what happened last night, in your own words." Shark spoke softly, trying to reassure her.

Marissa looked up at him briefly, but her eyes studied the floor as she said, "There really isn't much to tell. I got a call from Daniel Lawrence at Coastal Development. He made me a very generous offer for Marcus's business. I wanted to discuss it with B.J. before I gave him an answer."

"Why couldn't you just do it over the phone?" Dell asked.

"Because I was going crazy here by myself all the time. Shark, you were the one who told me to get out more. To go shopping or something. So I decided just to drive up and talk to B.J. in person. He agreed to meet me for dinner."

"What was his reaction to the offer?" Shark asked.

"I asked if he was interested in continuing his father's business, or if he thought we should go ahead and sell it. He didn't even hesitate. He said we should get rid of it as quickly as possible. All he seemed to be interested in was how soon he would get the money for his half. Said he was planning to go to Europe, as soon as his inheritance came through."

"Do you know when that will be?" Dell asked.

"I'm not sure," Marissa said hesitantly. "In a week or two, I think."

"Go on," Shark said. "What happened next?"

"Anyway, B.J. said something about traveling around Europe for awhile and maybe even taking some art classes. Said he always liked to paint, but Marcus thought it was a waste of time. I encouraged him to finish school, but I could tell fairly quickly that his agenda didn't include getting his degree. He asked me what my plans were. I told him I hadn't made any yet. I also asked him about Marcus's yacht. Did he want it, or should I go ahead and sell it too. He told me to do whatever I wanted, that he planned to stay in Europe for a long time, maybe even permanently. That's about it." Marissa leaned forward and repositioned the starfish paperweight on the coffee table.

"You were at dinner for approximately two and a half hours, according to the Clemson police. Surely there was more conversation than that," Dell said sharply.

"We discussed the details of the offer for the business and we *did eat dinner*. Really, that's all the conversation I can remember."

"I understand B.J. was drinking quite a bit. Tell me about that," Shark said.

"He had three Jack Daniel's and Coke before we even started the first course."

"What about you?" Dell asked.

"I had one glass of wine. When the soup arrived, B.J. ordered a bottle of the Merlot I was drinking. He started in on that and ordered a second one halfway through the main course. I tried to object, but he ignored me."

"How much of the wine did you drink?" Shark asked.

"I had a second glass with dinner."

"So, how did he seem after all that alcohol?"

"At first he was okay, but right before we left I noticed he was slurring his words a little. I offered to drive him back to his dorm, but he just laughed and said he was fine. He said it would take a lot more than that to get him drunk."

"Tell us about what happened in the parking lot," Shark said.

Marissa glanced at him, then quickly averted her eyes. "So, you know about that." Marissa took a deep breath, and let it out slowly. "About halfway through the main course, B.J. started coming on to me. He said it had been several weeks since Marcus had died, and I was probably getting pretty horny by now. Then he groped my leg under the table, said he'd be glad to stand in for his dear, departed dad. I told him he made me sick. I settled up the bill and left him at the table, but he must have followed me out. While the attendant was getting my car, he continued his crude remarks. Before I could get into the car, he grabbed me and kissed me. I slapped him across the face and left. That's the last time I saw him."

"Did you go directly back to your hotel?" Dell asked.

"Yes. I took a long shower and watched a little TV. The heater was blowing cold air, so I called the front desk and changed rooms. The next thing I knew, it was morning, and the police were knocking on my door. They insisted I come to the station, then they told me about B.J. I was shocked. I still can't believe it. If only I hadn't let him drive, maybe he would still be alive."

"Did B.J. say where he was going, after he left the restaurant?" Shark asked.

Marissa thought for a moment. "No. I assumed he was going back to his dorm, but I don't think he actually said that."

"When you were talking over dinner, did B.J. make any reference to anyone hassling him about his gambling debts?" Shark asked.

"No, he didn't say anything about that, but he did keep asking if I could do anything to hurry up the disbursement. Shark, you have to believe me. I've told you everything. Why can't you all just leave me alone?"

"Mrs. DeSilva, in view of the fact that you will now inherit B.J.'s portion of the estate, I'm sure you can understand why we need to make sure his death was an accident and that no foul play was involved." Dell threw it out not so much for reassurance, but to see how she'd respond.

Marissa's head jerked up. "Are you telling me it *wasn't* an accident?"

"We don't know yet," Shark said.

"I had nothing to do with *anyone's* death, not my husband's and not B.J.'s. I already had enough money to be comfortable the rest of my life. I can't believe you could even suggest such a thing." Marissa rose. "I want you to go now—both of you. You can find your own way out." She left the room, her back ramrod straight, and climbed the stairs to the second floor.

"Great, Dell," Shark said as he stormed out the door, leaving his partner to close it behind her. "Piss her off, why don't you? That really makes people more cooperative."

Dell didn't respond until they were settled in the car. Before Shark could reach for the ignition, Dell punched him hard on the arm. "You slept with her!"

"How do you figure that?"

"That scene in the garage and the way you look at each other. Tell me I'm wrong. And don't you dare lie to me."

Shark closed his eyes, glanced away momentarily, then looked his partner directly in the eye. "Yes and no. I did spend the night with her, but we slept fully clothed in front of the fireplace. Nothing happened, I swear."

Dell looked at him, brow furrowed. "Did you kiss her?"

"Ah, Dell."

"Did you?"

"Just once," Shark said, turning away and starting the car.

"Never in a million years would I have thought that you would compromise a case. Thank goodness I wasn't born male, it obviously impairs one's common sense."

Shark could have dealt more easily with her anger than with her disappointment. "The case has *not been* compromised," he said. "Don't you get it? There *is no case!* We have jack shit. I don't think we're ever going to know who really killed Marcus."

"Maybe you don't *want* to know, did you ever think of that? Well, I'll tell you this. *I* intend to find out the truth. With or without your help!"

They drove the rest of the way back to the office in silence. Neither of them even said goodnight, when he dropped Dell off. All kinds of thoughts raced through his head as he mechanically pointed the car down the familiar road toward Beaufort. Had Marcus's death been an accident after all? Was B.J.'s death related to his gambling debts, or had it been simply a drunk driving accident? Was Marissa really a black widow, or just a victim of circumstances? What was he missing? Nothing seemed to add up. And last, and most painfully, was Dell right? Did he subconsciously hope the case would never be solved, because of his unspoken fear Marissa might in fact be involved?

He suddenly realized he was crossing the Broad River Bridge into Beaufort. He didn't remember much of the drive, which was scary. He spotted the Citgo gas station where he used to buy his cigarettes and slowed down as he approached. He *really* needed a nicotine hit. It always helped him think better—at least that's what he told himself. He slowed almost to a stop at the entrance, then accelerated on past and turned at the next street toward home.

Shark unlocked the front door, threw his things on the table in the foyer, and headed directly to the kitchen. He grabbed a cold beer, and chugged it standing in the open door of the refrigerator. He took another and sat down at the kitchen table.

"That's great. Trading one addiction for another." He might as well have stopped and bought a pack of cigarettes. No, not a pack, a carton! He really missed having a cigarette with his beer.

He was so tired. Emotionally, more than physically. He knew Dell was really pissed at him, and rightfully so. What could he have been thinking spending the night with Marissa? He wondered if Dell would tell Sheriff Grant. That would definitely get him removed from the case. He knew it would take a long time to win back Dell's trust and respect. He hoped to hell he could. But it didn't keep him from wanting Marissa. He had had to force himself not to take her in his arms and comfort her. Was he in love with her, or was it just lust? Would she stay here after all this was settled? Did she care about him at all, or was it just convenient to be spending time with the cop investigating your husband's death? How had his life gotten so screwed up?

He opened another beer and headed wearily to the shower.

Chapter Seventeen

Friday morning Marissa moaned as she forced herself to get out of bed. Another day with nothing to do and no one to talk to. Maybe she should call Jason McCalvey and see about getting her old job back, at least temporarily. It would get her out of the house, which she desperately needed. But it was such a rinky-dink little station, and Jason and everyone else there were such amateurs. She carried a mug of coffee with her out to the beach. She needed to make some decisions about what she was going to do and where she was going to live when all this was over. Did she want to stay in Hilton Head? The weather was okay, though not as warm in the winter as she would like. Summers were really hot and humid, but she really didn't mind the heat. The real problem was that, without the tourists, it was really just a small town. And she'd had enough of small towns. She missed the rush, the vitality of the city, especially the nightlife, the clubs, the theater. She used to love it when she and Eric would fly to New York and see a different play every night. Marissa thought about having enough money to live anywhere she wanted. She began to feel a rising sense of excitement. Did she want to go to Europe? How about a cruise around the world? She could choose Hong Kong, Tokyo, or Australia. As a child, she had dreamed of visiting all those places. She smiled to herself as she skipped away from the water lapping at her feet. *Decisions, decisions!* Not bad for a poor little girl from Hazard, Kentucky.

It was cool and overcast. High was only going to get in the mid 50's today. Thanksgiving was next week and she dreaded the thought of spending it alone. And the approach of the Christmas holidays was hanging over her head. She had no one to go shopping for and the thought of Christmas Eve and Christmas Day alone was almost more than she could bear. If only . . . But it was no good to think like that. Her dad had raised a realist. And she knew she was a survivor. She would just have to figure out something. After all, why should she think this Christmas holiday should be any better than almost all the previous Christmases in the past? Her childhood wasn't filled with happy memories of gifts and family gatherings, but a drunken father and cowering mother, who tiptoed around trying not to upset her father. No turkeys or ham for them, usually a fried rabbit or squirrel or whatever else her mother could scrounge up.

She chased the memories away; it was better not to remember. She longed for Marcus's estate and investigation to be settled, so she could put everything up for sale and get off this island. In spite of its beauty, she realized she really hated it. Chilled to the bone at this point, she headed back to the house, or rather Marcus's house. That's how she would always think of it.

When Shark walked into the office Friday morning, Dell completely ignored him and continued working. Shark greeted her, but got no response. He opened the case file on B.J., picked up the phone, and got to work.

From his office, Sheriff Grant watched the two of them ignoring each other for over two hours. Finally he stepped out into the hall and yelled, "Morgan, Hassler, in my office now!"

Shark tried to catch Dell's eye as he got up, but she wouldn't look at him. They stood uneasily in front of the Sheriff's desk.

"Did you talk to Marissa DeSilva?"

"Yes, sir," Dell replied quickly.

"And?"

"Pretty much the same statement she gave the Clemson Police. We found no discrepancies from what she told them," Shark replied.

Sheriff Grant stared at the two of them, the tension palpable in the air. He had never seen them act like this. "Do you think she was involved in any way with B.J.'s death?"

"No, sir," Shark said quickly, just as Dell said. "That's yet to be determined, sir."

The sheriff leaned back in his chair and looked from one to the other. Both were staring down at the floor. "What's going on with you two today?"

"Nothing important." Shark paused a moment but apparently Dell wasn't going to help him out. "Just a difference of opinion," he added.

"Dell, anything you want to tell me?" Grant asked.

Dell still wouldn't meet his eyes. "No, sir."

"Then quit acting like a couple of kids in the schoolyard and get back to work. And keep me informed," he called, as they turned and left the office.

They both worked steadily through the morning. Shortly before noon Shark picked up his car keys and approached his partner. "Let's go get some lunch."

"I'm not hungry."

Shark leaned over, his voice pitched so only she could hear. "Damn it, Dell, we need to settle this. Frankly I don't care if you eat or not, but we're going to talk. So get your ass out of the chair and come on."

In silence, Dell picked up her purse and followed him out.

Sheriff Grant smiled as he watched them leave. "Wish I could be a fly on the wall," he muttered to himself.

At The Barbecue Hut, Shark asked for an end booth, where they could have some privacy. He ordered two barbecue plates and two iced teas. He occupied himself by cleaning off the crusty tops of the salt and pepper shakers, until the waitress had sat their drinks in front of them.

"I know you're really pissed at me, Dell," he began, "and you're right. I've been an ass. I can't tell you how much I appreciate your not ratting me out to the sheriff this morning. I promise you, I can still be objective about Marissa. If we come up with proof that she's implicated in *any way*, in either death, I'll be *first* in line to put the handcuffs on her. I don't know what else I can say."

Dell sat quietly, playing with her silverware.

"Please talk to me," Shark said softly.

Finally, she met his eyes. "I'm just so disappointed in you. I never imagined you would let yourself become involved with a suspect. I've trusted and respected you and counted you as my best friend. Now I feel as if I don't really know who you are."

"I'm still your friend, and I intend to win back your trust and respect. But you can't put people on a pedestal and not expect them to fall off at some point. I'm not perfect, Dell. And I have the same flaws as everyone else you know. I'm sorry I disappointed you. I'll try not to do it again, but I probably will. Are we going to be able to get past this and continue to work together, or do you want a new partner?" Shark held his breath, not sure he wanted to hear her reply.

"No, I don't want a new partner," Dell said quickly. "I just want my old one back. I want the same guy I've known and worked with all these years. I don't want to have to wonder about him." Dell resisted the urge to reach out and touch his hand. "I know you've suffered a lot since Laura died, and I want you to have a loving relationship with someone. It just can't be Marissa DeSilva. She's poison to anyone who becomes involved with her. I think she's a rich, conniving snake that preys on unsuspecting men—you included. Try to look at it objectively for a moment. Do you really think she would let herself fall in love with a poor cop whose whole social life centers around his damn fishing boat? This woman is geared for playing the socialite scene. She runs in different circles than you and I. And we still haven't ruled her out as a suspect!"

Shark fastened on the one thing she had said that could get them back to work. "Okay, I'll grant you motive, but that's all I can find so far. She has a perfect alibi in Marcus's death, and we don't even know if B.J.'s was anything more than an accident. So tell me what I'm missing here."

"Gut instinct. You always told me to go with my gut, remember? You're the one who said that nine times out of ten it would prove to be right."

"My, how my words come back to haunt me. So how do you see it going down then?"

"Maybe she has a male partner who actually does the dirty work."

"Not bad, but why a he? Women shoot rifles, too."

"I just see her partner as a man. If the point of all these deaths is to accumulate enough money to set the two of them up for life, then I have to assume they plan on spending it together. Just promise me you'll keep an open mind about her as a possible suspect, and stay the hell away from her."

"Okay, okay, I promise to behave."

The waitress brought their food then, and there was little additional conversation, except for the oohs and aahs about the meal.

"So you think plying me with my favorite food is going to get you out of the doghouse?" Dell used her fingers to pick up the last scrap of barbecue off her plate.

"Well, I figured maybe it was a start. And I was hoping this would get me all the way out." He grinned when the waitress slid the plate of gooey dessert in front of Dell. "And I promise not to ask for a single bite."

"Sinfully Chocolate! When did you order this?" Dell groaned as she picked up her fork and dove in.

"Before I left the office."

"I'll admit, it does score you some points."

Sheriff Grant could tell as soon as his two top detectives returned from lunch that whatever had been going on between them earlier had been put to rest.

Around four that afternoon Shark received a call from Detective Longfellow. "We've examined what remains of DeSilva's car. There is a dent in the back bumper, but we can't tell if it occurred during the accident or before."

"Do you think someone could have run him off the road?" Shark asked.

"With the condition the car is in, there's really no way to tell. The coroner also confirmed the identity. Since there's no blood available to do a blood alcohol level, we'll never know how drunk he was at the time of the accident. We haven't had much luck tracing his movements after he left the restaurant. His roommate said he didn't have a steady girlfriend he might have been visiting, so we're left checking the bars. Have you talked to Mrs. DeSilva yet?"

"Yes, as soon as she got home last night. Told us basically the same thing she told you."

"Well, if you come across anything we can use, please get in touch."

"I hear you. We do plan to attend the memorial service for B.J. on Sunday. I'll let you know if we learn anything."

Shark plopped down in the chair across from Dell and put his feet up on the end of her desk. He repeated his conversation with the Clemson detective. "You sure been burning up the computer all afternoon," he said when he finished. "What've you been working on?"

"I've been taking a closer look at Devon Phillips, Marissa's first husband."

Shark's feet dropped to the floor. "Why?" he asked, sitting up straighter.

"Because if she really is a black widow, he doesn't fit the pattern. He's still alive."

"God, are you back on that black widow thing again?"

"Just hear me out. After the divorce Devon Phillips moved to San Francisco. His degree was in accounting, but he took a job as a waiter in a fancy restaurant out there. Six months later he married a wealthy widow, twice his age. They were honeymooning on her yacht, when they supposedly got caught in a terrible storm. Phillips made a May Day call, said the boat was taking on water and gave their location. They found him with a life jacket, floating on a piece of wreckage."

"What about the wife?"

"Gone, along with the boat. He claimed they'd both abandoned ship, but he lost track of her in the storm. Her body was never recovered. After a pretty thorough investigation, her death was ruled accidental."

"It's almost quitting time, so is there a point to this story?"

"The point is, Devon Phillips inherited six million dollars! He used it to open a fancy restaurant and wine cellar, on the bay. Then he bought two more upscale restaurants. And he's never remarried."

"I thought you said you were getting to the point."

"Two years after Devon's tragic loss, Marissa's husband conveniently dies in a fall from a horse, and she inherits millions. Three months later Phillips, who's supposedly strapped for cash, opens a fancy catering business. Don't you see a pattern here?"

"Frankly no. What I see is someone trying very hard to manufacture one. But, if it makes you feel better, by all means pull Marissa's phone records and see if they're any calls to San Francisco."

"I've already requested them," Dell said softly. "And I'm going to see if I can determine if Devon Phillips was in San Francisco the day Marcus died."

"Go for it," Shark said. "I'm heading home."

That evening he sat in bed playing with the remote control and thinking of Marissa. Could he be wrong about her? Were she and Phillips in this together? Shark wondered if her attention had been intended only to throw him off. Despite everything, he still couldn't see Marissa as anyone but a victim of terrible circumstances. Maybe because that's the way he wanted to see her. He longed to pick up the phone and hear her voice, but he wouldn't let himself. He had already disappointed Dell enough.

Chapter Eighteen

B. J.'s memorial service on Sunday at the First Presby-
terian Church was restricted to family and close friends.
Shark and Dell sat in the back row, waiting for the service
to start. Shark looked around the huge church and observed
the stained glass in the large cross hanging behind the pul-
pit. Organ music played softly. He wished he could feel
the sense of peace that religion seemed to offer to many
people. But, thanks to his father, that wasn't the case. While
he did believe in a Supreme Being, he still felt uncomfortable in any house of worship.

Five minutes before the service was to start, Marissa,
dressed all in black, quickly made her way up the aisle to
one of the empty pews on the left-hand side of the sanctuary. Immediately, people began to point and whisper. Diane DeSilva turned to see what was going on and spotted
Marissa. She was on her feet and screaming before anyone
thought to restrain her. "Murderer! How dare you show
your face here! Get out!"

Rachel Wells, Marcus's sister, stared over at Marissa coldly. Family members rushed to Diane's side and tried to calm her.

"I had *nothing* to do with B.J.'s death," Marissa said emphatically, then rose and hurried down the aisle to the foyer. She stared straight ahead, not even glancing at the two detectives.

"Wow," Dell whispered. "I can't believe she showed up here."

"She was his stepmother after all. Wouldn't it look a little strange if she *didn't* show up?"

Family members quickly returned Diane DeSilva to the front pew, and the service began.

It was almost dark as Shark was putting away the last of his tools. He had been fine tuning the engine on his boat, the bizarre scene from this afternoon's service playing over in his head, when a black Porsche roared to a stop in front of his house.

Marissa sat in the car, waiting to see if Shark would approach her. When he didn't, she opened the door and made her way across the lawn to him. "Can I talk to you for a minute?"

Shark didn't respond for a moment, just reveled in the sight of her. Then he said, "I'm not sure talking *here* is a good idea. Maybe you should come to the office tomorrow." He wiped the grease off his hands and threw the rag onto his workbench.

"Please, Shark. I can't talk to you when that partner of yours is around. She doesn't like me. Can't I come in for just a few minutes?"

Against his better judgment Shark nodded, and Marissa followed him into the house. He washed his hands at the kitchen sink and offered her a beer.

They sat at the kitchen table. Shark took a long swallow from the cold bottle and waited for her to begin.

"Shark, I had nothing to do with Marcus's or B.J.'s deaths. Someone has got to believe me. Please tell me *you* do."

Shark ran his finger around the rim of the bottle. "Marissa, what do you want me to say? There's no evidence *at this time* to implicate you in either death. If there was, you wouldn't be sitting here right now."

"That's not the same as saying you believe me. I thought you, of all people, would be able to look me in the eye and tell me that. When is this going to end?" Her voice cracked and Shark watched her full lower lip begin to tremble.

He was a sucker for tears. Women who cried always appeared so defenseless. For the first time he noticed Marissa had lost weight. Her clothes seemed to hang on her, and there were dark circles under her eyes. Before he realized it he had put his hand over hers. "Try to get hold of yourself, Marissa. Tears won't help."

"But that terrible scene at the memorial service today. You were there. You heard them. Everyone thinks I'm guilty. I just want to leave Hilton Head Island and never come back. How soon can I get away from all these bad memories?"

"I honestly don't know. Not for a few weeks at least. Until the Clemson Police know for sure whether B.J.'s death was an accident, and until we finish checking out some things in Marcus's case, you'll have to stick around."

Marissa's head jerked up. "Do you have some new leads? What have you found out?"

Shark paused, weighing carefully what he was about to say. "Nothing in particular. We're just continuing to check out every remote possibility."

Marissa relaxed and took a sip of beer. "Why doesn't your partner like me?"

"What makes you think she doesn't?"

Marissa chuckled. "It's written all over her, as surely as if she wore a sign around her neck saying, 'I don't like you even one little bit.' I don't understand why I've always had trouble making friends with women. Never men, just women."

"Maybe because they're all jealous of you. You're beautiful, talented, and wealthy. All the things most of them aren't."

"And I'd give all of it up in a minute, to have a loving husband and family and a best girlfriend."

Shark wanted to believe her. But she'd just given him the perfect opening to ask about Devon Phillips, and he couldn't pass it up. "Well, we can't turn back time, but maybe if you and your first husband hadn't gotten a divorce, none of these other things would have happened to you."

"Don't you think I've thought about that?" Marissa picked up the beer bottle, tracing the wet circle it had left on the table. "If I could turn back time to before I ever met Devon, I would. Marrying him was a big mistake."

"How so?" Shark prompted.

Marissa looked up. "Because he was a druggie. Heavy into cocaine."

"Didn't you know that before you got married?"

"Oh, I knew he'd done some coke at parties, but I didn't know he was addicted, until too late. Not only did he blow every dollar he could get his hands on, but he'd sleep with anyone, male or female, who'd give him a hit. I tried to get him into rehab, but he was in complete denial about his addiction."

"Where is he now?" Shark asked casually.

"I don't know. Right after graduation, he said he was heading for San Francisco. For all I know he could be dead of an overdose by now."

Shark tossed his empty bottle in the trash and retrieved another beer from the refrigerator. Marissa seemed to be waiting for some response, but he didn't know what to say. It all sounded perfectly plausible.

"Is there anything you can do to hurry things along, so I can leave? I don't think I can face the holidays here. I feel that everywhere I go people are pointing and staring at me. I hardly leave the house, except to walk on the beach. I just want to turn the house and yacht over to brokers and let them sell everything. I've already told Daniel Lawrence, I'd sell him the business. I just want to get out of here and start over."

"Where will you go?"

"I have no idea. I haven't gotten that far yet. If you could tell me approximately when I can leave, it would help."

"I'm sorry, Marissa, I just don't know."

"I guess I'd better go," she said, standing. "Thanks for talking to me." She leaned over and kissed his cheek. "Please help me clear my name. You're the only one who believes in me." She waited, her face close to his, to see if he would kiss her back.

He didn't. "I'll do what I can, Marissa," he said, and opened the door.

On the drive in to the office Monday morning, Shark mulled over what Marissa had told him about Devon Phillips. For a brief moment he considered not sharing Marissa's appearance at his door yesterday. But by the time he pulled into the parking lot, he had decided he would keep no more secrets from his partner.

As soon as he stepped into the office, he went directly over to Dell's desk. "Let's go to Starbucks and I'll buy you a cappuccino."

Dell looked up surprised. "Why?"

"I need to share something with you. Privately."

"Okay," she said, grabbing her jacket and purse. In the car, she fastened her seatbelt and pulled on her sunglasses. "What's this all about?"

"It can wait until we get our coffee."

When they were seated at a table in the corner, he said, "I had a visit from Marissa yesterday afternoon."

"What?" Dell said, her eyes widening in surprise. "How did she know where you live?"

Shark took a deep breath and decided to cleanse his soul. "Because it's not the first time she's been there." Reluctantly, he related the circumstances of her previous visit.

"My God, why didn't you tell me this before?"

"Because I knew you'd react just like you're doing now."

Dell shook her head in disgust. "So what happened yesterday?" When he'd finished relaying the gist of the conversation she said, "I don't think you should have mentioned Devon Phillips. It may have made her suspicious."

"I don't think so. One thing just naturally kind of led to another. She's more focused on how soon she can leave here."

"Well, I don't want her going anywhere for awhile. At least not until we can determine if there's any connection between the two of them now. I've got requests in for Phillips' phone records and credit card reports. I'm trying to establish if he was in San Francisco at the time of Eric Meier's and Marcus's deaths."

"Honestly, I don't know how much longer we can keep her here if something doesn't show up soon."

"And the thought of her leaving and starting this scam somewhere else, pisses me off." Dell winced as she swallowed a mouthful of the steaming cappuccino. "Anyway, thanks for telling me everything. That *is* everything, isn't it?"

The information on Phillips' and Marissa's phone records were waiting for them when they got back. They split them up, and each worked independently until late afternoon. "Not a single call to *anywhere* in California," Shark said with a smug half smile.

"Well, maybe she used a pay phone. Anyway, Devon's credit card charges show three transactions in San Francisco on the day of Marcus's death. But for the five days preceding Eric Meier's accident, there were no charges of any kind."

"Proving?"

"Nothing, I guess. There are three other times when several days go by with no charges at all. At first it seemed suspicious, but now I'm not sure."

"When were the other times?"

"Twice in the year after Marissa married Eric, and once since his death."

"Well, it looks like we've just wasted our time," Shark said as he threw down the pencil he'd been chewing on. He still missed his cigarettes.

"Let's call it a day. I've got a date tonight."

"The guy from Charleston? I thought maybe that was off. I haven't heard you mention him lately."

"He's been out of the country working on a project. He just got back."

"Working out of the country, huh. That's pretty impressive."

"Hey, I know how to pick em," she said as she grabbed her purse and sashayed toward the exit.

Chapter Nineteen

Jo Parker grabbed her aching side and crept quietly out of bed. She stood for a moment, holding her breath, to make sure that Bubba was still asleep, then tip-toed into the bathroom. She barely inhaled, trying to keep the pain at bay. She thought he might have broken a couple of ribs this time.

From the linen closet, Jo took a bathtowel, folded it, and bound it tightly around her ribs. That seemed to help a little. Her hand shook as she opened the medicine cabinet. Stifling a groan, she lifted her arm to retrieve the bottle of Advil from the top shelf. The slightest movement sent pain shooting through her side. She swallowed three tablets. Carefully, she set the glass back down on the sink. Even stone drunk, Bubba could be awakened by the slightest noise.

She hardly recognized the woman staring back at her from the mirror. She had been a pretty girl. Now she looked fifty, instead of just barely thirty-one. She dabbed at a small cut on her lip. All over a few lumps in the gravy.

Jo knew things were getting worse. It used to be that Bubba only hit her occasionally, but lately it was happening two or three times a week. She was having increasing difficulty hiding Bubba's abuse. Even Reverend Hart had begun to ask questions. Of course she denied everything, always coming up with some kind of excuse about her clumsiness. But she knew she wasn't fooling him or anyone else. Even the lady detective had called.

Jo lowered the lid on the commode and sat down. When had things gone so wrong? It hadn't always been this way. In the beginning they had laughed and danced and gone out for romantic dinners. It was hard to imagine that was only five years ago. It seemed like another lifetime.

What had she done to make him treat her this way? That first year Bubba and a friend of his had owned their own auto repair shop. Business was good, and they had no problem paying their bills on time. They even talked about saving money for a down payment on a house. Then his partner cleaned out the business account and disappeared. Bubba had been the mechanic, his partner, the businessman. Bubba closed the shop and went to work for someone else.

He became angry at the world, drinking heavily and accusing her of flirting every time they went out. So they stopped going. Slowly, he cut her off from her family and drove away all her friends. He made her quit her secretarial job because he didn't want other men talking to her. He sold her car. Slowly, her whole world became confined to Bubba and the small house they rented in Bluffton.

Jo lifted the red-splotched Kleenex away from her lip. She ran her tongue across the cut, not surprised by the familiar coppery taste of her own blood.

As Bubba's drinking escalated, he began having difficulty holding a job. The first time he hit her was the night he got fired, for the first time. He apologized profusely and promised it would never happen again. She told herself it was just because he was so upset. But a month later, the next blow knocked out a tooth.

Now he was drunk almost every night, and the smallest thing sent him into a rage. She had begged him to let her get a job, since they were so behind on their bills, but he refused. The implication that he couldn't support them had earned her a black eye. In a rare moment of guilt, he had finally agreed to let her accompany another woman to church and volunteer there once a week. Now he was threatening to take that away, as well. She wasn't sure she could hold on to her sanity if he did.

Jo knew she had to do something. She wished she could talk to her sister. But it had been two years since she had seen Rene, and she didn't even know how to contact her.

If only she had some money. But Bubba controlled it all. She couldn't even skim anything from the grocery money, since he drove her to the store and paid the bill himself. Occasionally, when she did the laundry, she found a few crumpled dollars in his pants pockets. Probably change from the bar or liquor store he'd been too drunk to remember about. She'd hidden away a grand total of thirty-six dollars, maybe enough to buy a bus ticket, but certainly too little to get them far enough away to start over. Through swollen lips, Jo smiled, and her hand went instinctively to her stomach. "Hush, little one. I'm not going to let anything happen to you. I'll figure something out."

She had cried two days earlier when the home pregnancy test came out positive. She had always wanted a child, but God knew this wasn't the right time. She had almost made up her mind to leave Bubba, but now she knew it was impossible. She had to stay with him, at least until the baby was born, so his medical insurance would cover the costs. Otherwise, how would she be able to afford it? Surely not with thirty-six dollars.

She hadn't told Bubba about the baby yet. He always referred to kids as "snot-nosed brats." Would it be any different with his own? Jo didn't think so. She was afraid . . . for both of them.

Jo crept quietly into the kitchen and made lukewarm tea with water straight from the tap. She eased herself down at the kitchen table and tried to think. Maybe she should go to one of those shelters for a few days. If she could hide her pregnancy long enough, she might be able to get a job and some insurance, before it was time for the baby. Then she remembered someone talking about a woman who changed jobs before she found out she was pregnant, and the new insurance wouldn't pay.

No, she'd have to stay until after the baby was born. But then what? It would be even harder to get away from Bubba afterwards. And if she did manage to escape and find a job, who would take care of the baby? And then there was the threat that Bubba screamed at her every time he hit her now—that if she ever tried to leave him, he would kill her. She dropped her head onto her folded arms and prayed silently.

What was she going to do?

Two days before Thanksgiving, Marissa was in the middle of an aerobics workout when the doorbell rang. Surprised, since she hadn't called in a pass for anyone, she slung a towel around her neck and rushed to the door.

She opened it to find Jason McCalvey and a young boy standing on the step. The child, who had to be Jason's son since they looked so much alike, held a cardboard box covered with a pink blanket.

Jason's eyes traveled the length of Marissa's body, admiring every curve of the leopard print leotards. "Hi! Marissa, this is my son, Derek. Forgive us for barging in on you like this unannounced. I had a friend who lives in this plantation call in a pass so we could surprise you. Looks like you were working out."

"Yes, but I'm always looking for a good excuse to stop."

"Now, Dad?" Derek asked, looking up at him.

"Not yet. Just be patient."

"I don't know where my manners are. Please come in," Marissa said, motioning for them to enter. "Have a seat in the living room, and I'll join you as soon as I change."

"Wow," Derek whispered as they sat down on the couch facing the ocean. "I've never been in a fancy house like this before where you can see the beach. Do you think I can go down there later?"

"Maybe. We'll have to wait and see."

Marissa returned dressed in black jeans and a red turtleneck. "Okay, Derek, let's go to the kitchen and I'll get you something to drink?"

"Now?" the boy turned to his father as they followed her down the hallway.

Jason laughed. "Sure."

Derek held the cardboard box out to Marissa. "We brought you a present."

Surprised, Marissa accepted the box. "But it's not my birthday, and Christmas isn't for a few weeks. Are you sure this is for me?"

"Yes, ma'am. It's because you been sad since your husband died and all."

Marissa fought back tears as she gazed into the boy's upturned face. "Thank you, Derek. Let's put this down on the floor, and I'll open it right now."

Jason and his son carefully knelt on the floor as Marissa gingerly lifted a corner of the pink blanket and looked inside. A small Dalmatian puppy, with just the hint of a spot or two, snuggled in a corner of the box on a pile of shredded newspaper. Her hand froze.

Another kitchen . . . another box. A nine-year-old Marissa, and a cocker spaniel puppy. At last something to love . . . to love her back. Rolling and giggling and wet floppy dog kisses until Daddy found his pipe, gnawed like an old bone. Then Rascal, yipping and straining at the rope as Daddy pulled him into his old red pickup, never to be seen again.

Derek reached in, gently picked up the puppy and held her out to Marissa. "This is Pepper—don't you like her?"

"What? Oh, yes, of course. Of course I like her."

"But you can call her anything you want. My dog, Salty, had eight puppies a few weeks ago. Dad said I couldn't keep all of them. So we brought you one to cheer you up."

Marissa hesitated then snuggled the puppy against her cheek. "I love her. I've never had a dog." The puppy woke up and began to lick Marissa's hand.

"She likes you," Derek said excitedly.

"I think she does," Marissa said as she looked up. "Jason, how thoughtful of you."

"Well, I thought she might be good company. Someone to walk with you on the beach, and love you unconditionally."

"Thank you."

"Can we take her to the beach now?" Derek asked, jumping up.

"I think that's an excellent idea. You hold her for a minute while I grab a jacket."

A few minutes later, they were all laughing as Pepper struggled to run with her short legs in the sand. She sniffed at shells and tried to chase the sea gulls, without much success. She would waddle down to the edge of the water, then run back up the beach when a wave lapped at her paws. Before long she lay sprawled, totally exhausted, on the sand.

"She'll get more spots as she gets older," Derek explained as he gazed fondly at the puppy.

"I bet you're really going to miss her," Marissa said softly.

Derek hung his head. "Yeah, but Dad said maybe you'd bring her with you on Thanksgiving so I could see her."

"Thanksgiving?"

Jason cleared his throat. "Uh, we were hoping you would join us Thanksgiving Day for dinner, if you don't have any other plans. There's just going to be the two of us. Derek usually spends holidays with his mother, but she and her husband are on a cruise. Please say you'll come. I'm a pretty good cook."

"Please, please, please come," Derek chimed in.

Marissa looked over at the boy and smiled. "I'd love to. Thank you for inviting me. What do you say we take this tired puppy up and get her some water, and I'll fix us some hot chocolate?"

"Great!" he said, jumping up and brushing the sand off his pants.

They sat around the table sipping hot chocolate and watching Pepper asleep on the pink blanket. Marissa asked Derek about school and learned that his favorite hobby was soccer.

"Maybe you can come to one of my soccer games sometime."

"I'd like that."

"Well, Tiger, I think it's time to get you home so you can do your homework," Jason said as he carried their cups to the sink.

"Aw, Dad, can't we stay just a little longer? I don't have much homework."

"Not this time. Go tell Pepper 'bye, and let me talk to Marissa for a minute."

"Okay."

"Thanks for agreeing to come for Thanksgiving. Let me write down the directions to my house. It's easy once you get on Lady's Island."

Marissa rummaged in a drawer and came up with a notepad and pen from a local real estate agent. "Jason, thank you for the puppy. I love her already."

"Good. Now I only have to find homes for four more," he said with a chuckle.

"Derek's a wonderful boy. You've done a good job with him."

"Thanks. That means a lot. It's not easy, with working and everything. Fortunately, I have a good housekeeper, who by the way, will really be doing most of the cooking for Thanksgiving."

Marissa laughed. "What can I bring?"

"Nothing, just yourself."

"But I want to. How about dessert?"

"Okay, if you insist."

Marissa walked down to the car with Derek and Jason.

"Oh, I almost forgot. I brought you a little dogfood to get you by till you're out the next time," Jason said, handing her a sandwich baggie.

"Thanks." Marissa leaned down and gave Derek a squeeze. "Don't worry, I won't forget her on Thanksgiving."

"Great," he said, squirming out of her embrace.

Then she turned to Jason, reached up and kissed his cheek.

He ran his hand up and down her arm, careful to keep the contact brief. "We'll see you in a couple of days. Call me if you need anything before then."

That night Marissa lay in bed, with Pepper curled up next to her, and for the first time in weeks, had no trouble falling asleep.

Chapter Twenty

Thanksgiving Day, Marissa arrived on Jason's doorstep, with a pecan pie in one hand and a large chocolate cake balanced in the other. Derek answered the door before she could even ring the bell.

"Hi!" he said, looking at both her hands expectantly. "Didn't you bring Pepper?"

"Of course I brought Pepper. She's in the car. I just didn't have enough hands to carry everything. Why don't you get her for me?"

"Okay," he said, racing down the steps.

Jason appeared at the door wiping his hands on a dishtowel. "Here, let me help you. "Come on in."

Marissa laughed at the white chef's apron tied around his waist. "I like your new look. It suits you. If the guys at the station could only see you now."

"You don't have a camera hidden in that big purse of yours, do you?"

"No, but I wish I did."

"In that case, welcome to my home. I'll put these in the kitchen, while you take off your coat."

"Smells scrumptious in here."

"The turkey should be done in about an hour."

Derek came in carrying Pepper. "She looks bigger already."

Marissa laughed. "It's only been two days since you've seen her."

"Has she been crying at night? I forgot to tell you to put a clock or a radio in her bed."

"Well, actually she's been sleeping with me, so she hasn't been crying at all."

"Cool! I wanted to sleep with all of them, but Dad wouldn't let me."

"Dad wouldn't let you do what?" Jason handed Marissa a glass of white wine.

"Sleep with Salty and all her puppies."

Jason chuckled. "There wouldn't have been enough room for you in the bed."

After meeting Salty and her family, Marissa was treated to a tour of the house, conducted by Derek, who insisted she spend most of her time in his room looking at his aquarium and collection of Pokemon cards.

Jason found the two of them sitting on the floor, heads bowed in deep concentration over a checkerboard. "Dinner in ten minutes."

"Can we finish this game first, Dad?" Derek asked without taking his eyes off the board.

"As long as you can do it in ten minutes."

They feasted on turkey and dressing. Marissa was surprised that Derek filled his plate not only with candied sweet potatoes, but also with green bean casserole and cranberry sauce as well. "I've never had potato salad with turkey before. Is this an old southern tradition?"

Jason slathered butter on a warm roll and said, "Beats me. But Lucille, my housekeeper, insists it's not Thanksgiving without it."

Finally, Marissa pushed back her chair. "I don't think I can eat another bite. Everything was delicious."

"Well, you've lost too much weight. We need to put some meat back on those bones. Would you like dessert now or later?"

"Now," Derek said at the same time that Marissa said, "Later."

They burst out laughing. "Okay, you can have some now, and Marissa and I'll wait for a little while. Do you want pecan pie or chocolate cake, as if I didn't know?"

"Chocolate cake! And can I have some ice cream on it?"

"Sure, why not."

"I'll clear the plates while you fix his dessert," Marissa said as she stood up.

"You don't have to do that."

"I know, but I want to."

"If you insist. Just stack them on the counter for now, and I'll put them in the dishwasher after we have our coffee."

They relaxed over coffee and watched Derek consume a huge bowl of cake and ice cream. How fortunate Jason was to have him. She wondered what it would be like to have a child of her own.

Marissa filled the dishwasher while Jason tried to cram all the leftovers into the refrigerator. "Let me send some of these home with you. Derek and I can't possibly eat all this food."

"Maybe just a little white meat. I love turkey sandwiches."

"I'll fix it up," Jason said, pulling several plastic containers out of the pantry.

After getting the kitchen back to some semblance of order, they returned to the living room to find Derek and Pepper curled up on the couch, both sound asleep.

"Come on. Let's go out back, and I'll show you my retreat." Jason quietly slid open the glass door to the deck. They walked down the stairs into the back yard. Marissa looked around with surprise. It was laid out like an English garden. In the distance, she could see a small building surrounded by tall green plants and blooming flowers. They meandered down a gravel path and settled onto benches in the gazebo. Off to the side, a small waterfall trickled into a gold fishpond.

"This is beautiful," Marissa said, captivated by the serenity. "Did you do all this yourself?"

"All but the fish pond. I had that built."

"It must have taken years." Marissa trailed her fingers across a late-blooming hibiscus.

"Ten, as a matter of fact. I started with just a few plants the first year I moved in, and it gradually evolved."

"But how do you keep it like this, with the hot summers here?"

"Many of the plants are drought resistant, and I have an irrigation system. Eventually I want to add a small greenhouse. I'd like to try my hand at raising orchids."

Marissa realized she really didn't know this man. He seemed so different from the person she used to work with. "I never would have figured you for a gardener."

"There's a lot of things you don't know about me, Marissa. You never gave me a chance outside the office."

"You were my boss. It didn't seem appropriate."

"But I'm not your boss now. Maybe we can start by just being friends for the time being."

Marissa paused. "I'd like that."

A sleepy-eyed Derek, with Pepper at his heels, appeared down the path. "Hi. I think I fell asleep for a minute. When I couldn't find you in the house, I knew you'd be here."

Jason chuckled and motioned for his son to climb up in his lap. "Actually, I think you slept a little longer than a minute."

"What are we gonna do now?" Derek asked as Jason finger-combed his mussed-up hair.

"I don't know. Marissa and I are enjoying the garden. What do you have in mind?"

"I thought maybe you guys might wanna play some badminton. Marissa, I'm pretty good. You could be on my team."

"I haven't played badminton in years. Are you sure you want me on your team?"

"It's okay if you're not very good. I'll help you."

"That sounds like a challenge to me," Jason said, glancing at Marissa. "Are you sure you're up to it? You don't have to, you know."

"Come on, Derek, we're going to make him beg for mercy," Marissa said, jumping up.

They split the first two games. The third was neck and neck, but Derek and Marissa finally pulled it out by one point.

"We're the champs!" Derek cried.

"You don't have to rub it in." Jason sprinted around the net and chased his squealing son across the lawn.

Marissa followed, smiling at their foolishness, and found them collapsed in laughter at the kitchen table. She poured large glasses of sweet tea, while Jason cut slices of rich pecan pie for the two of them and another piece of cake for Derek.

It had been a wonderful day but Marissa knew it was time to go.

"Jason, thanks for inviting me to share the day with you and Derek."

Jason took both her hands in his. "I'm so glad you came. You made it special for us, too."

Reluctantly, Derek shuffled over and held the puppy out to her. "Can I come and visit Pepper sometime?"

"Of course, anytime you like."

"I've been thinking." Derek stared at the floor, his hands shoved deep in his pockets. "If you and Dad got married, you and Pepper could live with us."

"Derek!"

Marissa laughed. "Don't scold him. I think he just misses the dog."

Jason helped her on with her coat, then handed her a bag with several containers of leftovers. "Thanks again for a lovely day."

As the black Porsche roared to life Marissa waved and backed down the drive. *Marry Jason McCalvey? Sorry sweetheart, not in this lifetime.*

Shark anchored his boat in Mackay's Creek and forced down a bologna and cheese sandwich. *Hell of a Thanksgiving dinner*, he thought. Dell was off in Greenville at her sister's house. Last year they'd shared a Pilgrim sandwich at their desks while working on a case. One of the worst things about being single was spending days like this alone. He could understand why the suicide rates skyrocketed during the holidays.

He wondered what Marissa was doing. Was she sitting alone today, too? Last night it had taken all his willpower not to call and invite her out for Thanksgiving dinner at one of the local restaurants. He knew Nick's Seafood House served a free meal to anyone who was spending the day alone. It had been a tradition, and he'd heard they served eight hundred people last year. But that wasn't for him, eating with strangers. No, he'd rather dine on bologna alone out on the ocean he loved so much.

He missed Laura. He remembered one Thanksgiving when they'd cooked a seventeen-pound turkey and all the trimmings, just for the two of them. As they were preparing to sit down to eat, his beeper had gone off, and he had been called out on a case. Laura never complained. She knew the drill well—her father had been a cop. When he finally stumbled in around midnight, she just reheated everything. They ate, then left the dishes piled in the kitchen sink. Collapsing on the bed, they made love till dawn.

Through a mist of tears, Shark raised his eyes to the empty sky. "Why did You have to take her from me so soon?"

Oh yes, he believed in God. Not the righteous loving Father of his Sunday school days, but the cruel vengeful God of the Old Testament.

Would he ever find someone to love him again? Even with all his quirks and baggage, didn't he deserve to have a wife and kids like other people? Surely, he wasn't destined to go through his remaining years alone. If he thought that was the case, he would be tempted to jump overboard right now.

Off to his left, he heard the distinctive whoosh, and turned to see two dolphins break the water as they surfaced to expel air through their blowholes. Even those beautiful creatures always seemed to travel in pairs.

He knew he was on the verge of falling into another of his blue funks. It was a state he had lived in for over a year after Laura died, a place he desperately did not want to return to. He remembered it as a time when he took too many risks in his job, because he didn't care if he lived or not. At night he would drink himself into a stupor so he could fall asleep.

He took out the pack of cigarettes he'd bought on the way to the boat landing this morning. All day he'd resisted. Now, he ripped them open, tapped the pack on his hand, and shook one out. He pulled a lighter from his tackle box and lit up. The first wave of nicotine hit his blood stream like a bowling ball. God, how he'd missed this!

Shark checked the bait on both lines, then settled back into the cracked leather captain's seat. He knew he was spending too much time alone, just like before. But the only woman he wanted to see, to hold in his arms and make love to, was off limits. Even if she were totally cleared of suspicion, did he really think she would be interested in him? Dell's words that day at the restaurant had hurt, but he knew she was probably right. He and Marissa didn't move in the same circles. She had simply needed someone at that particular moment, and he had been handy.

The wind was picking up dramatically, piling up heavy clouds over the mainland. He decided it was time to pull his lines and head to the dock. It was nearly dusk anyway. The long day was almost over. He had survived another Thanksgiving alone.

Chapter Twenty-One

Friday, for lack of something better to do, Shark went to the office and pulled out all his notes on Marcus's case. Was he missing something or had Marcus's death truly been an accident? Dell had learned that Rachel Wells was, in fact, having a lot of financial problems. Apparently, the manager she had hired to oversee the operation of the travel agencies had done a lousy job. Still, he didn't see her killing her brother.

On Monday, Paige Bishop, Marcus's old girlfriend, was supposed to be back in her office. She had been in Europe on a buying trip for her decorating business, so it would be their first opportunity to question her.

He reread every interview and notation in the file and still came up with nothing. Shark threw his pen disgustedly across the room. He missed Dell.

Sheriff Grant stepped out of his office and reached down to pick up the pen. He tossed it onto Shark's desk, then plopped down in the chair across from him. "What's happening?" he asked.

"Nothing. That's the problem. I've gone over everything on the DeSilva case and I've still got zip. I just feel like I'm missing something."

"I don't know if this is going to help any, but I got a call from the Clemson Police. They found the bar where the kid went after he left the restaurant. Apparently he kept right on drinking. For the time being at least, they're calling his death accidental. Maybe it was the same with the father. We might never know for sure. I don't think we can hold up the settlement of the estate much longer, unless you come up with something soon."

"I know. That's why I just went over everything again."

"We won't be able to prevent the widow from leaving either, if she gets it in her mind to go."

"Oh, she has it in her mind all right. Today wouldn't be soon enough for her."

"Well, don't say anything. Wait until she pushes it."

"I hear you."

"Did you have a nice Thanksgiving?" the sheriff asked.

"No, Ben, I didn't. Spent it alone out on the boat."

"I'm sorry to hear that. You spend too damn much time by yourself. You need to find another wife. I thought you and the coroner were an item."

"Nothing serious. How was your holiday?"

"Great. All the kids and grandchildren came. I tell ya, those grands are something else. You better get started so you can get you some one of these days."

Dell returned, bubbly and full of energy.

"So I guess you had a good one," Shark said, as he handed her a cup of coffee.

"The best. Josh went with me. Of course, my sister can't cook worth a damn, but after enough alcohol, it really didn't matter. How about you?"

"Spent it on the boat. It was okay."

"Okay, my ass. Looks like I'm going to have to find you a girlfriend. You're not doing so good on your own."

"Spare me please. I can imagine the kinda girl you'd pick for me."

"I'm hurt, Shark, truly hurt. As a matter of fact, Josh has an older sister who just got divorced. Maybe I could set you up with her. What do you think?"

"Not in this lifetime."

By ten-thirty, they were seated in Paige Bishop's office. She was a tall blond with large breasts, a tiny waist, and fire-engine red fingernails, so long that Shark wondered how she could dial a phone. "Thank you for seeing us on such short notice," Dell said, as she moved fabric samples out of the chairs, so they could sit down.

"I'm extremely busy, so can we make this quick."

"Okay, what can you tell us about your relationship with Marcus DeSilva?" Shark asked.

If Paige Bishop was surprised by the question, she didn't show it. "It was great until little Miss Newscaster came along. Then it was as if he didn't even remember my name."

"How long had you and Marcus been dating?" Dell asked.

"About nine months."

"Do you know anyone who had a grudge against Marcus?"

"Gene Branigan comes immediately to mind. He was really upset over their breakup. And I heard him bad-mouthing Marcus one night at Reilly's Bar. I really don't think Diane cared that much. They seemed to get along, as well as exes usually do, whenever I heard them talking on the phone. Can't think of anyone else right off the top of my head."

"When did you leave for Europe?" Dell asked.

"A couple of days before the wedding. I couldn't stand the thought of being here on the big day. Besides I needed to make some acquisitions for the store."

"What airline did you use?"

"Delta. You don't think I had anything to do with Marcus's death, do you? Let me tell you something. If I had been the one doing the deed, that little tramp Marissa would be the one scattered all over the ocean, not Marcus. She's a gold-digging lowlife, as far as I'm concerned. It wouldn't surprise me if she were the one behind it. Have you checked her out? She *is* from Kentucky. You know how those hillbillies are. Do anything for a buck."

Back in the car, Shark said, "If we could only learn how to convert hatred into an energy source, that woman could make us rich."

Dell laughed. "I'd say she doesn't like Marissa very much."

"That's an understatement. Now, if Marissa had been the victim, we could probably close this case right now."

"At least her story checks out with what we had already learned from the airline."

"Yeah, but just in case, let's make sure she didn't reenter the country in time to be at the wedding, after all."

Marissa took Pepper and headed to the beach, even though it was cool and overcast. As she walked, and watched the puppy waddle, she began to formulate some plans. She would call a real estate agent and list the house, so that when the police allowed her to leave, she would at least have that out of the way. She would also contact a boat broker and turn the yacht over to him. The closing on Marcus's business was in two days. Daniel Lawrence seemed as anxious as she was to complete the transfer.

She had been trying to narrow down the list of places she might like to live. She and Eric had taken a vacation once to London. That was the only place in Europe she'd been. Of course the weather was lousy there this time of year. Maybe she should go someplace warm, like Mexico or an island in the Caribbean. But what would she do there, besides lie or walk on the beach? She'd had about enough of "life at the beach" for awhile.

A few drops of rain splattered onto the sand, so she scooped Pepper up in her arms and jogged back to the house. After showering and changing, she settled herself at Marcus's desk and put in a call to the law offices of Baker and Silverstein. Once connected with Mr. Baker, she asked, "When will the funds from Marcus's estate be disbursed? I'm anxious to leave the island, as soon as possible, and obviously, I can't till all the legal matters are resolved."

"I understand, Mrs. DeSilva. As you know, we were preparing to release the funds when Mr. DeSilva's son died. At that time, the police asked us to delay settlement, and we haven't heard anything more from them since. I'd be happy to check with them today and see if they will allow us to proceed. We will have to make some adjustments, in view of the fact that you will now inherit the son's share, as well. Perhaps I can call you tomorrow, after I've had an opportunity to talk to the police."

"I would appreciate that. Thank you."

Marissa swiveled in the chair to watch the rain, now being blown in sheets against the window. *Definitely someplace warm.*

The next few days found Dell and Shark drowning in work. Someone had shot a clerk at the Starvin' Marvin convenience store, just down the street from their office. A heavy-set white male had been seen driving away in an old white Toyota pickup, by a customer who had pulled up for gas, around the time of the shooting. He'd used a credit card to pay at the pump, so he hadn't entered the store, but had come forward when he read about the killing in the newspaper. It wasn't much to go on.

They didn't know if the guy in the Toyota was the shooter, or just a customer who'd been lucky enough to leave just before the robbery went down. Or he could have entered the store after the shooting, but didn't want to get involved. They just knew they needed to find him.

Frustrated and getting nowhere, Shark dragged himself home Saturday evening, plopped down in his recliner, and twisted the top off a beer. He reached in his pocket, pulled out a cigarette, and lit it. He was already working on his second pack of the day.

How quickly we fall back into old habits, he thought. He wondered what Marissa was doing. Halfway through his second beer he dialed her number.

"Hello," a voice said gaily.

"Hi. It's Shark. You sound good. What have you been up to?"

"Oh hi. Jason and his son Derek brought over pizza, and we're playing with Pepper."

"Pepper?"

"Oh that's the Dalmatian puppy Derek gave me. He came over to visit her."

How cozy, Shark thought, wishing he had given her a present like that. "Well, I just wanted to check in and see how you're doing."

"I was planning to give you a call and thank you. Marcus's lawyer contacted me and said they'll be disbursing the funds from the estate next week. And I understand that my travel is no longer restricted. I don't know if you had anything to do with that, but thank you if you did."

"Not really, Sheriff Grant made the final decision. So when are you planning to leave? You know you need to leave a number where we can contact you, in the event something comes up with Marcus's case."

"I understand. But I'm still trying to decide where to go. Once I make up my mind, I'll let you know. I've got to finish clearing up some things here with the house and furnishings."

Shark could hear a young boy in the background, calling Marissa's name. "I won't keep you any longer. Will I see you before you leave?" He tried not to make it sound as important to him as it was.

"I'd like that. Thanks again."

Shark stared at the phone for a moment, then placed it gently back in the charger. "Well, that's that," he said.

Chapter Twenty-Two

Ten days before Christmas, Marissa DeSilva, with two suitcases and a carry-on bag at her feet, locked the front door of the sprawling mansion that had so briefly been her home, for the last time. The shuttlebus, waiting to transport her to the Savannah Airport, stood idling in the driveway. She placed the key under the doormat, so the realtor could place it in the lockbox the next time she showed the house, and hurried down the steps.

The boat and the house and its entire contents had been turned over to brokers. She had gotten a good price for the Porsche, and Derek McCalvey was taking care of Pepper until she got settled somewhere. She had given the Sheriff's department an address and phone number where she could be reached for the next few weeks. Marissa was sure she had probably forgotten something, but she wasn't going to worry about it now. She was finally leaving the island, and with considerably more than when she'd arrived.

Her excitement grew as the van approached the airport. She debarked and quickly checked her luggage at the Delta counter, then made her way to the gate. A half-hour later, she was airborne for Atlanta. It took only long enough for the stewardess to offer a beverage and quickly return to pick up the cup, before she arrived at the terminal where she walked briskly to her connecting gate.

Once the plane was in the air, Marissa let out a deep sigh. Finally, she could relax. She had been convinced something would happen, at the last minute, to prevent her leaving. She wouldn't have been surprised if Shark or his odious partner had grabbed her by the shoulder and dragged her from the jetway back to Hilton Head. Now she could put all this behind her and move on.

She relaxed into the soft leather first-class seat and accepted a glass of champagne from the hovering stewardess. Marissa took out *Fodor's Complete Guide to Spain* and settled it on her lap. She would plan an itinerary so she wouldn't miss any of the important sights of Madrid.

When the plane landed safely, almost eight hours later at Barajas Airport, Marissa cleared customs and claimed her luggage. As she emerged into the cool, overcast Spanish afternoon, her heart was racing, and her palms sweaty. *The adventure begins.*

She hailed a cab and handed the driver the paper on which she had written the address of the Ritz Hotel, at Plaza de Lealtad 5. She didn't trust her rusty high-school Spanish.

The twelve-mile journey into the city was punctuated by blaring horns and screeching brakes, as the taxi wove in and out of an endless stream of traffic. Marissa was captivated by the graceful old arches and huge statues that dominated every corner. When they finally came to a stop, it was in front of a structure that looked like a palace, at least to a girl from Hazard, Kentucky. Marissa paid the driver and stood gawking on the sidewalk.

She'd read in the guidebook that when Alfonso XIII was preparing for his marriage to Queen Victoria's granddaughter, he'd realized, to his dismay, that Madrid did not have a single hotel up to the exacting standards of his royal guests. So the King had personally overseen construction, and the Ritz had opened in 1910, furnished with rare antiques in every public room, hand-embroidered linens from Robinson and Cleaver of London, and all manner of other luxurious details. But it also had modern amenities as well, a restaurant, bar, beauty salon and health club.

And with one hundred and fifty-eight rooms, it was large enough that she would not stand out.

Marissa jumped, as the bellman reached for her luggage. Closing her gaping mouth, she entered the lobby. Marble floors, magnificent chandeliers, and columns all added to the opulence. She made her way to the registration desk and checked in.

Her suite, done in pastel peach with an intricate gold and glass chandelier and a huge four-poster bed, seemed like a soothing oasis. Yawning, she kicked off her shoes and threw herself on the white silk duvet. Though she was anxious to begin exploring the city, she knew she needed to rest. Her internal clock needed to be reset. She stripped off her wrinkled suit then wrapped herself in a luxurious white and gold bathrobe that had *Ritz* embroidered on the pocket. Lifting aside the heavy drape, she was pleased to see she had a good view of the Prado Museum. It was one of the places she was eager to visit, and one of the primary reasons she had chosen Madrid.

She dropped the curtain back into place and turned toward the bathroom. A quick shower and a short nap and she would be ready to explore.

As Shark drove home through the deepening twilight, his thoughts turned to Marissa. How exciting it must be to travel, with the finest accommodations, to any place in the world you wanted to go. He wondered what Spain was like. He'd never ventured outside the old U. S. of A. And the farthest west he had been was St. Louis.

He arrived just as a UPS truck was backing out of his drive. He honked his horn, and the truck pulled back in. When he got out, he saw the driver struggling with a huge crate about the size of a refrigerator box. *What in the world?*

"Wait, I think there's a mistake. Before you wrestle that thing any farther you better recheck the address. I don't think it belongs here."

"It's addressed to Shark Morgan, twenty-six Pleasant Farm Court. That's not you?"

"Yes, but I didn't order anything."

"Well, maybe someone sent you a surprise. Would you help me get this onto the hand truck? It's really, really, heavy."

They struggled with the crate, and Shark grew more curious. He unlocked the front door and told the driver to put it in the living room. As soon as the man left, Shark walked all around the thing. There was no return address. It would require tools to get it open.

Ten minutes and a lot of sweat later, Shark was finally able to see inside. He was flabbergasted. It was the Wyland sculpture of the dolphin and pedestal, from Marissa's bedroom. He touched its cool surface with reverence. Tucked into the crate was a white envelope.

Dear Shark,

How can I ever repay you for all the friendship and kindness you extended to me after Marcus's death and while I was hospitalized? I know that if I had tried to give this to you before I left, you would have declined. But I truly want you to have it. It should be in the hands of someone who will appreciate its beauty, and I know that you will. I hope that someday you make it out to California to see the Whaling Wall.

I'm sorry I didn't have an opportunity to see you before I left, but maybe it's better this way. Take care of yourself.

Forever in your debt,
Marissa

Shark sat in a state of shock. He should return this to her somehow. But he knew, deep down inside, that he didn't want to. He had never, in his wildest imagination, ever expected to own a Wyland. And he made a vow to himself that his next vacation would in fact be to California to see his work. He cleared the packing away, picked up the heavy pedestal and began searching for just the right spot for it.

Refreshed after her nap, Marissa turned left when she exited the hotel and made her way to the Plaza Canovas del Castillo. With its Neptune's fountain, the plaza was the hub of Madrid's so-called "triangle of art." It was made up of the red brick Prado, spreading out along the east side of the boulevard, the Tyssen-Bornemisza Museum, across the plaza, and the Reina Sofia, five blocks to the south. Leaving them for another time, she continued north along the wide landscaped walkway that ran down the center of the Paseo del Prado to the Plaza de la Cibeles. It was home to the Fuente de Cibeles, a huge statue depicting the wife of Saturn, driving a chariot drawn by lions. It stood alone at the intersection of six streets.

For the next two hours, Marissa took in the flavor of the city, going through two rolls of film. Working on a blister from the not-so-sensible shoes she was wearing, she limped down old cobblestone streets back to the hotel. Dusk was settling over the city, and she admired the multicolored lights illuminating the fountains and arches. This city was even more beautiful at night. Already she loved it here. How different this was from any other place she'd ever been, and certainly a world away from Hilton Head Island.

As Marissa approached the hotel, the air felt heavy, almost as if it were about to rain. Hurrying inside, she stopped to pick up several brochures describing the major museums in the city. She hoped she would be in Madrid long enough to see all that it offered.

Marissa flung off her shoes as soon as she entered her

suite and collapsed onto the peach floral sofa. Her energy was waning, and she was hungry. She knew that dinner in this part of the world was usually not served until nine or ten P.M. and that it could go on for hours, depending on how many courses you ordered. Knowing she wasn't up for that, she decided just to order something from room service. She picked up the menu off the desk and groaned. Of course, it was all in Spanish, and Marissa recognized only a few things. She knew *saluda* was salad, and *la chuleta el cerdo* was pork chop. In her halting Spanish, she placed her order and included a bottle of "*el blanco el vino.*"

She had almost drifted off to sleep before the food finally arrived. She tasted the wine first, a little sweeter than she preferred, but still good. And the dinner wasn't half-bad either. She was just finishing when she heard the first peal of thunder. She walked to the window and gazed out across the city, illuminated now by almost continual flashes of light.

The weather mattered little to her plans. Tomorrow she would spend all day in the Prado, admiring famous works of art and waiting to see if the person she had sent the message to would find her.

Chapter Twenty-Three

The next morning Marissa took extra care with her makeup and wardrobe. If she did make her rendezvous, she wanted to look her best. After breakfast in the hotel's restaurant, Marissa walked casually out the front door and across the plaza to the Prado Museum.

She opened the brochure she had picked up in the lobby the night before. The Prado had been commissioned in 1785 by King Carlos III and was originally meant to be a natural science museum. But, by the time it had been completed in 1810, its purpose had been changed to exhibiting the vast collection of art gathered by Spanish royalty since the time of Ferdinand and Isabella. Marissa loved art and planned to begin collecting pieces she had admired for a long time.

She began her tour on the upper floor through a series of halls dedicated to the Renaissance, made her way through the works of El Greco, which didn't hold as much interest for her, and casually searched the crowd for that head of blond hair as she admired the works by Velazquez.

Still not finding the face she was searching for, she descended to the basement cafeteria to have lunch and rest her feet.

Marissa spent most of the afternoon in the halls dedicated to Goya. Since the Prado had not yielded the face she was searching for, Marissa headed toward the exit that would take her to the Botanical Gardens. A few steps from the door a woman dressed head to toe in a black abaya, with a black veil covering all but her eyes, stumbled into her. Marissa reached out her hands to prevent her fall. In the process Marissa's purse flew open, the contents spilling onto the floor. The woman, muttering unintelligible apologies, stooped to help her retrieve her belongings, then hurried away.

Marissa strolled leisurely through the Botanical gardens. When, after nearly an hour of wandering among the exotic plants no one had made contact, she sat down on a stone bench to rethink her plan. Maybe the person she was looking for hadn't seen her ad in the classifieds. Perhaps she should run it again and give a rendezvous date a few days from now, in a different location. Until then, she would continue to be a typical tourist and take in as many sights as she could. Marissa sneezed, and reached into her purse for a Kleenex. Her hand closed around a small envelope. She knew it hadn't been there when she left the hotel this morning. The woman in the abaya? Surely not. She started to unfold it, then decided she should read it in the privacy of her room. Quickly, she rose and hurried down the path that would take her back to the hotel.

As soon as she entered her suite, Marissa dumped the contents of her purse onto the bed, ripped open the envelope, and took out the note.

Hello my love,

No sign of a tail all day—think you're clean. Here's a train ticket to Cordoba. Leaves at nine in the morning. When you arrive, place your luggage in a locker at the station, wait thirty minutes, then take a cab to the Hotel Boston. Come directly to room 17. I'll be waiting. Pay for your suite in Madrid for another two weeks so you can call in for messages. Until tomorrow.

Marissa's heart began to flutter. It wouldn't be long now. She pulled her suitcase from the closet.

At midnight the phone shrilled loudly. Startled, she sat up in bed and looked at the clock. Something must have gone wrong, she thought as she picked up the receiver and tentatively said, "Hello?"

"Marissa?"

"Yes," she answered, fully alert now.

"It's Shark. Damn, did I wake you? I wasn't sure what time it was over there. I'm sorry."

"That's okay. Really, it's only midnight. Has something happened? Did you find out who killed Marcus?"

"I'm sorry, no. That's not why I'm calling. I wanted to thank you for the Wyland sculpture. It's beautiful, and I admire it more than you can imagine. But you shouldn't have. It's much too valuable. You need to take it back."

"No, I want you to have it. Consider it a Christmas present. And what would I do with it anyway while I tool around Spain, carry it in my luggage?"

Shark paused. "How about this. I'll take care of it for you temporarily. Then at some future date, when you settle somewhere, if you come to your senses and decide you want it back, I'll return it to you."

"Only on the condition that you won't try, unless I ask for it."

"That's a deal. So how's Spain?"

"Wonderful! I love what little I've seen so far. I spent the whole day at the Prado Museum. The art is unbelievable, and you should see all the fountains and arches in the city. Everything is so old, not like in the States. You should try and visit sometime."

"Yeah, sure. I'll be lucky if I ever make it out to California. So how long are you staying in Madrid?"

"I'm not sure. At least until I see all the things the city has to offer, and then I may rent a car and tour the rest of the country. There are so many cities here I'd like to explore. So how are you? Caught any sharks lately?"

"No. I haven't been out in the boat much." He paused, not sure if he should say what was really on his mind, then plunged ahead. "I was disappointed I didn't get to see you before you left."

"I'm sorry about that. There just seemed so much to do at the last minute, things I hadn't thought of."

"Are you ever coming back?"

"Maybe, for a visit. Once I get settled somewhere, I'll have to retrieve Pepper."

"I forgot about the dog. Who's taking care of her?"

"Derek. I don't think he really wanted to give her up in the first place."

"Well, I'd better let you get back to sleep. Send me some postcards so I can see all the exciting places you're visiting."

"I'll do that."

Shark hung up the phone and reached for a cigarette. He watched the smoke curling up toward the ceiling fan, glancing occasionally across the room to admire the sculpture.

Well, he hadn't gotten the girl, and he was surprised that he wasn't more upset about it. Marissa had just made it perfectly clear that their friendship had been nothing more to her than a way to escape the shock and loneliness of her sudden widowhood. And if he were honest, he hadn't really been in love with her either. Lust no doubt, strong enough to send him chasing after a woman for the first time since Laura died. He had almost lost the one thing that was still important to him, his career. Never again would he act so foolishly. He would just accept the fact that he was destined to spend the rest of his life alone and concentrate on catching the bad guys. He took another swallow of his beer and reached for the remote control.

As soon as Marissa boarded the train and settled into her seat, she began searching for the face. She didn't really think the person she was seeking would be on the train, but you never knew.

As they sped along through the countryside, she watched acres and acres of olive trees fly by the wide windows. At times the land was hilly, at others perfectly flat. She promised herself that she would come back and explore the many quaint towns and villages they were passing through. But at the moment she was eager to reach her destination.

Finally, hungry and curious to inspect every face she passed, she meandered down the aisle toward the dining car. Since tables were at a premium, Marissa was seated with an older gentleman, who was also traveling alone. Gold-framed glasses glinted between his full head of white hair and matching bushy mustache. Marissa admired the European cut of his dark blue suit, as he stood at her approach. She smiled, said hello, and picked up the menu.

"*Su Americano?*" His voice was deep and cultured.

"Yes, I am. Forgive me, but my Spanish is awful. Do you, by any chance, speak English?" she asked, glancing at him over the top of the menu.

"*Un poco*, a little." He shrugged and smiled. "*Donde* you live in the United States?"

"Recently, in South Carolina. Have you been there?"

"No. Only in New York, on business."

"What kind of business are you in?"

"I am seller for art and antiquities."

"How fascinating. I spent all day yesterday at the Prado. The paintings were unbelievable. My name is Marissa Langford," she said, extending her hand across the table.

"I am called Juan Perez."

"It's nice to meet you, Señor Perez." Marissa glanced down at the menu again and frowned.

"I may be of assistance?"

"I would be grateful. My high-school Spanish was a long time ago."

With his help, Marissa placed her order and accepted a Coca-Cola from the waiter. "I can't get used to the idea of warm soft drinks."

"You must ask for a glass with ice. I will tell him to bring one."

"Thank you. That would be nice. Do you live in Madrid?"

"Madrid is my home, but I travel much in my work. Did you not love my city?"

Over lunch, they discussed the beauty of Madrid and the wonders of the Prado. Juan Perez regaled her with stories and the glorious sights she should not miss in Granada and Seville.

Reluctant to end the encounter, but suddenly aware of a number of people waiting for tables, she reached for her bill. "No *Señora*, please, you must allow me," Juan Perez said, placing it with his. "To share such beauty is better than fine food."

Marissa smiled and thanked him. As she stood he touched her arm. "*Caución, Señora.* A woman alone is not good." He pressed an embossed business card into her hand. "My number."

"Thank you for your concern, but I'm meeting someone in Cordoba."

"Good. Adiós."

"Goodbye."

At Cordoba, Marissa reclaimed her luggage, put all but her carry-on in a locker as instructed, and made her way to the small coffee shop in the terminal. She wondered why she needed to wait half an hour before arriving at the hotel, but knew there must be a good reason. There always was.

She lingered over espresso, then hailed a cab. The Hotel Boston was not nearly as grand as the Ritz in Madrid, but she didn't care. Inside the lobby, Marissa paused to get her bearings, and turned down the corridor to her right. She found *diecisiete*, number seventeen, and knocked softly.

Immediately the door flew open and she stepped quickly into the room. He closed the door softly behind her and locked it. She knew not to speak. It was always the same. No talking until later. Slowly he slipped the strap of her purse from her shoulder and dropped it to the floor. Next, he took the carry-on bag from her hand and placed it gently on the carpet, his eyes never leaving hers.

He made no move to touch her, but she could feel his power and control over her just the same. His gaze drifted toward her mouth, cherry red. That tantalizing little beauty mark like a finger beckoning him closer. She looked up at him from under her lashes, and ran the tip of her tongue across her lips, inviting his mouth to settle on hers. Instead, he just gazed at her and gave her a long level stare with blue eyes the color of an Arctic wolf's. The intensity of his gaze made her feel as if he could read her innermost thoughts, which made him one dangerous man. His power frightened and excited her at the same time, and their unspoken words thickened the air like humidity.

Then he turned his back and walked halfway across the room before turning to face her again. His white dress shirt was unbuttoned. His wide chest was covered with a fine dusting of soft blond hair that trailed down the center of a six-pack of stomach muscles, then disappeared into the waistband of his jeans.

Marissa knew it was better not to need anyone, and certainly better not to need him, but it was too late for that. She had been stared at often in her lifetime, but it had never unnerved her the way it did when he looked at her this way. She had learned through the years that a smile or a flirtatious look would have most men eating out of her hand. But not this one, he was more likely to bite. She cursed the tingling along her nerve endings.

Still not a word had been spoken, just as he always demanded it be, after a long separation. It was as if he had to reestablish his control over her, remind her that he was the one real man in her life.

He motioned for her to turn around, which she did slowly. When she was facing him again, she started to take a step toward him. But his hand went up and motioned for her to stay, like he would with a well-trained pet.

Marissa's face flushed with anger, and she broke eye contact and looked down at the floor. She had forgotten how he enjoyed his mind games, and she had gotten used to being treated with respect.

Deciding he had pushed her to her limit, he finally motioned for her to come. She hesitated for only a second and then walked slowly across the room. He pulled her against him, let her press her cheek into the soft mat on his chest. He stroked her hair, and sighed. Marissa entwined her fingers in the soft down on his chest. With his free hand, he stroked her back lovingly. It was her signal that she could break the silence. "God, I've missed you," she said softly.

"You think it's been easy for me? Knowing another man was touching you, loving you? You're mine, and you always will be."

"He may have used my flesh, but he never captured my soul. Only you have that."

Two hours later, over a small feast of cheese, bread and fruit, Marissa asked, "So what's the plan now?"

"I thought we'd spend a couple of days here, then go on to Granada and Seville. Maybe stop on the Costa del Sol for one night. I've chartered a plane to take us over to the Canary Islands, where it'll be nice and warm. I've rented a house on El Hierro. Very few tourists there, not like on the larger islands. We can do some hiking and diving, and spend some time on the black sand beach."

"Sounds wonderful," Marissa said, yawning.

"Let's have a nap, and when we get up I'll take you out for paella."

Just as Marissa was about to drift off to sleep, she asked, "Devon, was that you in the black abaya and veil yesterday?"

He chuckled. "Of course. Good disguise, huh?"

"And were you on the train with me today?"

"Yes, but you didn't recognize me."

"Please tell me you weren't the man I had lunch with," she said sleepily.

Devon laughed. "No, that *wasn't* me."

"But why did I have to wait at the station before I came here?"

"So I'd have a chance to get out of my little old lady clothes and get here before you. We'll pick up your luggage when we go out to eat. I didn't want a bellman deciding to carry it to the room for you."

"You think of everything."

"I know."

For the next two days, they acted like all the other tourists in Cordoba. They walked through the Old Quarter and visited Mezquita, the famous mosque. It was hard to imagine that, even in the eleventh century, over a million people had lived in the city. And even more incredible that Moors, Christians, and Jews had lived together in harmony within its walls. Marissa found it fascinating that it was in Cordoba, that Queen Isabella had granted Columbus the commission for his first voyage to the New World.

For the first time in months, Marissa felt truly free. She wasn't constantly on her guard, looking over her shoulder. Hilton Head Island seemed a whole world away.

They played like teenagers, holding hands and acting silly. One of the things she had always loved about Devon was his ability to make her laugh. All through her childhood, she'd had to struggle—against her family's poverty, for an education, so that one day she could get out of Hazard, but mostly, just to survive. She had always been so serious, allowing nothing to stand in the way of reaching her goals. Never had she felt carefree, like the other kids. She had never known how to have fun, until she met Devon.

Marissa remembered when they were dating in college and Devon pulled her outside in a pouring rain just so she could feel *alive*. He had taught her how to live.

Devon had introduced her, as well, to the finer things in life. He had taken her to museums and art galleries, symphonies and the ballet. He had worked with her to lose her coarse Kentucky accent. It was as if she had been Eliza Doolittle. He had transformed her into a woman with class. In the process, Devon had also made her totally dependent upon him. He dictated the smallest details of her life, from how she wore her hair to the style of her clothes.

For Marissa's part, she would do anything to please him. She needed Devon to validate her, not only as a woman, but also as a person. She didn't feel whole unless she was with him.

It was shortly after they were married, when Devon began to talk about what he wanted out of life. Houses in the Carribean and the south of France. To travel the world, collecting priceless art and Chinese antiquities. He dreamed of a vineyard in California, cases of slender wine bottles bearing his name. They would never have to think about money, just enjoy life—together.

Gradually Marissa came to believe it might be possible, this waking fantasy, so far removed from Hazard, Kentucky. The night he told her how they could achieve all those things, she didn't believe he was serious. They had been drinking all evening and she was sure it was the wine talking. Slowly, over time, Devon had worn down her reluctance. After all, she wouldn't be the one taking the risks. All she would have to do was be her beautiful, charming self. Devon would be the producer and director, and Marissa simply an actress playing a part. Then, after a "couple of performances," they would have enough money to spend the rest of their lives, fulfilling their dreams. When he put it that way, how could she refuse?

Chapter Twenty-Four

Late afternoon on Christmas Eve, Shark and Dell sat at their desks, comparing notes. They had split up the list of names from the DMV of people who owned white Toyota trucks and had been out tracking them down all day.

"This seems like a waste of time. We don't even know if the owner of the truck has anything to do with the shooting at the Starvin' Marvin. Maybe he was there before it happened." She pulled out an emory board, frowning at the broken nail on her index finger.

"Or maybe he pulled up right afterward and saw the shooter." Shark leaned back in his chair and propped his feet up on the desk.

"We couldn't be so lucky."

"Or maybe he *is* the shooter," Shark said, pulling the list on his desk closer. "We only have eight people left to interview." He had already crossed off dozens of names. They had been working the list for several days. "Do you have a better suggestion?"

Returning the nail file to her center desk drawer, Dell said, "Well I'm not going to think about it anymore right now. We have two whole days off, and we'll just finish up the list when we get back."

"Maybe I'll try to catch a couple more who live in Beaufort on my way home."

"You will do no such thing. It's Christmas Eve. Just because you don't have plans this evening, doesn't mean other people don't."

"What time is Josh coming?"

"Around eight. Why don't you drop by and have a glass of wine with us?"

"No thanks. I don't want to intrude."

"You wouldn't be intruding. I wouldn't have asked you if I didn't want you there."

"That's okay. I'll leave you two lovers alone tonight. I'll get to meet him tomorrow anyway."

"Brunch is at ten. *Please* try to be on time, for a change."

"Yes, ma'am. I wouldn't want to spoil your quiche, or whatever it is you're cooking. Are you sure you wouldn't rather just spend the day alone with Josh? I can find something to do."

"Absolutely not! You are *not* going to spend Christmas out on that boat of yours, like you did on Thanksgiving. Anyway, I have a surprise for you," Dell said, grinning mischievously.

"Oh no. I don't like the sound of that. What are you up to?"

"Relax. Don't you know you're supposed to have surprises on Christmas? So give me a hint about the present you bought me."

"No way. Not after last year. I gave you one little hint, and you guessed it right off. Takes all the fun out of it."

"If I remember correctly, your little hint was 'It could save your life.' It wasn't hard to guess a new bullet-proof vest."

"Not fair. It could have been a box of condoms. Or a gun, or a first-aid kit, or any number of things."

"Yeah, sure."

"Well, at least I was thinking about your safety."

"Do me a favor. Get me something not work-related this year, okay?"

"In that case, I better return the Uzi."

Dell lobbed her pen at him. "I'm leaving. What about you?"

"I think I better get to the mall before it closes."

"You haven't even bought me anything yet, have you?"

"Wouldn't you like to know. Guess you'll just have to wait and be surprised."

"I don't understand why men always wait until the last minute."

Shark knew why he always waited. It was a ritual he had shared with Laura. They always shopped together on Christmas Eve. Again, he would have to do it alone.

At the liquor store in Main Street, he picked out two bottles of wine to take to Dell's. He didn't know what Josh drank, but figured he couldn't go wrong with a fifth of Jack Daniel's. The clerk offered to gift-wrap them, which was good, because he had two left hands when it came to tape and ribbons.

The parking lot was half full as he pulled into the Mall at Shelter Cove. At least he wasn't the only one who had procrastinated. He wandered through the aisles at Saks, not finding anything that was within his budget. How could such small pieces of cloth cost so much? He paused at the jewelry counter. He knew Dell liked earrings, but that was probably too personal. He didn't want Josh thinking they had anything more than a professional relationship. He considered perfume, until he spotted the skinny guy standing guard over the display of exotic-looking bottles. In black leather pants and a red satin shirt, the man's long, bleached blond ponytail revealed delicate ears, each bearing at least three studs. Shark didn't even slow down, just headed for the exit.

He turned into the Williams Sonoma store. Dell would kill him if he bought her a toaster or something practical like that, but he knew she couldn't object to the cappuccino machine that caught his eye. She was addicted to the stuff.

Carrying his foil-wrapped package, he walked on past Victoria's Secret. He had loved shopping there for Laura, once he got over his initial embarrassment. The crowd was beginning to thin. Most of the remaining shoppers were men, like him, wandering alone, postponing the moment when they'd have to face their empty houses, their empty lives.

In Belk's he found a beautiful crystal ornament with the year engraved in gold that he knew Dell would like. She always insisted on having a "real" Christmas tree and spent hours decorating it. The smell of cranberries drew him to a display of candles. Laura had always loved them. He chose a fat red one and waited in line for his gifts to be wrapped.

Pleased with his purchases, Shark walked back into the mall. In the window of Walden's Book Store he noticed a new book by John Jakes, a resident of Hilton Head and one of his favorite authors. After scanning the jacket cover, he decided it would hopefully keep him occupied through the long evening.

Traffic was unusually light as Shark drove toward Beaufort. He wondered if Marissa was spending Christmas Eve alone, as well. Although it was probably already tomorrow in Spain.

At ten o'clock, Shark closed the Jakes book. He had finished a little over a hundred pages, but had little memory of what he had read. He kept remembering his last Christmas with Laura.

The afternoon of Christmas Eve, they had gone to the mall in Savannah and shopped until the stores closed. Laura had been flushed with excitement when she met him at the exit, barely able to carry all her packages. Christmas was her favorite holiday. She always started baking the first of December and filled Christmas baskets with all kinds of homemade goodies for neighbors and friends. She worked for weeks, making kahlua, hot fudge sauce, cranberry chutney, and about a dozen different kinds of cookies.

Laura always insisted on dragging him to the Christmas tree farm to pick out the perfect tree. They would spend days decorating it and the house. She had painted over forty pieces for their miniature Christmas village, which was now boxed up in the attic, and hadn't been out since she died. He couldn't stand to look at it.

When they had left the mall that last Christmas, they had been famished but all the restaurants had been closed. The only place open was the Krystal hamburger joint. They bought a dozen of the mini-burgers, fries, and milk shakes and inhaled the food on the drive home. Wrapping presents until midnight, Laura had gotten a little tipsy on the champagne she loved so much. She always said it made her horny, so he used to buy it by the case. Then they had gone to bed and tried to make a baby. Tears spilled onto his cheeks when he realized he could no longer remember how her body had felt beneath him. He closed his eyes and willed himself to retrieve her image. The beautiful eyes and quick smile of her well-loved face floated just out of reach. How long before that too would fade?

"Merry Christmas, my love," he whispered softly.

"Let's quit." Marissa propped her bare feet on the low stool and turned toward Devon. Across the narrow strip of beach that separated their porch from the ocean the setting sun hovered on the edge of the horizon. "These last few days here have made me want to be with you all the time. Besides, I don't think I can go through this again."

"*You* won't have to. I've made a new acquaintance back home. She's worth a fortune."

"Devon, no! We have more than enough money. Why take the chance?"

"You can *never* have enough money. And she's primed. I've played tennis with her a few times at the club, and she can hardly keep her hands off me. Anyway, I'm enjoying the game."

"No, I want to stop. We've been lucky so far. But it may be running out. It's beginning to look like a pattern. Even those two redneck detectives were starting to get suspicious. We *have* to quit. And what do you mean you're enjoying *the game*? I thought the point was to make enough so we could be together for the rest of our lives."

"We will be together, and soon, I promise you. It's just that this one is too good to pass up. We'll never have to think about money again. Then we can live out our dreams."

Marissa rose from the wicker chair and walked to the edge of the porch and gazed out over the darkening water. The sun had almost completely disappeared and the first few stars had begun to appear overhead. It wasn't often that Devon frightened her. But lately she wondered just exactly what her role really was. Did he love her, as he claimed, or was she simply the means to his end? Her beauty and her willingness had made her the perfect partner. But what would happen if he no longer needed her? One of the first things they'd done was to execute wills in each other's favor. What would stop him from killing her, at some point, and having all the money for himself? Her hand shook as she turned to the table and picked up her wineglass.

"What's her name?"

"You know better than to ask that."

"Then tell me about her."

"She's in her late fifties. Not a bad body, works out a lot. Old money. Her husband died five years ago. He was into oil. Trust me, she's ripe for the picking."

"How will you do it?"

"Darling, you know never to ask me that," he said, frowning up at her.

"So what am I supposed to do, while you seduce the lonely widow?"

"Whatever you want. Take a trip around the world. We can afford it."

"But I don't want to do that alone."

"So what do you have in mind?"

"Nothing, that's the problem."

"So find something that interests you. Collect art, go back in the TV business, write a book. Whatever makes you happy."

"What would make me happy, is for us not to be separated again. How long will that take? How long will I have to be alone this time?"

"Just give me six months, eight max. Maybe less. Then we can be together for the rest of our lives. I promise."

"Devon, please, let's stop now before somebody figures it all out. We've already taken too many chances."

"But Darling, what chances? Eric simply fell off his horse, and Marcus's death appears to have been a terrible accident, as well. Isn't that what everyone thinks?" he asked.

She knew he was taunting her and it made her angry. "Maybe so, but you drowned your wife out on that sailboat."

"Do you know that for sure? Were you there? Or was it simply another senseless tragedy? Now, no more talk about business. We only have a few days left before I have to be back in California."

Marissa didn't resist when he pulled her roughly onto his lap.

Chapter Twenty-Five

Christmas morning Shark mounted Dell's front steps at exactly ten o'clock. A tall, good-looking man answered the door.

"Hi! You must be Shark. I'm Josh. Come on in. Let me help you with those packages," he said.

Shark let him take the large box from his arms, carrying the two smaller ones, along with the wine, over to the beautifully decorated tree. The sweet scent of pine brought back memories of past Christmases.

"Wow, I'm impressed. You're actually on time. This must be a first," Dell called from the dining room. The table was overflowing with steaming casserole dishes, Dell's best china, and a lush centerpiece of fresh flowers and greenery. "So I guess you did the introduction thing already."

"Yes," Shark answered. Turning to Josh he said, "Dell tells me you're an architect. That must be interesting work."

"I really enjoy it. I specialize mostly in historical restoration. And that is a never-ending process in Charleston.

There are so many really old, neat houses that need to be returned to their former glory. But it's pretty boring compared to your job."

The door to the powder room opened and a tall woman, with the same dark hair and olive complexion as Josh, stepped out. She was dressed in a red suit and white turtleneck sweater. Sheer black stockings and three-inch heels drew attention to her long, slim legs.

"Shark, I'd like you to meet Jasmine Delacourt, Josh's sister."

Shark took the offered hand and forced himself to smile pleasantly. "Hi," he said. "Nice to meet you, Jasmine."

She had a strong handshake. "My friends call me Jazz."

Up close he could see the little scar over her left brow. Dark, sparkling eyes studied him back, and her full lips twitched at the corners, as if she were trying not to laugh. He didn't think beautiful was an appropriate description, but nice, real nice.

Against his direct orders, Dell had set him up, but maybe it wouldn't turn out to be so bad, after all.

"Come on, everybody. Let's eat, before things get cold." Dell avoided her partner's eyes, uncertain whether or not he was upset.

Over eggs Benedict, blueberry muffins, and fresh fruit they exchanged stories of childhood presents they had destroyed within an hour of opening. Shark was unusually quiet. He watched the interplay around the table, pleased to see that Josh really cared for Dell. He and his sister seemed close, and Dell apparently liked her, too. Jazz had a quick wit and laughed easily at herself. He learned that she was an attorney, his least favorite profession. But at least she worked in the prosecutor's office in Charleston.

After they finished eating, Dell shooed Jazz and Shark into the living room with instructions to get better acquainted while she and Josh cleared the table. Jazz settled onto one end of the couch and placed her coffee cup on the table. She crossed one long leg over the other and smiled across at Shark, slouched down in the easy chair. "You got ambushed, didn't you?"

"What do you mean?"

"You had no idea I was going to be here today."

Shark smiled. "It's okay, really. It was a nice surprise."

"If Dell hadn't invited me, I'd be spending the day alone."

"Divorced?"

"Yes. It was final about three months ago, but we'd been separated for almost two years."

"I'm sorry."

"Don't be. I'm not."

"Do you have children?" Shark asked, reaching for his coffee cup.

"No. That's the one thing I do regret. What about you?"

"No, I don't have any kids either."

"Dell said your wife died several years ago."

"Yes," Shark said, avoiding her kind, but direct gaze.

"That must have been terribly difficult."

"It was."

"Do you think of her often?" Jazz asked softly.

"Sometimes, but not as much as I did in the beginning."

"Holidays must be especially hard."

"They do bring back memories," Shark said, trying not to let the pain show in his eyes.

"Memories are good. Don't run away from them. You should embrace them and hold them close. They can help you through the tough times."

In the uncomfortable silence, Shark searched for a way to change the subject.

Sensing his discomfort, Jasmine did it for him. "Why do they call you Shark? Are you a con man, a pool shark, or do you eat your prey?"

Shark smiled. "None of the above. I spend all my spare time shark fishing. I don't suppose you like to fish?"

"Only if I catch something," Jazz said with a half-smile.

"Please don't get her started talking about fishing." Josh carried the coffeepot into the living room and refilled their cups. "She'll be bragging about winning the Spanish Mackerel Tournament in Charleston last summer, or about holding the spot tail bass state title for females, etc., etc., etc.. But you should see her handle a boat. Better than most men I know."

"You own a boat?" Shark asked, suddenly a little more interested.

"Just a little one, a thirty-foot Grady White."

"She's the only lady boat owner at the marina. You should see her slide that baby right up to the dock, just like a pro."

"Ignore him," Jazz said, embarrassed by her brother's obvious pride.

"Who are we ignoring?" Dell slipped her arms around Josh's waist.

"Josh was just telling me about what a good sea captain his sister is."

"Oh God, don't get Shark started talking about boats. He can go on for hours. Let's open presents." Dell knelt in front of the Christmas tree and pulled Josh down beside her. "Come help me play Santa."

Dell seemed really pleased with the things Shark had bought for her—for once. She had given him a boat grill, a tacklebox, and a fine filet knife. He had been surprised to find that Jazz had brought him a twenty-four-pack of beers from around the world.

Jazz picked up the box holding the filet knife. "Do you mind if I look at this for a minute?"

"Don't tell me you clean fish, too!" Shark said, grinning. "Of course."

"A woman after my own heart! Thanks again for the Christmas gift. If I'd known you were going to be here I would have brought something for you. You sound like the kind of gal who would appreciate a few eels or a pound of squid."

"Bait's always good. You don't have to worry about the size or the color. Don't worry about it," she said, slipping off the jacket to her suit.

He admired the way the white sweater clung to her. "Would you let me take you out to dinner sometime to make up for it?"

Jazz met his eyes, then said, "That would be nice, as long as it's not sushi."

Shark had never met a woman, except maybe for Dell, who could deflect the jabs as fast as he could throw them. "When are you going back to Charleston?"

"Probably sometime tomorrow afternoon, or early evening, if I can tear Josh away from your partner. I have some briefs I need to go over when I get home."

"I have an idea. Why don't I pick you up for breakfast and let the lovebirds have some time alone."

"That would be great. I do feel sort of like a fifth wheel."

"How about nine o'clock?"

"Sounds good."

They watched football all afternoon, then ate turkey with all the trimmings for dinner. Afterwards Dell broke out the cards, and they drank beer and played poker until midnight.

At the door Shark hugged Dell and brushed a brief kiss across her cheek. She leaned up and whispered, "Forgiven?" in his ear.

"I'll let you know after breakfast," he said, turning to shake hands with Josh. Jazz offered to walk him to the car.

He put his packages in the backseat. Jazz hugged her arms, shivering in the cold. Shark pulled her close and wrapped her in his coat. "I'm really glad you were here today. I'm looking forward to breakfast."

"I had a great time too. But one thing's been bothering me all day."

"What's that?" he asked. Their faces were just inches apart.

"I've wondered all day if you're a good kisser." With her hand on the back of his neck, she lowered his mouth to hers.

The kiss was tender, gentle. He made no move to touch her. Jazz looked up at him. He had the sweetest smile on his face. It reminded her of how she felt sitting on the boat, the soft marsh breeze caressing her.

Shark knew it was better not to need anyone. But he couldn't bear the idea of going home to an empty house. He had been alone too long. He wanted to get to know this woman. Slowly, layer by layer as if he was peeling back the petals of a delicate flower.

"Come home with me," he said without thinking, and immediately felt her pull back. He reached out and touched her arm gently. "Wait, it's not what you think. I have a spare bedroom. I'd just like to get to know you better, no strings attached. Besides I'm sure Josh and Dell wouldn't mind having some time alone. What do you think? Remember, you did promise to have breakfast with me."

His voice was as soft as baby's hair.

Jazz relaxed again. "Can you keep a secret?"

"Of course, cops know everyone's secrets."

"Josh plans to pop the big question tonight. Maybe it would be a good idea to give them some privacy. Let me get my overnight case and my coat."

Shark relaxed his tense shoulder muscles and grinned like a woman eyeing a box of Godiva chocolates. "Want me to come with you?"

"No, just warm up the car. I'll be right back."

Shark started the engine and hoped he wasn't making a mistake. He'd been sincere when he told her he just wanted to get to know her better. Perhaps she felt the same. He'd just take things slow and see how it went.

Dell and Josh just grinned at each other as the door closed behind Jazz.

On the drive to Beaufort, they speculated on what Dell's answer would be. While Shark was certain she cared for Josh, he also knew his partner to be a competent, independent woman. It remained to be seen how much of that freedom she'd be willing to give up.

Jazz talked easily about herself, relating stories about growing up in Wilmington, North Carolina. She and Josh had no other siblings. Their father was a retired judge, and their mother had died several years before.

Shark felt a little apprehension as they turned into his driveway. He shut off the engine and hurried around to open the car door. He hadn't done that for a woman in years. Inside the front door, he flipped on the lights, hoping he'd remembered to throw all the empty beer bottles in the trash.

"Welcome to my humble abode. Let me show you your bedroom, so you can put your overnight case away," he said, turning down the hall. He was glad there were fresh sheets on the bed, and the room was in half decent order. It should be, he never used it. "There's probably lots of dust, I'm sorry."

"It's fine. I think I'll change into something more comfortable if you don't mind."

"Sure. Can I fix you a drink?"

"I've had enough alcohol. Do you have any decaf?"

"I think I can scrape some up," Shark said.

"I'll be out in a minute."

He raced into the kitchen and grabbed the phone. *Come on, Gary, be there. Who the hell drinks decaf instead of the real stuff?*

"Hello."

"Gary, it's Shark. Sorry to call so late, but I saw your light was still on. Do you have any decaf coffee?"

"Yeah, why?"

"I need to borrow some. I'll be right over. Thanks, pal."

A few minutes later Jazz walked barefooted into the kitchen. The mauve silk nightshirt hung just below her knees. "Coffee smells good."

Shark admired her shapely feet and trim legs.

"Do you want to take it into the living room?"

"Actually, here's fine for me. Why don't you go get into some sweats or something—make yourself at home?"

"Ah, I think that's my line," he said, setting the brimming cup in front of her. "Do you take anything?"

"And ruin a good cup of coffee? No thanks."

When Shark returned, in black sweat pants and a white Sheriff's Department T-shirt, he found Jazz with her feet propped up on the kitchen chair looking exactly as if she belonged there. "So tell me about your work," she said, pouring him a cup of coffee. "What makes a death investigator different from a homicide cop?"

They exchanged war stories, Jasmine having no trouble topping Shark. Even in a city as small as Charleston, the ways people found to kill each other never ceased to amaze her. As Shark reloaded the coffeemaker he told her about the DeSilva case, and his frustration at being unable to solve it. Despite asking several probing questions, in the end she was unable to offer any viable solution. She was convinced, however, that he would eventually catch a break, and probably when he least expected it.

They drank and talked and time disappeared. How long it had been since Shark had sat at his own kitchen table, talking about his work with someone who was genuinely interested. *Not since Laura*, and for once the thought of her came without pain.

They left crime, moved on to boats, bait, and a hundred other things. He liked her. She made him laugh, something he hadn't done much of in a very long time.

Jazz stifled a yawn and looked at her watch. "My God, it's five o'clock in the morning. I can't believe we talked so long."

"I know what you mean," Shark said, as he stood up and stretched.

Jazz hugged him briefly. "Thanks for the great conversation, and the bed. I guess I'll see you in a few hours."

Shark leaned down and kissed her softly. "Remember, I promised you breakfast in bed. What time would madam like it served?"

"I won't even be human before noon."

As Shark climbed naked into bed he thought of Jazz just down the hall. *A lovely lady sleeping only a few feet away, and here I am alone. But that's okay. For now.*

Shark didn't surface until a little after ten. He crept silently down the hall and eased open the door to the spare room. Jazz still slept, her dark hair splayed out on the white pillowcase, one shoulder and a tantalizing curve of breast visible above the sheet. He had been wrong—she *was* beautiful. He wanted to kiss the tiny scar above her eyebrow and learn how she had gotten it. He wanted to know her favorite food, her favorite music. He wanted to know ... everything.

Quietly he closed the door and tiptoed to the kitchen. He started coffee, the real stuff this time, and pulled bacon, eggs, and cheese from the refrigerator. He was buttering the toast when he felt her arms slip around his waist. "Something smells heavenly. I think I could eat a cow."

Shark turned in her arms and held her close for a moment. She smelled like toothpaste. "Get back in bed, and breakfast will be served shortly."

Jazz eyed the two TV trays on the counter, turned, and headed toward the bedroom.

Passing the living room, she stopped abruptly. "What a beautiful Wyland," she said, moving to inspect it closer. She ran her hand lovingly over the sculpture.

Shark followed, a tray balanced in each hand. "You know Wyland?"

"Of course. Mine is much smaller, though," she said, standing back to admire it from a different angle.

Shark raised his eyes to the ceiling. "Thank you, God, for sending me this woman." Then, "To bed, wench, your breakfast is getting cold!"

"Yes master."

They spent the rest of the morning propped up on pillows in bed talking. He learned she had gotten the scar when a three-year-old Josh had tossed a rock at her. She liked classical music and the blues, loved seafood, hated lamb, and wanted at least three kids. And when she retired, she wanted to buy a boat and sail around the world. By noon he was afraid he might be falling in love, and it scared the hell out of him. He couldn't believe he had only known her twenty-six hours.

Dell called at three. "Hope I'm not interrupting anything, but I couldn't wait any longer to tell you."

"Tell me what?" Shark asked, pulling Jazz closer to the phone.

"After you left last night, Josh asked me to marry him."

"And?"

"I said yes, of course. Can you believe it? I'm getting married!"

"Congratulations, Dell, that's wonderful. I'm really happy for you. When's the big day?"

"I don't know yet. We haven't picked out a date. I just got off the phone with my parents. My mom still can't believe it. You should see my ring."

"Poor Josh, I never had a chance to tell him how really nasty you can be before you've had your coffee."

"Go to hell. So how are you and my future sister-in-law getting along?"

"Wonderful, just wonderful," he said, smiling over at Jazz.

"So I guess you're not mad at me for surprising you. A lady fisherman, I knew you two would hit it off."

"I hate to admit this, but I think I will be forever in your debt."

"Wow, things are going that well? Anyway, tell Jazz that Josh will pick her up around six."

"So soon?"

Dell was laughing as she hung up the phone.

Jazz lay her head on Shark's chest. "I take it she said 'yes.' "

"Was there every any doubt? She's thrilled. She can't wait to show me her rock."

"I helped him pick it out. I have excellent taste in jewelry."

"I'll keep that in mind."

"I'm really happy for my brother. He said the first time he saw Dell he knew she was the one for him."

"So you believe in love at first sight?" Shark asked, his fingers stroking her hair.

Jazz paused. "Until yesterday, I would have said no."

"Look at me," Shark whispered. She was soft, sweet, but independent as well. She was all that he had imagined, and more than he had ever hoped to find again.

Chapter Twenty-Six

T he next day Dell and Shark were back, working the list of people with Toyota trucks. They still had eight names left to check.

"I still can't believe it about you and Jazz. I figured you guys would have lots in common, but never in a million years would I have guessed you would get along so well."

"Me either," Shark said, grinning. "So how are you coming on a date?"

"I always wanted to be a June bride, but Josh doesn't want to wait that long."

"So I guess you'll be moving to Charleston, and I'll have to find another partner."

"We talked about that, but we've decided to live in Beaufort. Josh does a lot of his work at home anyway, and it's only about an hour's drive when he does have to go to the city. That way, I won't have to leave the force. So I guess you're stuck with me."

"Damn, I had this cute little Sergeant, in traffic, all picked out."

"Would that be the one with the brown belt in karate? Get out of line with her and your sorry butt would be sprawled on the floor in a heartbeat."

"Promises, promises. Now let's get back to work. We'll each take half the list and see if we can't finish it today."

Before they could begin, the phone rang on Shark's desk. He listened for a minute, then grabbed a pen and began to make notes. "Okay. We're on our way." He pulled his coat from the back of the chair. "A body on the beach at the Westin Hotel. Young, white female. Let's go."

The partially clad body had been found under the lifeguard stand. Beach chairs had been stacked on it, and sand mounded up along the sides. Hotel security guards kept onlookers at bay while the detectives examined the scene. Shark could tell the young redhead had been pretty. The only noticeable marks were the dark bruises on her throat. The buttons had been ripped off the green silk blouse, and her bra had been cut away, revealing her small breasts. She was naked from the waist down except for the narrow gold bracelet encircling her childlike ankle. A trickle of blood had dried on her inner thigh.

Michelle Dupree had been reported missing at eight that morning. The parents were staying in one room, and she and her nine-year-old brother, Matt, in the one adjoining, The mother had panicked when she discovered the girl's bed hadn't been slept in, although Matt had insisted she was there when he went to sleep around ten-thirty. Security had launched an immediate search, finally discovering her body on the beach.

Anna Connors dusted sand from the knees of her coveralls. "Looks pretty cut and dried at this point. I'd say she was sexually molested, then strangled. I don't think the autopsy will give you much more than that."

"Time of death?" Shark asked.

"Can't say for sure right now. I'll have to factor in the temperature last night. Can you find out from the parents what time she ate dinner? That should help?"

"I'll do that," Dell said, moving away.

Anna stepped out of her protective jumpsuit and pulled off her surgical gloves. "So how do you see it going down?"

"She may have gone for a walk on the beach and gotten jumped by a stranger. Or maybe she arranged to meet someone. She was a pretty girl. Who knows? Anyway, future Christmases are sure going to be hell for her family."

Anna glanced up at Shark, surprised by the pain in his voice. "So how about you? Did you have a good holiday?"

"One of the best I've had in a long time," he answered with a half-smile. "And you?"

"Okay I guess." Anna paused, groping for a way to put the feeling into words. "You seem different. Calmer or something." She stepped closer. "I've missed you. Come to dinner tonight."

He put a little distance between them. "I appreciate the invitation, Anna, but no thanks."

"You've met someone, haven't you?"

"Yes, I have."

"Who is it?"

"You don't know her. She's from Charleston."

Dell approached them, hesitating, not sure what she was interrupting. "Dinner was at seven, and her brother said they shared some potato chips about nine-thirty"

"Thanks." Anna turned abruptly, trudging away through the loose sand.

"What was that all about?" Dell asked.

"Let's just say Anna wanted to pick up where we left off. We're going to need some additional officers over here so we can start interviewing the guests. This is going to be a nightmare. We've got to get to people before they begin checking out. I hate investigations involving tourists. Where are the Duprees from anyway?"

"Madison, Wisconsin."

Shark groaned. "Why couldn't it have been Savannah or Columbia?"

After numerous interviews, they learned that the dead girl had been seen, earlier in the evening, talking to a young man by the pool. Todd Bergman, however, had an alibi. Room service confirmed they had delivered champagne to his room around midnight and that he had not been alone. The waiter remembered, because the woman had been barely dressed, and the guy had tipped him a measly dollar.

A local contractor, who was having a drink in the small lounge off the lobby, supplied the only other interesting piece of information to emerge. Around twelve-thirty, the girl had perched herself on a barstool and attempted to order a drink. When they refused to serve her, she left quietly.

Which was why, after interviewing the parents, the brother, and the other hotel guests, Dell and Shark found themselves sorting through credit card receipts in the back of the bar. So far they had come up with four names that did not match the hotel register.

"So we track down these people and find out if any of them saw the girl after she left here. But what about anybody who paid cash?" Dell asked, rubbing a knot in the back of her neck.

"A good bartender should remember the faces, especially that time of the morning. There can't have been that many," Shark said.

The Human Resource department supplied an address for the bartender, a villa in Shipyard Plantation. The young man who answered the door was medium, in every way. Dressed in a pair of navy sweat pants and white T-shirt, he looked as if they had gotten him out of bed.

"Yeah, what do you want?"

"Michael Murphy?" Shark asked.

"Yes."

The sight of their badges woke him up. Inside, Shark informed him about the body on the beach and showed him the picture of Michelle Dupree they'd gotten from her parents.

"My God. That's the girl who came in last night just before closing. She ordered a strawberry daiquiri. When I asked her for ID, she said she'd lost her wallet. She was obviously underage, looked about sixteen, so I refused to serve her and she left."

"And that's the last time you saw her?" Shark checked out Murphy's bare arms, but saw no signs of any scratches or bruises.

"Yes."

"We went through the credit card receipts at the bar. We found four names of people who weren't guests at the hotel. Can you tell us how many cash customers you had last night?" Dell asked.

"Let me think for a minute. I can only remember two. One was an older guy, probably in his fifties. Bald, big diamond on his left hand. Drank Chivas. The other one was around my age, late twenties maybe. A couple of Coors Lites, and he nursed them."

"Were they both alone?" Shark asked.

"Seemed to be. The bald guy had been in the previous night, so he may have been staying at the hotel. I'd never seen the younger one before. But the faces change nightly. He could have just checked in or he might have wandered in off the street."

"Can you describe him?"

"Big, about six-three. Light brown hair, muscular build, like he worked out a lot. Didn't say much. I tried to ask him questions, like where he was from, but he just said 'around.' Definitely not the chatty type, so I just left him alone."

"What percentage of the people in the bar are usually staying at the hotel?" Dell asked.

"I'd say at least ninety percent. Most of the locals hang out at Callahan's or one of the other sports bars on the island."

Shark showed him the list they had gleaned from the credit card receipts of people who were not guests at the hotel. "Recognize any of these names?"

"Sean Mallory is a college student who works in the health club in the summer. He was home for Christmas break and dropped in for a couple of drinks. This guy, Halpin, was with him. I don't recognize the other two names."

"Had you seen the girl around the hotel the last few days?" Dell asked.

"No, I'd never seen her before she came in the bar."

"Did you notice anyone follow her out when she left?"

Murphy looked off into space for a moment. "I think the Coors guy left a while later, but it definitely wasn't at the same time she did."

Shark left his card in case Murphy thought of anything else.

The following day, they learned from Anna Connors that the victim had been a virgin at the time of the assault. There was evidence of tearing of the hymenal ring and trauma to the vagina and rectum. Death was from manual strangulation.

"Anything under the nails?" Shark asked.

"No, and physical evidence isn't going to be helpful. Any hair or fibers could have come from the sand or the beach chairs that were stacked on top of her. And there was no sperm, so either the perp wore a condom, or he didn't ejaculate."

"How about the time of death?" Dell asked.

"Between one and two I'd judge, based on the stomach contents. And she had a small amount of alcohol and traces of marijuana in her bloodstream. Afraid that's all I've got for you." She tossed the file onto Shark's desk.

"Thanks for dropping the report off," Dell called to her retreating back and was rewarded with a half-hearted wave.

"So where did she get the alcohol and the grass?" Shark asked as they settled into the unmarked car.

"Maybe she was partying with someone on the beach. Or the marijuana could have been hers, and she slipped away from mom and dad to have a smoke."

"Yeah, that would make sense. I can see her meeting up with someone, having a drink and sharing a joint. I think whoever gave her the alcohol, probably killed her."

"I think you're right. And if she met him on the beach he could have come from anywhere. Port Royal Plantation is practically next door, and you have villas all along the shore in the other direction."

"This is impossible. Couldn't we, for once, have a plain ordinary homicide with at least a *few clues* to go on?" Shark asked, shaking his head.

"Not sure we'll ever get this one solved, especially since all the hotel guests turn over every few days. I squeezed those four addresses out of the credit card companies. Let's start with them," Dell said, chewing on a hangnail.

"Let's leave the guy who worked there and his friend till last, talk to the others first."

"Okay. Timothy Bronsky lives in Sea Pines. Let's start with him and work our way back. The other guy is in North Forest Beach."

But those, like everything else connected with this investigation, proved to be a dead end. Added to the frustration of the DeSilva case, it made Shark, who usually hated being forced to take time off, almost look forward to New Year's.

Chapter Twenty-Seven

It had been a beautiful day on El Hierro, the temperature hovering in the low seventies. Quite a change from other New Year's Eve's Marissa remembered from her childhood in Kentucky. She and Devon had just returned from a walk on the black sand beach and now sat companionably on the porch, sipping wine and watching the sun march toward the horizon.

Marissa knew they were never to discuss a job once it was over, but the question had been nagging at her ever since they'd reunited. Casually she asked, "Why did you have to kill Marcus on our wedding day? You ruined a perfectly good dress, and I was really looking forward to the honeymoon. I've never had a proper one, you know, not with Eric, and certainly not with you."

Devon looked hurt. "Poor darling, I never knew it was that important to you. But here's the thing—*I* didn't kill Marcus. Someone beat me to it."

"What?" The wineglass slipped from her hand and shattered on the wide boards of the porch. "You *are* kidding me, aren't you?"

Devon burst out laughing. "You mean all this time you thought *I* did it?"

"Well, of course. But if you didn't, then who did?"

"I have no idea, but I salute him." Devon raised his wineglass and drank a silent toast.

Marissa rose from her chair and retrieved another glass from the kitchen. Slowly she poured more wine, her mind churning.

"I don't believe you," she said, stepping around the broken glass and settling in once more next to Devon. "You're just pulling my leg."

"No, dear, I'm not. This time someone else made you a millionaire."

"What about B.J.? Did you have anything to do with his death?"

"The boy? Nothing whatsoever. That would have been stretching coincidence a little too much, don't you think? It would have thrown too much suspicion on you."

"I just can't believe this. I know I'm never supposed to know when it's going to happen so I can appear genuinely shocked. And I certainly wasn't acting that day at the wedding. I guess I just assumed it was you since you're the one who chose him out of our three possible marks. So who could have killed him? And you really believe we were lucky enough to have B.J. run his car off the road on his own?"

"Apparently so. Or maybe he had a little help from the loan sharks he was dealing with. Frankly, I don't care. More money for us, my dear."

Marissa shook her head. "This is too bizarre. Do you know that for a while the police actually thought that *I* might be the target?"

"But who would want to kill you, darling?"

"No one, I guess. It just makes me nervous to think about it."

By late afternoon, Shark and Dell sat at their desks, having run out of ideas on the Michelle Dupree murder. "You just have to accept the fact that we've come to a dead end in the investigation," Dell said. "We've done all we can at this point."

"I'd just like to close one case, for a change. Since DeSilva, it seems as if we have nothing but open files, except for that murder/suicide in Port Royal. And that was so obvious a rookie could have figured it out. It's beginning to make us look bad."

"Well, it's New Year's Eve, and I'm not going to worry about it. Jazz and Josh should get here around eight, and our dinner reservations at the Gaslight are for nine. So don't be late!"

"I wouldn't dream of it."

"I think I'm going to check out the last two names on my list of these people with white Toyota trucks. Since they both live in Bluffton, I can do it on the way home. That way, when we come back, at least I'll have that marked off my 'to do' list. What are your plans for this afternoon?"

"Maybe I'll run down the last two names on my list, too. Then we can start on something fresh when we get back."

Jo Parker leaned against the kitchen sink, peeling carrots for the roast she'd planned for dinner. It was one of Bubba's favorite meals. She tried to still her shaking hands. Bubba had been in a drunken rage for the past two days. He had lost his job again, for drinking at work. And he hadn't left the house since. As usual, he had been taking his frustration out on her, and her battered face and bruised body were evidence of his handiwork.

So far she had been successful in shielding her abdomen, protecting the life that grew inside her. But she didn't know how much longer she could absorb this kind of punishment and live. She had to find a way to escape from Bubba. She rinsed the carrots and was adding them to the pan when Bubba yelled from the living room, "Bring me another beer."

Jo dried her hands and grabbed a Budweiser from the refrigerator. She rushed into the living room and handed it to him. "I'm fixing your favorite dinner," she said softly.

"Good," he muttered, flipping channels with the remote control.

Jo hurried back to the kitchen, anxious to be out of his way. When, a few minutes later, she heard a car pull up outside, she groaned in despair. Since she had no friends, it had to be one of Bubba's drinking pals. He was always meaner when he had an audience.

Bubba, too, heard the car. He hauled himself out of the sagging recliner and walked to the window. He didn't recognize the woman, so she had to be selling something. He flopped back into the chair and yelled, "Some woman is getting out of her car. Must be peddling something. Get rid of her."

Surprised, Jo hurried past him, just as the bell rang, and pulled open the door.

"I'm sorry to bother you at dinner time, but I'm Detective Hassler with the Beaufort County Sheriff's department. I need to speak to Reginald Parker." Dell watched fear leap into the eyes of the hunched woman with the black eye and bruised lips. "Wait a minute, don't I know you? You work with Reverend Hart."

"Please, just go away." Jo's hands clutching the dishtowel to her waist shook uncontrollably.

"I'm sorry, this will only take a second. I need to speak to Reginald Parker about that white truck over there. Can I come in?"

"No! He's not here." Jo backed away, trying to push the door closed.

Dell grabbed the knob. "I don't believe you. Is he the one who gave you that shiner? Just let me come in. Maybe I can help."

"No, please just go!"

"Shoulda listened to her, witch!" Bubba roared as the shot rang out.

"Noooo," Jo screamed. Her ears rang from the explosion, and the sulfurous smell of the gunpowder made her gag. She stood frozen in the doorway, staring at the lady deputy crumpled at the bottom of the porch steps, until Bubba yanked her back inside and slammed the door. He still clutched the ugly black revolver in his hand.

"Damn!" he screamed. "Get your purse! We've got to get the hell out of here!" Bubba dragged her into the bedroom.

"Why did you have to kill her?" Jo sobbed.

"Because she was here to arrest me, you stupid witch," he said, backhanding her across the face and knocking her to the floor. "Get up!"

"Arrest you for what? I don't understand." Jo tried to stand, but her legs refused to obey.

"It doesn't matter," he growled, aiming a kick at her ribs. "Come on. We've got to get out of here."

"No! I'm not going with you!"

"Oh yes you are. One way or the other." He kicked her again, this time full in the stomach.

"Stop, please stop! I'll do whatever you say. Just don't hurt the baby."

"Baby?" he said with disgust. "Whose bastard is it? Tell me!" He pummeled her, and she rolled into a fetal position, her arms protecting her child.

"It's yours!" she screamed, "It's yours!"

"Oh no, not mine, whore! You know I can't have no kids, you've known it for years. Whose is it? It's that preacher, ain't it?

"No. I swear it's yours," Jo whimpered as he picked her up by the hair and threw her into the wall.

"I knew you were sleeping with him! I missed him the last time, but I won't make that mistake again. This time I'll kill the guy, for sure!"

It took a minute for Bubba's words to register. Had she really just heard him say he had tried to murder Reverend Alan Hart? And then she realized, in the moment before she lost consciousness, that her husband had just confessed to killing Marcus DeSilva.

Shark was heading north on Highway 278, close to Belfair Plantation when he heard the call on his radio. "Shots fired at Twenty-eight Burnt Church Road. One victim in the yard. All units in the vicinity respond." His heart raced as he swung his car into the median, bumped up into the southbound lane, and pushed the accelerator to the floor. Twenty-eight Burnt Church Road. Why did that sound so familiar? And then it struck him—it was one of the addresses on Dell's list of white Toyota truck owners. The hand that reached for the radio was slick with sweat.

"This is Unit Sixteen. Detective Hassler was planning to stop at that location on her way home. Do we know who the victim is?" He flipped on the siren and watched the traffic ahead of him peel off to the sides of the road as he raced by.

"Checking," the dispatcher replied calmly.

And then Shark began to bargain with God.

"Unit Sixteen. The vehicle parked in the drive matches Detective Hassler's. An ambulance is en route."

Shark didn't respond. He needed both hands on the wheel as he took the corner onto Burnt Church Road at fifty miles per hour.

Bubba picked up the box of ammunition, and stuffed car keys and wallet into the pocket of his sagging jeans. Jo lay slumped on the floor. He grabbed her by the arm and dragged her, unresisting, into the living room. He heard sirens approaching fast. He pulled back the sheer curtain on the front window and peered outside. *Good, the witch outside hasn't moved. She must be dead. I gotta hurry.*

When he bent down to pick up Jo, she suddenly sprang to life, her thin arms flailing and punching. He tried to restrain her, but she fought like a cornered animal. He didn't have time for this. And he shouldn't have let it slip, about trying to kill the preacher. She and her bastard would have to die. He backed away, raised the pistol, and squeezed the trigger.

Bluffton police chief Freddie Marks heard the shot as he climbed out of his car. He had pulled in to block the driveway, and now drew his weapon, crouching down for protection behind the open door. Two other Bluffton police cars slithered to a stop right behind him. In the first sweep of his headlights across the front of the decaying house he'd spotted the body at the foot of the porch and wondered how many others might be inside. Within the next minute an ambulance arrived, followed closely by several Beaufort county deputies.

Chief Marks deployed several officers to the back of the house to keep anyone from slipping away into the woods. The rest of the deputies took up defensive positions. Their weapons trained on the peeling front door. The paramedics stood helplessly by, waiting for the Chief to declare the scene safe, before they could rush to the victim.

As soon as Shark cut his engine, he was out of the car, gun drawn. He recognized Marks and moved up to crouch beside him. "Cover me," he said. "I'm bringing her out."

"Are you nuts?" Marks grabbed his sleeve and pulled him back down.

"That's my partner up there," he shouted, trying to wrench his arm free.

But he was no match for the 6'5" Marks.

"We haven't verified that."

"I have. That's the coat she wore to work today."

"Well, even if it is, you're not going to do her any good by getting yourself shot too! And we don't even know if she's still alive. I heard another gunshot as I pulled up. What was she doing here, anyway?"

"A guy in a white Toyota pickup, like that one over there, was at the scene of the convenience store shooting a few weeks ago. She was just here to ask if he had seen anything."

When Sheriff Grant pulled up, Shark filled him in. Though no one had seen any sign of movement from Dell, they continued to plan their strategy on the assumption that she was still alive.

With the house now completely surrounded, Chief Marks used a bullhorn to demand Reginald Parker's surrender. Beside him, Shark checked his watch. If the bastard didn't show in two minutes he was going after his partner.

Bubba Parker sprawled on the floor of the kitchen, drinking straight from the bottle of Jack Daniel's. Through the fog of alcohol and disbelief he could hear someone outside yelling, but he couldn't seem to understand the words. He knew he'd really screwed up this time. Not only had he killed a cop, but his wife as well. That he regretted. He really had loved her, in his own way. Maybe the kid *had* been his, but it was too late now. He couldn't surrender. He'd been in jail once, and he wasn't going back.

How had they known he'd shot that store clerk? He took another slug out of the bottle and told himself that when it was empty he would "do it." *No use to waste good whiskey,* he told himself. He leaned back against the cabinet, his legs splayed out in front of him, and studied the gun in his hand. He noticed a couple of rust spots on the barrel and remembered how his old man used to yell at him when he didn't take care of his things. Then his gaze shifted over to Jo's body, crumpled on the living room floor. He thought about when times had been good and wondered where it had all gone wrong.

Shark could hardly breathe. He desperately wanted to go to Dell, but the Sheriff was practically glued to his hip. Grant knew Shark well and had even gone so far as to threaten to handcuff him to the steering wheel, to prevent him from doing something irrational.

Again, Chief Marks shouted through the bullhorn, but only silence echoed back.

"Chief, I think we need to consider storming the house. I want to get my wounded officer out of there."

"But we could have hostages inside. I believe the man has got a wife, maybe kids," Marks said.

"Hold it," Grant shouted, but Shark had already leaped around the car door and sprinted toward the porch. When the shot rang out from inside the house he dropped and rolled. The night erupted in gunfire as the deputies surged forward.

Chapter Twenty-Eight

Jo Parker opened her eyes. Her throat hurt and she was thirsty. She had no idea who the man was slouched in the chair next to her bed. But maybe he would get her a drink. "Excuse me," she whispered, and he was immediately on his feet.

"Mrs. Parker, I'm Detective Morgan. You're going to be fine."

"Water?" she said, through parched lips.

"Oh, sure." He held the plastic cup, with its flexible straw, to her mouth.

"Thank you." Then her hand went to her stomach, and panic flashed across her face. "The baby!"

"I'm sorry," Shark said, wishing it hadn't fallen to him to tell her. "You were shot and they had to remove your spleen. I guess the shock was just too much for the baby."

A solitary tear slid down her cheek. "And Bubba?" she asked quietly.

Shark cleared his throat. "We tried to get him to surrender, but he shot himself. He's dead."

Jo closed her eyes for a moment. "I know I should be sorry, but I'm not. He tried to kill Reverend Hart, but he shot that Mr. DeSilva by mistake."

"What?" Shark said, his eyes widening in disbelief.

"He thought the Reverend and I were sleeping together. That's why he tried to kill him. Then when I told him about the baby, he just went nuts. He swore it wasn't his, but it was. There was nothing going on between the Reverend and me. I was always faithful to Bubba."

Shark tiptoed into Dell's room, leaned over and kissed her on the cheek, being careful of the gauze bandage on her forehead. "Hi," she said softly, opening her eyes.

"Hi yourself. Don't you ever scare me like that again, you hear?" He covered her hand with his.

"Did you really think I was dead?" she asked groggily.

"I don't even want to talk about it." He looked quickly away, so she wouldn't see the tears. "The doctor said you have a mild concussion from falling down the stairs, and a badly bruised heart and lung, but you're going to be fine. If old Bubba had been standing any closer, the bullet would probably have gone right through the vest. It saved your life. What made you wear it?"

"I don't know. I just grabbed it and slipped it on, as I got out of the car. Someone up there must be watching out for me. I guess that was a pretty good Christmas present last year, after all. Jeez, it feels like there's an elephant sitting on my chest. How long do I have to be in here?"

"The doc said a couple of days at the most. Just till they make sure you don't develop any heart irregularities. And while you've been lying here, taking it easy, you'll be happy to know I solved the DeSilva case."

"How? Who?" Dell struggled to sit up.

Shark repeated Jo Parker's story of her husband's confession.

"I'll be damned. So the *minister* was the target. Didn't I tell you that in the beginning?"

"And it looks like the gun that shot you was the same one used on that clerk at the Starvin' Marvin. So, two closed cases for the price of one."

"That'll help our stats. Any way we can tie him to the killing on the beach, too?" Dell asked with a hint of her old grin.

"I think that may be stretching it," Shark said, laughing.

"I'm glad Jo Parker is going to be okay, but I feel awful about the baby. I just wish she would have listened to me and left that son of a bitch the first time I talked to her. It would have saved us all a lot of grief."

"Well, don't beat yourself up about it. It's all part of the job."

"Which she won't have very long, if she's going to marry me." They both turned at the sound of Josh's voice. He was across the room and had gathered Dell into his arms, before either of them could respond.

"Help!" Dell mouthed over his shoulder.

Epilogue

Marissa carried a glass of mint iced tea and the mail out onto the deck of her oceanfront home. Maui in April had been a good choice, she thought, stretching out on the chaise lounge. She had spent the previous three months traveling all over Europe and Asia and was glad to be no longer living out of a suitcase. She closed her eyes for a moment, savoring the sound of the surf crashing on her private beach below.

Marissa reached for the mail and sorted through it, setting aside a couple of bills to open later. The blue envelope was addressed to Marissa Langford, her maiden name, which she always resumed. She turned it over, but there was no return address. Curious, she tore it open and pulled out a newspaper clipping from the *San Francisco Examiner*, along with a small note. The clipping announced the wedding of Amanda Spencer and Devon Phillips. The note read simply, *I'll be adding approximately twenty million to our kitty soon!*

261

Marissa smiled as she tore them both into small pieces and let the soft tropical breeze scatter them across the foaming water.

At last.